$7000, DEAD OR ALIVE

It was on all the reward posters, but there wasn't a man in the West wanted to try and collect it.

"He's a kid," they scoffed. But they whispered when they said it.

"He's little. He's a runt," they jeered. But a stick of dynamite's only eight inches high and Coyle was the same stuff.

"Hardcase" they called him—the outlaw who would gamble his life against any odds—and laugh as he did it!

Bantam Books by Luke Short
Ask your bookseller for the books you have missed

Richard

LUKE SHORT

HARDCASE

❦

HARDCASE
A Bantam Book

PRINTING HISTORY
Serialized in CHICAGO TRIBUNE April-June 1941

Doubleday edition published March 1942

Sundial edition published April 1943

Bantam edition / October 1955

2nd printing .... October 1955	5th printing .. September 1960
3rd printing .. November 1955	6th printing ...... April 1965
4th printing .... January 1956	7th printing ...... April 1977

8th printing

ISBN 0-553-10232-X

Published simultaneously in the United States and Canada

PRINTED IN THE UNITED STATES OF AMERICA

I

YELLOW JACKET'S post office was a rack of pigeonholes in the front corner of Badey's Emporium. Around eleven o'clock each morning after the mail stage from Sabinal got in the loafers lounged on the dry-goods counter while old man Badey sorted out the mail.

This morning the procedure was no different than usual. In the drift of idle talk and low laughter from beyond the rack of pigeonholes old Badey squinted through his bifocals at the topmost letter of a stack he held in his left hand, and with his right hand he deliberately placed it in its correct box. Fred Curtis, the clerk, was taking care of the trade beyond the post office.

Nobody saw old Badey when it happened. He had just read the address of a letter and had his hand halfway to the general-delivery cubbyhole when his hand paused. And then as the name he had read sank into his consciousness he dropped the letter like he would have dropped a hot iron. Gingerly he picked it up again and read: "Mr. Dave Coyle, General Delivery, Yellow Jacket, New Mexico Territory. Hold till Sept. 1, and return."

Old Badey's panic was immediate and complete. The first thing he did was natural enough. He poked his head out of the wicket and surveyed the loafers in the store. He knew them all, men, and women, and children, and still he was uneasy. The second thing he did was explainable; he looked at the feed-mill calendar on the wall behind him, and it said August 31. The third thing he did was pure instinct. He called up to the clerk, "Finish sortin' this mail, Fred," and left the store, taking the letter with him.

Across the wide and dusty street, wedged in between two wooden-awninged buildings, was the sheriff's office, and old Badey made for it. He tramped into the small office to find Sheriff Harvey Beal, his feet cocked up on the roll-top desk, in conversation with his deputy, Ernie See.

Old Badey put the letter on the desk and said hoarsely, "Take a look, Harve."

Beal was a bland-faced, heavy-set man whose wide and innocent blue eyes were trusting and affable. He was also a slow-moving man, but now, because he read the excitement in old Badey's face, he moved with alacrity. He picked up the letter, read the address, and came out of his chair like he'd been kicked out.

"Where'd you get this?" he demanded swiftly.

Old Badey, besides being testy, was scared, too, and he said truculently, "It's got a stamp on it, ain't it? I didn't print it. It come in the mail."

Ernie See reached over and took the letter from the sheriff's hand. Ernie was a slow reader, but it didn't take him long to read this name, because it was familiar enough to him. He dropped the letter and said, "Wow!" and looked blankly at the sheriff, his young face surprised.

Beal said, "Did you look at the crowd in the store?" Without waiting for an answer he went to the door and looked swiftly up and down the tie rails on both sides of the street, then closed the door.

Badey said, "I knowed everyone in the store."

"Ernie," Beal said swiftly, "you go camp on Badey's counter till I get this fixed up."

"Not me," Ernie said slowly. "Hunh-unh. I got a three-day vacation comin', Harve. I'm takin' it—startin' now."

Beal eyed him with deceptive mildness. "You're a deputy of this county."

"That's right. A live one," Ernie said. "I aim to stay alive too."

Beal stepped over to the desk and pulled out a lower drawer and rummaged in it. He was a somewhat ridiculous figure to a stranger, a fat and rotund and polite man in outsize pants, half boots that were run over at the heels, and a buttonless black vest over a too-small calico shirt. But a careful man might consider this: Beal's hands were soft and uncalloused, which argued he had done no manual work in a long time. Which argued he had been sheriff for a long time. Which argued, since Yellow Jacket was a cattle county with a reasonably high homicide rate, that he and his office managed to take care of any trouble that came up. And since he seemed anything but a scrapper, a careful man might consider the deputy. He would have been right, too, for Ernie See was the sheriff's office.

Beal found what he was looking for and laid it on his desk and looked at his deputy. "Read it," he said.

"I read it," Ernie said stubbornly. "Hell, I know it by

heart. Seven thousand dollars, alive or dead, for Dave Coyle."

Beal wheeled to face old Badey. "You read it."

"I got one in the post office," Badey said sourly.

"Well, divide it by three and see what each of us'll make," Beal said.

Old Badey looked carefully at him and said, "Harve, I'm goin' to be sick tomorrow, sick in bed. I'm already sick now."

Beal looked from Badey to Ernie and back to Badey. "One of you on vacation and one of you sick," he murmured scornfully. "Where's all the men in this town?"

"I know where they will be when you tell 'em," Ernie said. "They'll be out of town."

"He ain't so tough," Beal countered.

"If I was you I'd whisper that," Ernie said dryly.

"He's little. He's a runt," Beal said.

"A stick of dynamite's only eight inches high," Badey said. "He's over five feet, and the same stuff."

"But he's a kid—just a tough kid," Beal insisted. "You afraid of a kid?"

Ernie said dryly, "Don't look at me. I didn't print that reward notice. It's the U.S. commissioner that's afraid of him. Me, I just don't aim to bust up a three-day fishin' trip to meet him."

Beal said grimly, "All right, Ernie. But make your trip longer than three days. Make it three months. Make it three years. Why not? Because you don't have to get back to work."

"I'll get back to work," Ernie retorted. "I've got a date here for September second."

"Not here."

"No, I'll call at your house."

Beal looked blank. "Why?"

"That's where a funeral usually starts, ain't it?" Ernie said. He waved his hand at Sheriff Beal, grinned, and stepped out onto the walk. Badey started after him, and Beal said, "Wait a minute, Badey. I'll go with you."

"No, you won't," Badey said. "I sleep in a single bed, and that's where I'm goin'."

Sheriff Beal settled down into his chair and watched Badey leave. He didn't feel exactly cheerful himself, and he looked around to see if the door was closed. There was a kind of hot and greedy urgency within him, but he knew this would take a little thinking out. As long as the letter, the bait, was in his possession, Dave Coyle couldn't get it. He put the letter in his pocket, just to make sure, and then considered.

Was it a fake? He didn't know, but it seemed as if Dave Coyle had told somebody he'd drop in at Yellow Jacket before September 1 to get his mail. That was the way Dave Coyle did things—like the time he'd gone into the Governor's mansion the night of the inaugural ball and picked the blossom from a century plant of the Governor's wife to wear in his buttonhole during the dance. He'd do anything that took gall, preferred to do it that way, and somehow this letter business seemed typical.

Beal pictured seven thousand dollars in gold. That was a lot of money. For ten dollars apiece he could get twenty men to watch Badey's store day and night, and when Dave Coyle called for his letter it would be like shooting a clay pigeon.

Sheriff Beal thought of something then. He remembered the return notation on the envelope. He pulled it out and looked at the back of it, where the return address was given.

"Return to Box 73, Wagon Mound."

Sheriff Beal grinned faintly then. The return was wrong. It should have read, "Return the box to Wagon Mound," the box, of course, meaning the coffin. He went out, then, to start gathering recruits.

Just after dark that night a man rode up to the outskirts of Yellow Jacket and dismounted in the deep shade of a cottonwood tree that overhung the south road. He stretched with the smooth clean movements of a cat, then set about a job that came easily to him. He knotted the reins, looped them over the horse's neck, slipped the bit, lifted the stirrups and tied them together with a piece of string over the pommel, and let out the cinch an inch or so.

Afterward he walked away, for this wasn't his own horse he'd been riding. He didn't like to own a horse, hadn't owned one for years, and didn't intend to. It was a borrowed horse, which he had taken in the last town. When he got ready to leave here he would borrow a fresh one.

He scuffed along silently in the dust of the road, a slight and shadowy figure, and long before he reached the section of town where the stores lighted the street he paused and studied it.

To a man less concerned than himself with the appearance of things the scene looked typical enough. There was usually one store in any town that stayed open at night and whose lamps laid bright squares of light far out into the street. But it went beyond that here. There were, he noticed, lights on only one side of the street. And why weren't there horses at the tie rail in front of the store? And why weren't people moving in the street; why were they all loafing, sitting around? It all shaped up into the old familiar face of trouble, but he wanted to be sure. He vanished in an alley.

Some minutes later he again looked upon the street, this time from a position in the narrow weed-and-bottle-cluttered space between two buildings. He had already tried three similar spaces farther up the alley and had found men with rifles across their knees squatting in each of them. He already knew what to expect; all he wanted now was to make sure this brightly lighted store was also the post office. Through Badey's window he could see the mail racks, and he turned and went back to the dark alley.

A man was walking up the alley, coming toward him. The man stopped. He stopped too.

"I'm gettin' sick of this," Dave Coyle said in the utter darkness. "Why don't he come?"

"You and me both," the other said. "What are you usin'?"

"A shotgun. I loaded her with washers."

The man laughed. "That ought to take care of him."

"I reckon," Dave said. 'So long." And he walked down the alley, the man forgotten. There was a letter for him over there in the post office, sure enough. But instead of minding their business and letting him call for it, this bounty-hunting crew wanted trouble. He didn't want trouble, though; he only wanted the letter. He was tramping down the alley when he caught a whiff of something that hauled him up in his tracks. It was the smell of warm ashes, of coal gas, and the faint lingering scent of burned hoofs. He followed the smell and came up to a large door that he knew was the rear of a blacksmith shop.

He found the door unlocked, went inside, pulled the door to after him, and struck a match.

The flare lighted a face that had graced a triple printing of reward dodgers. It was burned that same deep brown that had blurred the picture on the dodger and had made him look almost black. In shape it was a tough face, tight-knit, flaring a little at the jaw hinge, and then sweeping in a clean line to a pointed chin that was faintly cleft. The nose, thin and high, had a faint white scar across the bridge, but it was the mouth that people noticed. Maybe that was because, on the reward dodger, it had been grinning crookedly, insolently, so that half the sheriffs who had gazed upon it had felt uncomfortably mad and had sworn under their breaths. It was that kind of mouth, shaped into a sneer, the upper lip lifted in one corner, the whole tilt of it derisive. The eyes were a perfect foil—wide-spaced, gray without a trace of blue—whose habitual innocence confounded people and was intended to.

No reward dodger had ever carried a full-length picture, and for want of a better word, he had been described therein as "small." It was true only if a man didn't associate the word "puny" with the description. Right now a sun-faded blue shirt, worn levis, and scuffed half boots covered his lean smoothly muscled body, and nobody would have called it stocky. It had that long-legged, lazy grace that carried a hint of explosive possibilities. The gun, rammed carelessly into a wide and heavy shell belt, looked outsize against his small hand. A battered and curl-brimmed Stetson rode carelessly back-tilted on a shock of untidy blue-black hair.

Before the match flare died he had seen what he wanted. He went over to the forge, which was still warm, and tugged at the bellows rope. The small cup of glowing coals in the forge spread out now under the bellows wind, and when it was a cherry red he reached for the coal shovel. He scattered a thin layer of fine fuel on the coals, blacking them out. And then, swiftly, he shucked up two dozen shells from his shell belt and laid them on the black coal. Afterward he softly opened the double front doors, then retreated through the rear door into the alley.

It took him three minutes to walk down to the end of the alley, cross the street in the dark, and find the opposite alley that he was sure would lead past the loading platform of Badey's store. He did not approach close, for he was certain men would be back there too. He only hunkered down against a woodshed and began rolling a cigarette.

When he heard the initial spatter of gunfire his smoke was licked and pasted in one corner of his mouth. He listened. A man lunged into the light from the rear of Badey's store and stopped. He called, "Hear that? They got him!"

That was all that was needed. Six men materialized out of the darkness and pounded down the alley—bound for the blacksmith shop, where the forge's heat had finally exploded the cartridges.

Dave rose and walked slowly toward the store. He could hear men yelling out front and running on the boardwalk, and there were other shots now, the result of nerves gone edgy in the dark.

Dave mounted the steps, paused to light his cigarette, and then went into the store. It was brightly lighted and, of course, deserted. Seven thousand dollars, he reflected wryly, was too big a sum to keep a clerk on the job tonight. He walked the length of the store, hauled up at the mail rack, found the general-delivery cubbyhole, and sorted the mail there.

When he found his letter he pocketed it, put the mail back, and went out the rear door again. This time he headed up the alley, and when it emptied into the side street he turned left toward the main street. The corner building was the hotel. The clerk, like most of the other men in town, had deserted his post to run downstreet toward the gunfire that was still racketing.

Dave walked in, chose a room key from the board behind the desk, and went upstairs. His room, number eight, was a corner one, and he locked the door behind him.

After lighting the lamp, yawning, pulling the shades, and removing his hat he sat down by the lamp and opened the letter.

It began: "Dear Mr. Usher."

Dave stopped right there and stared at it. Then he leafed over the page and read the signature. It was signed "Carol McFee." That part was all right. He turned back to the beginning, the greeting still puzzling him, and began to read.

DEAR MR. USHER:

I am in receipt of your letter asking me to put you in touch with Dave Coyle. Do you think me stupid, or are you insane? Every child in this territory knows that each of you has sworn to kill the other. Do you think I would betray Dave, simply because you have a deal you think he'd like to talk over with you?

I am writing Dave tonight, warning him against you—if that's necessary, which it is not. Rather, I should warn you that he'll kill you on sight. I honestly believe that Governor Johns would pardon him if he killed you, so if I were in your shoes I would take warning.

Believe me, with all the ill will in the world, I am not sincerely yours and never will be.

CAROL McFEE

Dave stared at the note. He knew what had happened. Carol had written him and Will Usher on the same night and had put the letters in the wrong envelopes.

He thought of something then. Suppose Carol had mentioned his presence in Yellow Jacket in her other letter?

As soon as he thought of it Dave lunged for the lamp, wiping out the flame with his hand. The envelope, which had been in his lap, fluttered to the floor and planed under the chair.

And in that very instant there was a knock on the door.

Dave waited a moment and said softly, "Who is it?"

There was a throaty chuckle from the other side of the door.

"Who'd you think it would be, Davey? It's me—Will Usher."

II

DAVE SAID through the door, "I don't want trouble. Light a shuck."

"Listen a minute, Dave," Will said. "I want to talk to you."

"Drag it."

"Wait a minute." Usher's voice was urgent. "I haven't got a gun and this isn't a trap. Open the door."

Dave said softly, "I'll walk that door down and cut off your ears, Will. Here I come."

He went to the door, unlocked it, and opened it with his right hand. His gun was in his left. There was nobody there. He stepped out into the hall and looked down it, and it was empty.

He stepped back into the room again, locked the door, and lighted the lamp, a frown on his face. Carol, in her letter to him which Will Usher had received, mentioned Yellow Jacket, and Will was here. Beyond that, Will had the letter that Carol had written him, and he wanted it. He wanted the letter and he didn't know whether he could trust himself to take it from Will Usher without getting in a fight, but he decided he could if he held his temper.

He started across the room toward the door and was almost there when a knock came on the door again. He reached swiftly for the key, twisted it, flung the door open, and reached out and grabbed for Will Usher's coat lapels to yank him inside.

His hand was swifter than his recognition, for he already

was grasping the silk collar of a basque before he could stop himself. And then his his hand fell away, and he was confronting a girl who was almost as surprised as he was.

"Why—howdy, Carol," he stammered.

"Hello, Dave," Carol said softly, swiftly. "I'm coming in and close the door after me!"

She brushed past him, and Dave shut the door behind her, then turned and leaned his back against it. He saw a girl who was smaller than he was and whose thick hair was pale as his was dark. Her face, with its almost uptilted nose and its friendly mouth and deep violet-colored eyes, was too impudent to be beautiful and had too much character in it to be called pretty. Right now it was frightened, too, and Dave smiled faintly.

"You've grown up," he said.

Carol stamped her foot. "How can you joke now, Dave? Don't you know they're hunting you all over town?"

"Sure."

"You can't stay here. I'll——"

"Why not?"

"But they'll find you!"

"Not till I want them to," Dave said calmly. "Not till I've talked to you."

Carol sank down on the bed and put the flat of her palms to her temples. She shivered a little, and Dave looked at her curiously, his face impassive. He liked the blue color of the dress she was wearing, and he thought she looked nice, and he knew it wasn't because she was the first white woman he'd seen for a long time.

He said, gently for him, "What's the matter?"

Carol looked up. "I'm just thinking what an awful fool I am. First, I sent Will Usher the wrong letter, and he found out you were here. Second, I addressed your letter in your own name, so the whole town is hunting you. And now—well, Dad is with me. He's bound to find out you're here and he'll head a posse for three weeks just to hunt you down."

Dave said, "You're flustered, I reckon. You was flustered when you sent me word in Mexico. You still are. Why?"

"Dave," Carol said, "will you please go? Now? Will you please get out of town?"

"No."

"I—I sent word to you in Mexico because I needed help. You see, I didn't forget that stage trip we had together when I came home from school. I couldn't very well forget it, could I, when it was in all the newspapers in the territory that you saved me from that gang of Will Usher's kidnapers?"

"You shouldn't have told 'em who I was."

"But I thought Dad would plead with Governor Johns for your pardon! I—I didn't know they'd chase you clear out of the territory into Mexico."

"Neither did I," Dave said carelessly.

"Then when this—this trouble came up I sent for you because—well, I guess I thought you could help."

"What trouble?"

"Oh, it doesn't matter now!" Carol cried. "You can't help! All you can do is get out while you can!"

"What trouble?" Dave insisted.

"Dad's trouble. Haven't you heard that we're losing all our range on a forged deed?"

Dave scowled. "Who forged it?"

"Tate Wallace. He owns the Three Rivers Cattle Company."

The interest in Dave's eyes quickened. "Tate Wallace or Wallace Tate?"

"Tate Wallace. Why?"

"What's he look like?"

"He's a Texan. Tall, slim, over thirty, light hair and eyes, and a lazy way——"

"I know him," Dave said thinly. "How'd he do it?"

"He and his men just rode in and burned our line camps and drove our riders off and shoved the stock back. All we have now is the house. We fought, but there were too many of them. When the sheriff visited them they showed him the deed of sale from Dad. Now Dad's taking it to court, but it won't do any good."

"Why won't it?" Dave asked softly.

"They've got the fake witness to the deed—a liar named Sholto—under heavy guard. They're bringing him through here tomorrow on the way to Sabinal, where they'll take him by train to Santa Fe for the suit. We're on our way now too."

"What did you want me for?" Dave asked.

Carol blushed, but she looked him straight in the eye. "You won't like this, Dave. But you told me you were a gunman. Everybody said you were. I wanted you to come up and—and drive the Three Rivers outfit off our range."

"That's all right," Dave said tonelessly. "I would have too."

"But it's too late now! The message took so long to reach

you, and in between the deed came to light and Dad filed suit." She paused. "Now do you see? You can't help!"

Dave lounged erect from the door and walked into the middle of the room, his hands on his hips. His face was alert, still, curious.

"You think you tolled me into a trap and you're sorry," he said quietly. "Forget it. They can't take me and they can't hold me and they can't kill me, so quit worryin'. I want some questions answered."

"But——"

"Will you answer them, or do I have to go down the hall and ask your dad at the point of a gun?"

Carol stared at him, and she knew he meant it and she said quickly, "I'll answer them! Only please hurry!"

Dave grinned faintly, arrogantly, and said, "One. They must claim they paid your dad something for the land. Did they?"

"They've got a forged receipt to prove it. And they did." Dave scowled. "I don't get it."

"Last month our foreman quit, walked out. After he'd gone we found he'd deposited eight thousand dollars in the bank in Dad's name. We didn't know why. When we found that the Three Rivers outfit had shown Sheriff Beal a receipt signed by Dad for ten thousand dollars we knew where the money came from. The Three Rivers outfit had bribed Sam —our foreman—to deposit the money in Dad's name and leave, disappear. They claim, naturally, that they paid the money over to Dad and Dad gave it to Sam to deposit. They also claim Sam kept two thousand dollars of the ten thousand and jumped the country."

"Your Dad's signature," Dave said. "It's on the deed and on the receipt. What about it?"

"Dad had a fall from a horse two months ago that crushed his hand. It's still stiff. His writing isn't like it was—it's like a child's. They knew that. They could imitate it—and they did."

"And the foreman?" Dave said. "Is he gone?"

"Disappeared. He sailed for South America," Carol said briefly. She hesitated a moment, then said, "You see how hopeless it is? We're losing a range that would be a bargain at a hundred thousand dollars. But we can't win—not even with the lawyer Dad's got!"

"Who?"

"Senator Maitland, Dad's oldest friend. He's the best law-yer in the territory, Dave, but he says we haven't an even chance. And what could you do that he can't?"

Dave said, "Go to bed."

When Carol's face flushed and she came to her feet, in-dignant at his rudeness, he added, "Somebody may poke a gun through that window any minute. I don't want you hurt."

"Then you're going, Dave?"

"No."

"But——"

"Go to bed," Dave repeated.

Carol walked to the door, and Dave opened it for her. Carol paused and turned to him, a kind of hurt pride fight-ing with the friendliness in her face. "Dave, you were good to come. I didn't have any claim on your friendship. I was—well, just an acquaintance to you. But you see, you can't help. The time for fighting is over. I'm sorry you came up here. I'm sorrier about the letter. It's just—well, good-by." She put out her hand.

Dave took it. "Good night."

"Good-by."

"Good night, I said."

"But——"

Gently Dave placed his hand in the middle of her back and pushed her out the door and closed it. He leaned against it, listening. Presently he heard something like a sigh, and the sound of footsteps retreated down the hall.

He didn't leave the door, only moved to one side of it and waited. The knock he seemed certain was coming finally did. Dave said, "Walk in, Will."

The door opened, and a man walked into the room. He was a moose of a man, dressed in a black broadcloth suit that bulged at the shoulders. He had his hands raised far above his head and he didn't turn his head, only stopped in the middle of the room.

"I'll take your word for it, Will," Dave murmured. "You smell money. Put 'em down."

Will Usher let his hands sink to his sides and slowly turned around. He had the face of a Roman senator—the high, noble forehead, the wide-spaced and clean-looking blue eyes, the firm wide jaw, the well-shaped mouth, and a shock of beautiful iron-gray curls which he parted on the side. He was smiling now, and his teeth were white and even and strong. Standing there waiting for Dave to speak, he was every inch the high-born, intellectual aristocrat. But there was a flaw to his appearance, a flaw that he couldn't hide. His hands were not the long-fingered white hands of an aristocrat; they were the hands of a butcher—big, red, with thick fingers that were all approximately the same size. They were huge and hideous, stranger's hands, and even the soft buckskin gloves he affected could not hide them.

Dave said softly, "You don't mind takin' a chance, do you, Will?"

"You won't shoot me," Will Usher said confidently. "We need each other."

"The only thing I need you for is a target."

"Don't take that kidnapin' so hard, Dave. A man has to make a livin'."

"It drove me to Mexico, Will," Dave purred. "I don't love any man for that."

"That wasn't me; that was the——"

"Careful," Dave murmured.

They eyed each other a moment, and not like two dogs. It was more like two cats. In Dave Coyle's face was wary contempt, a careful, watchful disgust. In Will Usher's face, beneath the handsomeness of it, was the still fear of a man walking on dynamite.

Dave said, "Let's hear it."

"Can I sit down? This'll take time."

"No."

"All right. That McFee girl has——"

Dave held up his hand, and Usher ceased talking. Presently the sound of slow footsteps sounded in the hall. They came up to the door, paused, and there was a loud knock on the door.

Dave looked wickedly at Usher. Usher shook his head and shrugged his shoulders, denying any knowledge of who it was. Dave pointed to him, then pointed to the corner of the room against the front wall. Silently Usher tiptoed over to the corner and hugged the wall.

Dave twisted the knob and pulled the door open. He confronted a truculent-looking old man who had his hand raised to knock again.

"I heard you," Dave said arrogantly.

"Look here, young feller," the old man said. "You didn't register."

"You were out hellin' around."

"I was out——" The old man paused and peered closely at Dave. Then he licked his lips and took a step backward. "Ain't you——" he began, and his voice died. He tried again, weakly, "Ain't you Dave Coyle?"

"Yes."

For a moment the old man was confounded. He started to speak and couldn't and only stared. Then he said sharply, "You can't stay here!"

"Throw me out," Dave invited.

"Get out of here!"

"No."

The old man backed away and then raised a finger and shook it at him. "By gummy, I'll get you out!"

He turned and almost ran down the hall. Dave closed the door. Usher said dryly, "You better move quick, Dave."

Dave walked over to the bed and ripped off the blankets. He pulled off a sheet and while he was tying it to the bed-frame he said, "Take that other sheet and tie it to this one."

Usher moved swiftly too. When the two sheets were tied together Dave said, "Open the window." While Usher did, Dave shoved the bed over against it and then unrolled the two sheets out the window. To anyone entering the room it would be a case of simple escape out the window.

Dave said, "Where's your room?"

"Down the hall."

"Let's go there."

Usher led the way to it. Dave went in last and closed the door behind him and put his back to it. There was a sound of voices suddenly welling in the hall and then the heavy tramping of many feet. They pounded past the door and then stopped abruptly. Dave heard a man's voice saying, "I ain't goin' in there first. It's your job, Sheriff."

"Dave Coyle!" somebody called. "Come out of there! You're surrounded!"

No answer. Then there was a long period of silence, and suddenly a man bawled, "He's went out through the window!" Somebody shot.

Again there was a savage pounding of feet in the hall, and then it died as the crowd hit the stairs.

Dave looked at Will Usher, who was standing by the bed. "Make your deal," he said.

"That girl must have told you about——"

"She told me. What about it?"

"Don't get redheaded at this next, Dave. I'm only askin'. Do you like her? Do you want to help her?"

Dave, his gray eyes a little narrowed, said, "I want to help her, yes."

"And earn a fifty-fifty split on fifty thousand dollars?"

Dave said quietly, "Does it stink?"

"It's clean!" Usher protested. "Cleanest money I ever made!"

"It could still stink. What is it?"

"Look. The Three Rivers outfit is bringin' that witness, Sholto, through here tomorrow and takin' him to the railroad in Sabinal. Now——"

"How do you know that?"

"It's in the papers," Usher protested. "Anybody could read it."

"All right. Go on."

Usher grinned. "Well, don't you know now?"

"Sure I do. Kidnap him and let the Three Rivers outfit buy him back for fifty thousand."

Usher nodded, spread his palms, and smiled. "Simple, eh? And clean. They're a bunch of pirates. They're runnin' a pretty cagey sandy on Bruce McFee, and it's sewed up tight. But they need that witness. They're gettin' away with a hundred-and-twenty-five-thousand-dollar steal. They need Sholto, and they'll pay fifty thousand to get him back."

Dave nodded and said softly. "Why ring me in on it? Fifty thousand is more than twenty-five. Why split it?"

Usher shook his head and raised both hands, palms out. "Hunh-unh. Not me, Dave. I couldn't swing it. I'll take a fifty-fifty chance any time, and lots of times I'll take a sixty-forty chance. But I don't like these ninety-ten odds. You do."

Dave didn't say anything, only looked at Usher, and finally Usher said, "Well?"

"Got any ideas?"

"I've got a beauty. It's risky. Outside of that horse-faced Wallace and his Three Rivers crew there'll be a deputy U.S. marshal and Sheriff Beal and however many deputies he wants guardin' Sholto and the train. Now that you're in the country Beal will probably double the guard. That's the risk. Now here's the plan."

He told him, and Dave listened critically. When Usher was finished Dave said, "All right. I'll take thirty thousand; you take twenty when we get the ransom money."

"Wait a——"

"Take it or leave it."

Usher glared at him for a moment, then shrugged. "All right. It's a deal."

"Light a rag, then," Dave said coldly.

"What?"

"Get out. Vamoose. Drag it. Light a shuck. Hit the grit. Get out of here," Dave murmured.

"But this is my room! I sleep——"

Dave opened the door and stood aside. Usher glanced around the room, his handsome face sullen, picked up three cigars off the dresser, and put them in his breast pocket. He said, "You sure you know what you're goin' to do, Dave?"

"I'm goin' to kick you out of this room in about three seconds," Dave said coldly.

Usher hurried past him and went out, saying good night. Dave didn't answer him. He blew out the lamp, then lay down on the bed and stared at the ceiling.

Will Usher's plan was good as far as it went. It would get them money. But as soon as Sholto was back in Wallace's hands there was the same threat to McFee. The thing to do, of course, was to keep Sholto away from Wallace for good. But if he did that Wallace would claim that McFee and Dave Coyle were in partnership, and McFee would be prosecuted. No, he must help McFee and make it look as if he were helping only himself. And this was a start, small as it was.

He wondered, suddenly, why he had ridden six hundred miles and put a noose around his neck just to help a girl who had once ridden on a stage with him. He guessed it was because she needed him. Other women before had needed him —honky tonk girls, outlaws' women, little Mexican cantina girls—but never a girl like Carol McFee. Of course she had only wanted his gun prowess, but that was something. She was different, nice, strange, a lady. And some stubborn desire within him made him want to show her that he could be a friend to a lady too.

He went to sleep in Usher's bed, while outside in the night the sheriff's crowd was cautiously beating the alleys, looking for him.

III

SABINAL, TEN miles from Yellow Jacket, had an almost festive air today. It wasn't the kind of bright gaiety that is seen during a fiesta, when all the country people come in to drink and dance because their crops are in. It was a townsman's festivity, when hot black suits are donned, ties are worn, vest pockets stocked with cigars, and pants pockets are filled with half dollars to buy drinks. It was a politician's holiday, for wasn't Sheriff Beal and a posse bringing Sholto, the Three Rivers star witness, to the train? All the arrangements had been made at the Sabinal House to take over the dining room for the noon meal and the front suite afterward while they waited for the train to come in at three o'clock. Votes would be swapped, a lot of whisky drunk, and enough speculation on the coming court fight—McFee vs. the Three Rivers Cattle Company—to fill volumes. This was history making, for Mc-Fee had come into the country twenty years ago, a hardheaded and penniless Scot. And he had succeeded, with a born cattle-man's savvy, in building up a tidy empire, making a host of enemies and dumping along the way somewhere a trouble-some partner who had first put up the money to start them. Few people liked him, but everyone had respect for him, for his ruthlessness and his success. The Three Rivers outfit, headed by Tate Wallace, had set up shop next to McFee's range. They had fought in and out of court and in and out of three towns that bounded their range, but this was the first time it was ever intimated that it was going to be a fight to the death. Wallace claimed McFee, seeing he would be beaten, sold out to Three Rivers, and he had a deed to prove it. McFee claimed he had never signed the deed. One of them was lying. If McFee won his suit Tate Wallace would be in jail for many years. Most people hoped and thought Wallace would win it. And in that case, McFee was ruined.

It excited people, and they milled around the streets wait-ing for a sight of Beal's posse. Already two extra deputy mar-shals were lounging in the hotel, ready to swell the number of official guards offering safe conduct to the witness. The crowd was concentrated on the main street, for it was certain that Beal, good politician that he was, would give the towns-people a parade.

The back street next to the railroad track was naturally de-serted, and it was down this rutted street, around noon, that a team and wagon appeared. The team was a sorry-looking crowbait pair with their harness patched with rope. The wagon, its wheels atilt, was covered by a rotted canvas on hoops and was driven by a shabby Mexican in bib overalls. The wagon pulled up beside the railroad station, whose red paint was sun-blistered and peeled, and the Mexican dismounted. He glanced about him with some bewilderment, circled the place once, then walked up to the yawning door of the freight warehouse and took off his hat and stood there.

The men were lounging inside, one sitting on the scales and smoking a pipe, the other sitting on a box crate. Presently the man with the pipe caught sight of the Mexican and he called, "What you want, amigo?"

The Mexican smiled and said something in Spanish, and the man with the pipe said to his companion, "Come along, Joe. I don't savvy his gab."

The two men walked over to the Mexican and Joe said, "¿Como?"

The Mexican started to speak then in slow, measured tones. When he finished Joe said to the freight agent, "His father died last night. He wants us to ship the body to Socorro for him on the train."

The freight agent looked skeptical. "He does, does he? Tell him it costs money for that."

Joe told the Mexican; the Mexican answered, and Joe told the agent, "He says he's got money."

"I bet he ain't got enough for that. Tell him it will be twenty-four dollars." A sudden pity crossed the agent's face. "Ask him why he doesn't bury him here and save the money."

Joe talked again. Presently he told the agent, "He says he's got twenty-five dollars. He says all the Ochoas since DeVargas have been buried at Socorro, and that's their home. I reckon he just wants to do it."

"All right," the agent said gently. "I hate to take his money, though."

The Mexican spoke again and Joe translated. "He wants to know if it will go fast."

"Tell him express, as fast as we can send it."

The three of them went out to the wagon then. A plain pine box, a cross burned in its top, rested in the wagon bed, and when the two men saw it they removed their hats. The three of them stumbled up the platform with the box and into the freight warehouse, where it was deposited in an empty corner.

They went up to the office; the Mexican paid and left. The agent, watching his stooped figure disappear, shook his head and said, "Think of it, Joe. That poor old jasper has worked fifteen years savin' this money, and now he spends it all to get the old man back to his buryin' place."

"It's tough," Joe agreed.

A little before noon Sheriff Beal's posse arrived. At first glance it seemed a well-equipped army, with everyone carrying rifles and side arms. Tate Wallace, the Three Rivers foreman, was a shrewd man, and he knew that in putting up a howl for protection of his witness he was playing to Sheriff Beal's vanity. Beal had been more than glad to demonstrate that no witness in his county could come to harm.

Bruce McFee, from the upper-story room of the Sabinal House which he had taken in order to have some place for his daughter to rest after the ride from Yellow Jacket, looked down on Sheriff Beal's entry.

Carol, watching him from the bed, saw his face settled into grim lines. It was a rugged, craggy, over-proud face, the face of a domineering man just in his prime. There was bigotry and hardness in his eyes, too, and a kind of simmering rage that had been there since this affair. He affected the plain black suit and expensive boots of a prosperous cattleman, but it had been his boast once that he could top any horse or rope any steer that wore his brand. The trouble was, people said, he rode and hog-tied men with the same ruthless manner. And they had seen many instances to back up this belief. There was, for instance, the reward he slapped on Dave Coyle for saving his daughter from Will Usher's wild bunch. Also, there was that business about his old partner. Lacey Thornton. When Thornton and McFee, after a decade of killing work, had finally begun to make money, Thornton began to drink. Not much for that time and that day, but enough. Bruce McFee warned him, and when the warning wasn't taken he kicked him out of the partnership. Thornton claimed, in public and out, that McFee got him drunk and had him sign the release—a release which left Thornton very little money. McFee never bothered to answer him. His stocky body, overlaid now with a little fat, was somehow indomitable-looking. His right hand, which he favored since the fall, hung stiffly at the seam of his trousers, and the fingers twitched now with anger as he looked down at the street. His face was stiff with a cold, hating anger.

It was this anger that Carol saw now, and she said, "You knew it was going to happen, Dad. Don't get mad again."

Her father turned to her and pointed a stubby finger at the street. "But, dammit, don't you see what kind of a cheap insult it is? That damned play actin' out there, it's tellin' the whole world that I'd kill Sholto if I got a chance!"

"Wouldn't you?" Carol asked.

McFee's face got red and he started to speak. Then his eyes became reflective for a moment, and presently he smiled. "Why, yes, I reckon I would, the lyin', robbin', perjurin' tinhorn. I hadn't thought of that."

There was a knock on the door, and Carol went over to open it. She stepped aside to let in Senator Maitland, McFee's lawyer. He smiled at Carol and shook hands with McFee. He was an almost bald man, stocky as McFee, with the kindly and benign face of an overworked country doctor. His movements were deliberate, his speech slow, but under his almost bumbling and pompous demeanor was hidden the keenest legal brain in the territory. He wore a claw-hammer coat, white ruffled shirt, and black string tie, the indispensable uniform of the politician. His eyes were almost hidden in their deep sockets behind hooded lids. There was a simple air of honesty about him that won any man, and he had remained poor in the service of the people of the territory.

"Well, Sheriff Beal is playing it the politician's way, Bruce," he murmured. "See the parade?"

"I'm licked before I start, with that kind of stuff," McFee growled.

"Oh, I wouldn't say that," Maitland murmured. He put his arm around Carol and gave her a fatherly hug. "Can't you cheer him up, girl?"

Carol smiled sadly. "I'm afraid there's not much to be cheerful about."

Maitland shook his head. "That's a fact." He sighed. "Well, we aren't beaten yet. There are a few tricks in court I know that will have them guessing." He looked at McFee's gloomy countenance and smiled. "You might as well get ready for another jolt."

McFee looked puzzled, and Maitland went on, "Lacey Thornton is downstairs waiting for an interview with you. He insists that he doesn't want a quarrel but only wants an interview with you for that newspaper of his. He says the *Clarion* will print lies if it doesn't get the truth, so he wants you to give him the truth."

"Since when did he ever give me justice in the *Clarion?*" McFee growled. "Tell him I'll see him in hell first."

Maitland shook his head. "You'll need all the public support you can get, Bruce. You can't keep the habit of a top dog any more. Can't afford it. Go down there and hold your temper and tell him the truth."

"Do I have to?"

Maitland smiled gently. "Well, it's your lawyer's advice."

The three of them went downstairs, but not until after Maitland had taken the precaution of removing McFee's gun from the holster and putting it on the dresser.

The lobby was cleared of people, most of whom had stepped out into the street to watch Beal's parade. Only one man remained, and he rose as he saw the three of them coming down the stairs. Lacey Thornton, editor of the Sabinal *Clarion*, was a little terrier of a man, small, wiry, nervous, with a face that had a seasoned whisky flush in its wizened monkey's features. Ten feet from him his aura of good bourbon whisky was unmistakable. He'd been drinking today, Carol could see, as he came up to them.

He touched his hat to her, and McFee said coldly to his ex-partner, "You wanted to interview me?"

"That's right," Thornton said impudently. "How do you feel? Wait until I get my notebook." He drew out a sheaf of note paper, licked a pencil, and said again, "How do you feel?"

"Confident," McFee said coldly.

"He feels confident," Thornton murmured dryly as he wrote. Then he looked up and said, "Has your blood pressure increased?"

Maitland said gently, "There'll be no baiting, Lacey. An interview, yes, but no persecution."

Thornton made a mock bow to Maitland and said, "Only doin' my duty, Senator." To McFee he said, "How does it feel to hold the dirty end of the stick for once, Mr. McFee?"

"Let's go," McFee said curtly to Maitland.

"Oh, but my interview!" Lacey protested mockingly. "Think of the three hundred and ten readers of the *Clarion*, Mr. McFee. All of them hope you'll lose every dollar you've ever made, but they want to know how you're takin' it. What'll I tell them?"

"Anything you damn well please!" McFee shouted.

Lacey murmured as he wrote, "He's takin' it like a bear with a trap on each foot." He put his notes away and grinned and said, "Well, that covers it, I reckon—except for an expression of sympathy from the *Clarion*."

Carol said, "Sympathy?"

"Yes, miss," Lacey drawled. "Sympathy. The *Clarion* extends sympathy to Mr. McFee," he said mockingly. "We are all sorry, terribly sorry, that my esteemed ex-partner is going to lose his money. We all hoped he'd lose his life instead."

With a growl of rage McFee started for Thornton. Maitland grabbed his arms and held him. Lacey Thornton didn't move. He only stood there, the light of the devil in his eyes.

"Man alive," he murmured. "I'd just as soon die next week. I've lived to see everything in this life I wanted to see." He snapped his fingers in McFee's face. "When you're broke come around to the *Clarion* and I'll give you two bits for a drink. And I hope it'll choke you."

He laughed and walked into the dining room, not even looking back.

At that moment the lobby door swung open, and Tate Wallace stepped inside. When he saw McFee he stopped dead.

He was a tall man, a pale-haired, bleach-eyed Texan with a long bony face and the easy long-legged grace and spare movements of a man who has learned to be quick and swift-moving only in emergencies.

He paused in mid-stride as he saw the three of them, and then he turned and called over his shoulder, "Hide Sholto, boys. Here's McFee!"

There was a small commotion outside the door, and Beal stepped through, his gun drawn. He had the air of a courteous watchdog as he gallantly doffed his hat to Carol and pointed the gun at them with the other hand.

McFee spat contemptuously in Wallace's direction and stalked on through the lobby into the dining room, Maitland, with Carol, following. There was a gleam of inner amusement in Wallace's eye as they retreated, and then it vanished and his face was sober as he turned to Beal. "Much obliged, Sheriff. He looked pretty salty."

"Don't you worry none, Tate. We'll take care of you," Beal said in his professionally hearty voice.

Once inside the dining room McFee, Carol, and Senator Maitland took a table for three by the window and ordered their meal. Before it was served the posse filed into the dining room and sat at the long table provided for them in the center of the room. Sholto was ostentatiously seated in a chair where he was hidden, save for his head, by the bodies of the posse members.

Carol and McFee, since this was the first time they had seen the man who was supposed to have witnessed the signing of the famous deed, stared at him. It was this man who held their fate in his hands, for without him to swear he had witnessed the transaction, Maitland could prove that any child could forge McFee's signature. Carol's first thought was that he looked angry. He was thin, gaunt-cheeked, burned to a saddle color except for his forehead, which had a band of lighter flesh beneath the hairline where his hat had shaded him. Against her will she liked his face. It was melancholy, reserved, almost austere, and for one fleeting moment Carol wondered if her father had signed the deed and forgotten it. This man Sholto didn't look like a professional liar.

Sheriff Beal sat on Sholto's right, and he kept his eyes on McFee. The old boy wouldn't give him any trouble, he knew, but it wouldn't hurt to pretend he would. He was still watching McFee and Maitland, almost glaring at them, when a man stepped in between his chair and Tate Wallace's, who was seated on his right. It was Ernie See, his plain face preoccupied.

"Harve, I just ran into somethin' funny. You remember old man Badey's horse that was reported stole out of the feed corral this morning in Yellow Jacket?"

Beal nodded, knowing in his bones what was coming.

"Well, I just seen him in the corral down the street."

He and Beal looked at each other a long quiet moment, and then Tate Wallace, who had overheard Ernie, said, "Here? In Sabinal?"

Again Ernie nodded. Wallace put it into words, drawling angrily, "Well, Sheriff, it only goes to prove what I been tryin' to tell you. Box 73 at Wagon Mound is Bruce McFee's box. McFee and Dave Coyle was in Yellow Jacket last night. Dave Coyle never owned a horse in his life. He steals them whenever he wants to move. A horse is stole in Yellow Jacket this mornin' and it turns up in Sabinal this noon."

Sheriff Beal murmured, "Goddlemighty," and groaned.

Tate Wallace shoved his chair back and stood up and walked around to the table to face McFee. Sheriff Beal was at his heels, watching him anxiously.

"So you've throwed in with an outlaw now, have you, McFee?" Wallace demanded.

McFee's surprise was greater than his anger as he came to his feet. "What outlaw?"

"Dave Coyle. He's in town."

"What's that got to do with me?"

"You wrote him to meet you in Yellow Jacket!" Wallace said hotly. "You talked to him last night!"

Maitland said sternly, "Watch your language, Wallace, or I'll slap a libel suit on you to boot!"

McFee didn't even hear his lawyer. He said angrily to Wallace, "You're a liar on two counts!" His napkin was balled up in his fist.

"Gentlemen, gentlemen," Senator Maitland said. "Remember where we are."

"I'm tellin' you somethin', McFee," Wallace said savagely. "You're travelin' on the same train as we are this afternoon! We're takin' Sholto in the baggage car! And if I lay eyes on you or Coyle in that baggage car I'll gun you like the damn double-crossin' dog you are!"

McFee hit him then. He moved quickly, hotly, and there was a lot of solid weight behind the blow. Wallace cakewalked backward off balance until he was brought up against a chair, and then he sat down abruptly on the floor. For a half second he was immobile, and then his hand streaked for his gun. Sheriff Beal dived at him, and so did the man in the chair beside him. They caught him just as the gun was clearing leather, and there was a swift moment of grunting and wrestling, and finally Beal rose with the gun.

Wallace came swiftly to his feet. His face was pale with anger, and little lights danced wickedly in his bleached eyes. There was no inner amusement in them this time as he glared at McFee. His rawhiding had turned on him, and he didn't like it. He said softly, "I'll ruin you for that, McFee! And if I don't ruin you I'll kill you!"

He turned and stalked out of the dining room, and Beal followed him out. The members of the Three Rivers crew closest to their boss got up and followed Beal.

McFee, under the disturbed gaze of Carol and Maitland, who had said nothing during the fight, sat down and picked up his fork. He saw Lacey Thornton writing industriously at another table. He stabbed at some food and then slammed the fork down. He was murdering-mad, and there was no use trying to hide it.

"Eat, Papa," Carol said weakly.

"Eat, hell!" McFee roared. "I'm goin' up and get a gun and kill that curly wolf!"

The whole dining room heard him. He got out of his chair so abruptly that he tipped over the water pitcher and stalked out of the dining room; Carol and Maitland, a worried look on his face, followed him up the stairs. Already a pair of deputy marshals stood undecided in the door to the dining room, watching them. Lacey Thornton stood beside them, laughing.

In the room Carol grabbed hold of her father's shirt and beat his chest with her small fists. Maitland stood between McFee and the gun on the dresser.

"Dad! Dad! They'll murder you!" Carol cried. "Think a minute! Think!"

"I've thought too long!" McFee growled. "I'm goin' to get it over with."

"And what will happen to Carol, Bruce?" Maitland said gently. "Think of that, if you won't about killing a man."

It was that question that hauled McFee up. He stared at Maitland like a man coming out of a trance, but there was still fight in him.

"Dammit, the gall of that damn pirate!" he roared. "Me, throwin' in with that cutthroat of a Dave Coyle when I put up three thousand for his dead-or-alive reward! And now I'm supposed to be workin' for him."

"I know, I know," Maitland said gently.

McFee was shouting now, and Carol knew that when he did that the worst was over. Now all she had to say was "Yes, Papa," to everything he said, and he'd calm down eventually. He stalked to the window now and glared out as if he were trying to blacken the fall sun.

Senator Maitland looked at her, smiled faintly, and shook his head. Carol smiled back weakly. She was thinking of Wallace's accusation. Did they know she had talked to Dave Coyle last night? If her father found that out he would disown her.

If Dave would only keep out of it! He wouldn't, he couldn't, butt in now, after what she'd told him last night. But behind that thought was a creeping fear that he would. He was in town, because just before Wallace had come over to their table she had seen the expression on Sheriff Beal's face.

"O Lord," she prayed, "get us out of here without Dave Coyle doing anything."

The celebration had died like a wet firecracker. In the hotel and on the street the word went around that Dave Coyle was in town. Nobody knew where he was, but the straight of it was that he was helping McFee. And since the best way to help McFee was to kill Sholto everybody was uneasy. And Beal, who had counted on passing out cigars and drinks and reminding people what a good sheriff they had, was most uneasy of all.

He proclaimed an immediate search of the hotel. He put a

guard at McFee's door and one at Wallace's door. In Sholto's room he put a round dozen of his most trusted men. As for himself, he paced the lobby among the silent members of his posse. They were all recalling stories of Dave Coyle—how the very morning after the night the U.S. commissioner had raised the reward ante on him from three thousand to five thousand dollars Dave Coyle had begged a handout breakfast from the commissioner's cook. While the commissioner ate in the dining room with his wife Dave Coyle had eaten at the kitchen table. Finished, he had thanked the cook, walked into the dining room and thanked the commissioner and his wife, and had gone out the front door.

It was stories like that worried a man and made him jumpy. The hours from one till three were the tough ones. If he could weather them, Sheriff Beal thought, he would be safe, for Sholto would be on the train then. And nothing short of dynamiting a bridge would keep Sholto from reaching Santa Fe.

At two-thirty he sent a man down to see if the train was on time and with orders that it wasn't to leave until his party had boarded it. At ten minutes to three McFee, Carol, and Maitland came down the stairs, paid their bill in silence, and walked out. At five minutes to three, when he heard the train whistle, Beal sent word up to Wallace and Sholto.

The best plan was, he reflected, to put Sholto in the middle of the whole mob of men and walk down to the station, keeping an eye on second-story windows. They left the hotel about three and started the block's walk down to the tracks, and every man there had a gun in his hand, and every second-story window was suspect.

The crowd on the station platform was cleared off ahead of time so that the platform was empty except for the freight agent and his helper and the baggage truck. One truck, the contents of which were to be loaded, stood off to one side, while the other truck was being loaded at the open door of the baggage car. Beal glanced cursorily at the car, then stationed his men at six-foot intervals along the station platform, facing the crowd of townspeople gaping at the whole business. The unloading was finished, and the loading began.

The coffin was the biggest piece of freight on the truck. The black cross burned into its top with a hot iron and the shape of it told the curious what it was, although there were few curious about it now. The crowd was nervous, and there was no talk. If the break came it would come now. The coffin was taken in and placed on the floor in a corner of the seventh car. The rest of the freight and mail was loaded swiftly, and then Sholto, who had been standing in a group inside the warehouse, was hustled out and into the car. Twenty picked men surrounded him and followed him into the baggage car. Sheriff Beal stepped in last. He waved to the train crew, smiled at the crowd outside, and closed the door. The train pulled out, and back in the coach Carol McFee drew the first easy breath in three hours.

Inside the baggage car Beal sat down on the nearest piece of freight and mopped his face with a handkerchief. Nobody would ever know what a relief it was to get that door closed and the train moving. He said to Tate Wallace, "Are those doors locked?"

Tate grinned. "Both the end doors and the side doors. You ain't nervous, are you, Beal?"

"I am," Beal said. "I'll be nervous until we get over the grade and out of Yellow Jacket County."

Wallace sneered. "Dave Coyle may take chances, but not them kind of chances. The only way he could stop us now is by blowin' up the train."

"He won't do that," Ernie See said dryly. "McFee's on the train."

Beal shook his head doubtfully and looked at Sholto, who was sitting with his back to the mail racks, where the clerks were sorting out the mail. The other men were scattered in the back end of the car, their rifles leaned against the wall. If Beal was scared they were not, for they were talking and joking among themselves, conversing with the two deputy marshals.

Beal said to Sholto, "You never come closer to havin' a bullet in your back."

Sholto's face didn't change, didn't show any signs of fear. He said quietly, "I never heard of Dave Coyle shootin' a man in the back. I don't believe it."

Tate said meagerly, "Nobody's askin' you to believe it, Jim. You just listen."

Sholto looked up at Wallace, and for a moment a quiet, wicked hatred crept into his eyes. Than it died and he said, "Yes sir, Mr. Wallace."

Once out of Sabinal the train started the pull up the long grade of the high ridges that spread in a series of half circles around Sabinal to the north. The steady labored breathing of the locomotive could be heard distinctly, and the grade slowed the train's speed. The whole crew had relaxed now and were lounging about the car.

Somebody said, "I got some cards," and immediately a poker game started on the floor of the car. It was only a matter of minutes before a half dozen of them, seated in a circle on the floor of the car, were playing. The others, with the danger past, relaxed and stood or squatted behind them and watched the progress of the initial hand of stud.

Sheriff Beal and Sholto both stood up and watched. The mail clerks, their backs to the game, stuck to their business of sorting out the mail.

One of the deputy marshals, with aces back to back, turned over his hole card, grinned, and said, "My pot, boys."

At the same instant Sheriff Beal felt something hard bore into his spine, and a soft voice murmured, "Wrong, boys. It's my pot."

IV

EVERY MAN in the baggage car looked up then. Standing behind and to one side of Sheriff Beal and holding a gun in the Sheriff's back, stood Dave Coyle. There was a cold, jeering light in his eyes. His twisted smile was faint. He looked utterly relaxed and careless, but in his eyes was that unblinking watchfulness that kept every man there immobile.

Dave said, "Sholto, step back beside me." As he spoke he slipped the sheriff's gun out of its holster, cocked it, and took a step backward. Sholto, hands half raised, stepped back beside Dave. Slowly a deputy marshal put his hands on the floor in readiness to push himself up.

"Quit it," Dave said mildly. The man sank down on the floor again.

Dave said, "Sheriff, gather up those guns. Don't miss any, or I'm liable to get mad. Take an empty mail sack."

Beal, his face ashen, took one of the empty mail sacks on the rack and started collecting the guns. The only sound in the car was the clackety-clack of the wheels. Most of these men, for the first time, were beholding Dave Coyle in the flesh, and they did not like what they saw. He stood there, a sneer on his face, cocky, arrogant, his eyes jeering.

His glance finally settled on Wallace, who was watching

him warily. They observed each other a long moment, and then Dave said, "You've come a long ways since I saw you last."

Wallace frowned in puzzlement. "I don't get it," he said carefully.

Dave said, "You get it, all right. Two years ago in Dodge you were a tinhorn named Wallace Tate—a big wind from Texas. What's your name now?"

Tate Wallace's long face turned a shade darker. He said, "Tate Wallace."

"Well, well," Dave sneered.

All the men in the car now were watching Dave and Wallace. Dave said gently, "And you boss the Three Rivers outfit?"

"That's right."

"You come a long ways for a tinhorn," Dave said. "Just about as far as you're goin' to come too."

Ernie See grinned, and Dave looked at him. "What's your trouble?"

"You," Ernie said.

Beal stopped shoving guns into the mail sack long enough to look up and say to Ernie, "Be careful, you damn fool!"

Dave observed Ernie closely. He saw a plain-looking, pleasant-faced young man with outrage in his brown eyes and a stubborn set to his mouth. "Go ahead," he said softly.

Ernie said doggedly, "Who do you think you are? You think just because a little killer like you has throwed in with McFee that the law is goin' to fold up in this country?"

There was a moment's utter silence. Half the men there expected to hear a gun go off, and Ernie See would have paid for his rashness.

Dave only sneered. "You simple jug head. Would I help a stuffed Stetson like McFee that's put a price on my head?"

"Then what are you doin' now?" Ernie said hotly.

Dave glanced at Wallace and said coldly, "You tell him."

"I don't know," Wallace said.

"If you want Sholto back, buy him back," Dave sneered. He looked at Ernie. "That suit you?"

Ernie didn't say anything. Beal was finished gathering up the guns now. Dave tilted his head toward the door. "Throw 'em out. Leave the door open."

Beal pulled the big door back and dumped the sack of guns out the door, then stepped back among the others. Dave waited a moment, his head cocked as if listening to something. The train was gradually picking up speed now, and he knew they were on top of the grade, soon to start the long coast down the other side.

He said curtly to Sholto: "Stand in that door. When you see the horses, jump."

There was a moment of waiting, during which Sholto peered out the door up the tracks.

Ernie See suddenly blurted out, "How'd you get in here, Coyle?"

"I got mailed in a letter," Dave jeered.

There was another moment's wait, and then Sholto said, "I see them."

"Jump."

Sholto did, and then Dave walked over to the door. The sitting men came to their feet then, and Dave knew they were aching to rush him.

"Anybody feel froggy?" he taunted.

Ernie See said hotly, "You hurt Sholto, and we'll hang you by your thumbs, Coyle!"

"Boo!" Dave sneered. He looked at Tate Wallace. "Get some cash on hand for me."

Then he leaped through the open door. He hit soft sand, fell, rolled over and over, and came to his feet about ten yards from the train. The coach trailed past, and he saw Carol McFee at the window. She saw him, and for one instant there was surprise and fright on her face. Dave was too wise to wave at her, for other people were watching. He only smiled faintly, and then the coach rattled past.

He looked down the right of way and saw Sholto trudging toward him. The train ran on down the grade, gathering momentum each hundred yards. It would take a good five miles before it reached the bottom of the grade and could stop, and even then the posse would be without guns or horses.

Sholto came up to him. Dave stood there, hands on hips, observing the man whose perjury was going to ruin Carol McFee and her father. His inspection of him on the train had only been cursory, but he had been surprised then. He was even more surprised as he regarded him now. He had expected to find a shifty-eyed rat who would come crawling to him for mercy. But Sholto looked like a leaned-down and broke puncher. His gaze didn't falter as he came to halt in front of Dave.

Dave said dryly, "Ain't you goin' to thank me?"

"No," Sholto said quietly.

"That's funny," Dave drawled. "From that coffin back there

on the train you didn't sound like you liked Wallace much."

Sholto said nothing, and Dave scowled. "Want to ride off alone?" he asked presently.

Sholto shrugged. "Suit yourself."

"Where'll you go if I turn you loose?"

"Back to Wallace."

Dave, frowning faintly, jerked his head toward the horses. "Well, you're not ridin' off alone."

Dave walked a little behind him, frowning faintly, trying to figure out this man. He didn't look like a crook; and a moment ago Dave would have bet that Sholto was glad to be away from Wallace. But there was a spiritless resignation in the man now that had Dave troubled.

When they were almost up to the two horses tied at the edge of the cedar scrub Will Usher rode into the clearing and waited for them.

He was smiling broadly as they came up. "Have any trouble?"

"No," Dave said. "Did you stay hid?"

Usher laughed and eyed Sholto hungrily. "Trust me. I've got to find Wallace and collect the cash, don't I?"

"Go do it," Dave ordered.

Usher pulled his horse around and called over his shoulder, "I'll be at the line camp in two days."

Dave didn't even answer. He took the nearest horse, stepped into the saddle, and regarded Sholto. "I don't savvy just how slippery you are yet, Sholto. Suppose you go lead off." He nodded toward the near-blue bulk of the Corazon range to the west. "We're goin' over there. Keep to the rocky country and the streams and try to cover your sign."

Sholto led off without a word, and Dave rode behind, watching him. He had taken Carol McFee's story of the forged deed in utter good faith, but now he knew a moment of doubt. This man wasn't a crook, yet he seemed eager to testify against McFee. It almost looked as if Sholto had really witnessed McFee's signature and was only interested in seeing justice done. Dave put that out of his mind and observed the man's actions, his clothes, his mannerisms. He could tell from the way Sholto took advantage of the country that he had either been a lawman or an outlaw. He was smart at hiding his sign, and fast at it too. They continued toward the Corazon the rest of the afternoon, and when dusk finally came, when they were crossing a narrow stream, Dave called a halt.

They dismounted, unloosed the cinches, and let their horses

drink. Then Dave brought out some jerky and cold biscuits that Will Usher had provided in the saddle-bags, and they wolfed down their supper, squatting by the narrow stream. Finished, Dave took out a sack of tobacco and handed it to Sholto. "Smoke?"

Sholto looked surprised, took the tobacco, and rolled a cigarette. Dave waited until he inhaled, and, observing the deep luxurious mouthful of smoke the man dragged into his lungs, Dave said abruptly, "So Wallace ain't even goin' to pay you for lyin' for him."

Sholto looked at him coolly, and before he could speak Dave said, "Don't bother to lie. I know McFee never signed the deed. But I didn't figure any man was sucker enough to stick his head out for nothin', like you're doin'."

He could see Sholto's face turn darker in the dusk, and he knew the taunt had struck home. But Sholto kept silent.

Dave said abruptly, "How's your wife?"

Sholto started so that he dropped the cigarette from his fingers. He picked it up and slowly raised his head to look at Dave.

"I'm not married."

"You're a liar," Dave said flatly. "You like tobacco, but you don't carry it. I know the pants you're wearin' are two sizes too big for you, so they was given to you. I see your boots are rotten. You're broke. And if you're broke it's because Wallace ain't payin' you to lie. And if he ain't payin' you it's because he's got somethin' on you. And if he had somethin' on you and was holdin' you a prisoner you'd of been beggin' me the last four hours to let you loose. You didn't. That's because you're leavin' someone—a wife, mother, or a kid—where Wallace can get back at them if you duck out." He added coldly, "How do you like that?"

Sholto was trembling a little now, but he said steadily enough, "It's your story." He looked closely at Dave. "Besides, what do you care? You ain't helpin' McFee, you said. You're just after money."

Dave said, "I don't love Wallace. Neither do you."

Sholto looked away. "You'll get nothin' from me."

But Dave had got most of what he wanted. He was sure now that Sholto was being blackmailed by Wallace into perjury.

They set out again in the falling dusk, and this time Dave led the way. The Corazons were not really a range but two heavily timbered mountains. With their far-reaching foothills, their rough timbered slopes, and their rocky shoulders, they bulked as large as many ranges. Their two peaks, rounded and regular and matched, would have brought the name Squaw Mountains or Sugarloaf from a Yankee frontiersman seeing them for the first time. But a Spaniard had seen them first, coming on them in late afternoon when the heeled-over sun brought out every detail of the canyons. And from the flats, far out beyond Sabinal, the twin rounded peaks had seemed to be shaped like the top of a heart. The sun had touched the long slope of the canyons that met at a point in the foothills, and these slopes, taken with the peaks, had carried out the illusion of the heart. So he had named them the Corazon, the Heart.

It was for the point of this heart that Dave headed in the darkness, keeping to the streams which branched out from it. They climbed, hour after hour, the land lifting away from the foothills into the timber and the stream growing smaller.

Finally, long after midnight, they came to the mountain meadow that Dave was looking for. It was an old line camp, abandoned these weeks since the herds had been driven down for fall roundup. In a short time the snows would be here, but now it would be empty. Dave knew these things because he had to, because it was knowledge like this that let him live and camps like this that housed him.

They crossed the long meadow in dry grass knee deep to horses and pulled up in front of the line shack. It was dark, the door closed. Sholto offsaddled in silence and staked out their horses while Dave went behind the shack and picked up some lengths of wood. He came around, kicked the door open, and remembering where the stove was from the last visit, headed toward it in the dark.

He found it, laid the fire, found a match, and wiped it alight on his trousers.

He touched it to the shavings and watched them begin to burn. Sholto came in behind him and stopped. Then Sholto said, "Dave."

He said it in a way that held a warning. Dave whirled, and then his down-sweeping hand was arrested.

There, facing him, gun drawn, five other men backing him with drawn guns, was Will Usher.

"Well, Davey my lad," Usher drawled, "you did the job for me, all right."

V

DAVE LOOKED at him one brief second, and then his still face, its lips curled in contempt, settled into anger. "Put that thing down," he said softly.

Will Usher laughed. "I'm no woman, Dave. You move so much as a finger and we'll blow you through that wall."

He meant it, Dave saw. After lighting a candle on the table by Sholto, Usher skirted Sholto and edged closer to Dave, careful to keep himself out of the line of fire of his men.

For one desperate second Dave was tempted to make his play. But the odds were too great, and Will Usher knew it.

Usher reached out, slipped Dave's gun from its holster, then backed against the wall. He was smiling, his face handsome.

"So this is the pay-off," he gibed gently. "Wild Davey Coyle, the man who couldn't be caught." He laughed softly. "A sucker's trap. It was so plain you didn't see it, did you?"

Dave sneered, turning his cold eyes on Usher. "Take Sholto and get out of here before I get mad."

Usher only grinned, and Dave didn't like it. "And get only fifty thousand, when I could get fifty-seven thousand?" he asked gently.

For a moment Dave was puzzled, and then it came to him. Usher was going to collect fifty thousand ransom for Sholto. The seven thousand would be the reward money on him— Dave Coyle, wanted, dead or alive.

Usher saw that thought sink into Dave's awareness, and he smiled again. "So you were goin' to cut off my ears last night, Davey," he drawled. "I'll cut off your ears tonight. That's how I'll collect my bounty."

He looked at Dave. Dave said, "Will, I thought you were smarter than that."

"Than what?"

"Than to try and kill me. Better men than you have tried."

Usher's face flushed, and his gun, which had been sagging a little, came up again. "All I got to do is pull the trigger."

Dave shook his head. His hands were on his hips, his face arrogant, his feet widespread.

"Sure it is. But you won't do it now."

"Why won't I?"

"Because you'll want to rub it in first. You'll want to see me beg. You'll want to see me sweat and start to shake. That right?"

For a split second he wasn't sure whether Usher would pull the trigger or not. And then Usher said softly, "That's right, Davey boy. Maybe you better start beggin' now."

Dave had not had time to put the lid of the stove on, and now the fire was burning brightly, sending clouds of smoke into the room. Before he could answer Usher, Dave began to cough. He turned slowly, so that Usher would not be alarmed, and shoved the stove lid over the flames. But he still had a spasm of coughing, for he had been standing almost over the stove. Presently he ceased, and Usher smiled. "Ready to beg, Davey?"

Dave shook his head and said hoarsely, his eyes watering, "I got a proposition to make to you, Will. But give me a drink of water first."

Usher said, "Get him a drink, Sholto, from that bucket in the corner," without looking at Sholto, and then he sneered, "That's more like it, Davey. Beginnin' to crawfish, eh?"

Dave didn't answer, only coughed. Sholto got a cup of water, broke through the five men blocking the door, and came up to Dave, holding out the cup, Dave's left hand was already extended to receive the cup, his other hand at his mouth smothering the cough.

Just as he was about to take the cup he reached out, yanked Sholto to him, and at the same time whirled him. Usher's gun came up, and then it was too late.

Dave had pulled Sholto half around and now had his arms around him and pulled against his body so that Sholto shielded him.

Dave jeered, "Don't shoot your fifty thousand dollars, Will."

Usher hesitated, and so did the other men. To kill Dave they would have had to shoot Sholto too.

And in that second Dave acted. He put his back to the side wall and started moving along it toward the door, Sholto in front of him. He had traveled perhaps eight feet when Usher came to his senses. "Rush him, boys, he hasn't got a gun!" And he followed his own advice.

Dave pushed out from the wall with one leg and hurled Sholto toward the advancing men. And in the same movement he kicked the table, which tipped over the bottle with the candle and extinguished it. He let go of Sholto, hearing him collide with Usher, and threw himself at the feet of the others. He mowed one man down in the darkness, and the man shot. He rolled on, came to his feet, and dived for the door, tripping

over the sill. But he lit in the grass this time, rolled, came to
his feet, and ran in the darkness toward the meadow where
he had left his horse.

There was tumult in the cabin, and everyone was afraid to
shoot. He heard Usher cursing wildly, and then a voice bawled,
"There he goes! Through the meadow!" There was a scattering
of shots around him, and Dave dropped into the high grass
and crawled away through it from the spot where he fell. But
it was slow and exhausting work.

They had him now. He could hear Usher's voice yelling,
"Surround him!"

In the darkness a man's figure standing in the yellow grass
made a blob of black against a lighter background. He'd forgotten that. If he stood up he'd be a target for the six of them.

He lay there, breathing softly, wondering what he could
do. If they started to move in on him he might overpower one
man and get a gun.

But Usher had seen that, too, and now he was yelling,
"Don't move in on him! Stay where you are!"

Dave poked his forehead above the grass. He could see them
now. They were in a circle around him, a circle perhaps forty
yards in diameter.

Suddenly a match flared in the direction from which Will
Usher's voice came. The light died and then flared up again,
and it was bigger this time. The flame grew, and suddenly
Dave understood. Will was going to burn him out, set the
grass on fire. There was just enough of a ground breeze riding
off the peaks to fan the dry grass into flames, and Dave knew
that once it was started it would blaze with the heat of a blacksmith's forge.

"Shoot anything that moves!" Usher shouted, and then he
started out in the wake of the flames. They laid in a long line
now that was spreading. It didn't matter to Usher if he set a
forest on fire, just so he caught Dave.

For one panicked moment Dave wondered what to do.
Again he looked up, and now he counted the men. There were
seven of them, spaced at regular intervals around him, the
light from the fire picking them out. He sank down again,
cursing—and then something struck him.

Usher had six men, counting himself! He had counted seven.
That meant that Sholto was guarding too! Dave forced himself
to think back to what had happened in the shack. Sholto
hadn't struggled when he'd been forced to make a shield for

Dave. And it seemed to Dave that he had willingly smashed into Usher, upsetting his aim.

It was worth a try. And it was his only chance.

Again he raised up, studying these men's figures. They had the light in their eyes now and couldn't see him so well. He saw Sholto, off to one side, toward the middle of the meadow.

Dave ducked down and set off in the heavy grass on his hands and knees toward Sholto. A panicked family of field mice ran over his hands, oblivious to anything but the fire that was chasing them. Dave could hear it crackle behind him and knew that it was burning on a wide front and was fanned by the wind.

He paused and looked up again presently, and he saw Sholto twenty feet ahead of him, knee deep in the grass. The light touched up the man's face, and again Dave was reassured. This wasn't a killer's face.

He crawled on, and now he could see Sholto watching the grass that he was disturbing. And then he looked away, and Dave's heart leaped. He headed straight for him, and still Sholto was looking out toward the fire. Dave passed within inches of him, and still Sholto didn't look at him.

Dave stopped long enough to whisper, "Did they leave a gun in the shack?"

"No," Sholto whispered.

Dave vanished then. Usher, following the fire, was shouting instructions for them to watch closely. And Dave, traveling as fast as he could, headed for the nearest peninsula of timber that sloped down into the meadow.

In another two minutes he had achieved it, and he put the point of land between him and the fire, then disappeared into the timber.

Panting, he looked back at the scene. The circle of men still held, although the grass fire had eaten more than half-way through it. Those six men stood there with their guns drawn, waiting to collect their bounty on him. A sheepishness welled up in Dave as he looked at it. He'd been a sucker, just like Will had said.

He'd forgotten that Will traveled with a wild bunch, headed it, and that this was the sort of gall that needed men to back it. Well, he'd have to kill Will Usher now. He was a nuisance, a dangerous nuisance, but that could wait. In a few minutes these men would think of their horses, and Dave wanted to be away by that time.

He pondered a moment and decided that Will would have tied the horses to the windward of the shack, lest Dave's mounts, when they approached, catch the scent of other horses and give away their presence.

Therefore, he plunged into the timber, came presently to a ridge, crossed it, dropped down into a gully and walked up it, and found the horses in the dark. They were tied out in a thicket of scrub juniper, which they would tramp. The scent of evergreens would kill any other scent coming to them and keep them from whinnying.

Swiftly, then, Dave searched the saddles, and on one he found a carbine in the rifle scabbard. This was the horse he took, not even bothering to shorten the stirrups until he was clear.

Once he was away from the shack he dismounted, adjusted the stirrups, and considered his situation. Will had Sholto. He would collect ransom on him, just as they had planned together.

For one moment Dave pondered going back and taking Sholto, now that he had the gun. And then another thought occurred to him. Why not let Will Usher have all the grief of lugging Sholto around with him and sending a man for the ransom money? It would be easier to steal the money from Usher than steal Sholto from him.

And that meant that he'd have to hunt up Wallace and watch him. And Wallace had probably been out with the posse, which would return to Yellow Jacket.

He set off in the night, then, through the timber, headed for Yellow Jacket. Will Usher would keep. He was going to have a lot of fun with Usher before he killed him, and he wanted to figure out just what shape that fun would take.

VI

APPROXIMATELY TWENTY-FOUR hours after the kidnaping of Sholto, the posse, headed by Sheriff Beal, came home to Yellow Jacket empty-handed. Wallace, who had driven himself and his men until they were ready to drop, dismounted wearily at the tie rail in front of the sheriff's office alongside Ernie See and Beal. The posse members who had borrowed guns from the sheriff's gunrack returned them and scattered to their homes.

Wallace, as soon as he was inside the door of the sheriff's office, started the same song that Ernie had been listening to for twenty-four hours.

"I can't get over it," Wallace said bleakly, his voice still savage. "Just because you were so knot-headed you wouldn't look in that coffin, Beal, I'm goin' to have to pay out a sweet piece of money."

And Beal, harried and tired, gave the same exasperated retort he had been giving all night and day. "Dammit, man. You saw the coffin! If I'm a knot head, so are you!"

Ernie shucked off his shell belt and gun and said to Beal, "I'll be back after while." He went out, sick of Wallace's grousing, smarting under it because he was included as a knot head, too, and tired enough to fall asleep in the street. He cursed Dave Coyle with a bitterness that surprised even himself, and then he headed upstreet for a drink.

Bruce McFee, per Sheriff Beal's instructions, was in the custody of the two deputy U.S. marshals at the hotel here, but he would go free, Ernie thought bitterly. There was no excuse to hold him now. He had disclaimed all knowledge of Dave Coyle and had pointed to his posting of the reward money for Dave's capture as evidence of innocence. But all that was phony, Ernie thought. Who stood to profit most by Sholto's disappearance? McFee, and Ernie was willing to bet good money that none of them would ever see Sholto again. And while McFee was taking his ease in a hotel room, laughing at them, Ernie and the posse had been riding the legs off their horses. And for nothing. The trail had petered out.

Ernie tramped down the boardwalk, disgust riding his honest face. He wished fervently that both McFee and Wallace would drop dead.

"Did you just come from the sheriff's office?" a woman's voice said.

Ernie pulled up and turned. A pretty dark-haired girl in a rusty black dress stood beside him. Ernie didn't know her, but he liked her looks. He touched his hat. "Yes'm."

"Is Mr. Wallace there?"

"He sure is," Ernie said grimly.

"When will he be ready to ride out to the place?"

"I dunno, miss. Why?"

"Well, I—I work out there," the girl said. "I was going out with him."

Ernie looked at her closely. Then he saw the wedding ring on her finger. For a moment he wondered if Wallace was married, and then he knew he wasn't. Probably some relative.

Ernie said, "I wisht you'd take him out and give us a little peace around this place."

"Will you tell him I'm waiting."

"Sure," Ernie said. "What name?"

"He'll know," the girl said. She smiled her thanks and went down the street. Ernie watched her a moment, admiration in his eyes, and then started out for the saloon again. He had taken less than three steps when he heard someone call him again. "Ernie, oh, Ernie."

He stopped patiently and saw old Bitterman, the hotel clerk, hobbling toward him. Ernie looked at him with a baleful gaze. Likely there was a towel missing from the hotel, and old Bitterman wanted a blanket warrant sworn out for all the guests until the towel was retrieved.

"Well?" Ernie said disgustedly when Bitterman faced him.

"I found somethin' while you were gone. I didn't know whether to save it or not."

"What is it? A burned match?" Ernie asked sardonically.

Bitterman looked aggrieved, but he pulled a folded envelope from his pocket. "It's an envelope," he said.

Ernie took it, unfolded it, glanced at the writing, and then crumpled it up in his fist and threw it savagely in the gutter and said, "Ah, phooey!"

And then his face changed. He stood there a second, his face blank, and then he dived for the enevelope. Retrieving it, he smoothed it out and read the address again. It was the envelope of Carol's letter to Dave Coyle.

"Where'd you find this?" Ernie asked swiftly.

"Why, the chambermaid found it in that room Coyle was in the other night," Bitterman said righteously. "I told you it was——"

Ernie didn't even bother to hear him out. He turned and walked rapidly back to the sheriff's office, a plan already forming in his mind. And then his pace slowed. Wallace would still be there, and Ernie didn't want Wallace riding him on this business. He sauntered into the office. Wallace, his hat shoved on the back of his bony skull, was talking to Sheriff Beal, whose face was getting redder and redder.

"I tell you," Wallace was saying, "either you arrest McFee, Beal, or this is your last term of office!"

Beal spread his hands pleadingly and said, "On what grounds? In the name of all that's high and mighty and holy, on what grounds can I arrest him!"

Ernie interrupted lazily, "Did McFee and that girl of his sign them depositions?"

Beal glared at him. "How could they? This maniac hasn't even let me have a minute free since I got back!"

"I'll take 'em," Ernie said.

Beal fished around in the desk and got the depositions of McFee and Carol. They were merely statements that they had no part in Dave Coyle's kidnaping of Sholto.

Ernie took them and sauntered out the door, his message from the girl to Wallace forgotten. Wallace was talking again. Once on the street Ernie almost ran up to the hotel. He stopped at the desk long enough to take old Bitterman's inkpot and pen and then he went upstairs. A deputy, his chair back-tilted against the wall of the corridor by McFee's room, told Ernie McFee was in.

Ernie knocked and was bid enter. The room was a sitting room of the only suite in the hotel. Bruce McFee, his hands folded behind his back, was pacing the floor. He whirled at Ernie's entrance and said savagely, "How long am I going to be kept here?"

"Dad," Carol said, "be patient."

She was sitting at a table, playing a two-handed game of rummy with Senator Maitland.

Ernie took off his hat and said, "It won't be long, Mr. Mc-Fee. If you and Miss McFee sign these depositions I reckon the sheriff won't keep you much longer."

Maitland, always the lawyer, said, "Let me see them."

Ernie handed him the papers and put the pen and ink on the desk. His heart was beating wildly, and he hoped his face didn't show it. He stood there, hipshot like a horse, while Maitland read over the depositions.

"I think they're safe to sign," Maitland said. "They absolve you both of any complicity in the kidnaping of Sholto."

Ernie's face didn't change. He only picked up the pen, dipped it in the ink, and handed it to Carol. She signed, and Ernie handed the pen to McFee, who signed with a stiff hand his childish-looking signature.

Ernie picked up the two papers, backed off across the room, dropped McFee's deposition, and pulled out the envelope. It was Carol's writing on the envelope; he was certain now.

He went to the door and said to the guard, "Step in here."

When the bewildered deputy came through the door Ernie said swiftly, "Put your gun on them, and don't let them out of this room."

He bolted out the door and ran down the stairs. McFee, his face bewildered as the deputy's, looked at Maitland. "What did we sign?"

Maitland looked puzzled, too, but neither of them looked at Carol. If they had they would have noticed that she was as pale as the white lace collar of her dress.

McFee started for the deposition that Ernie had dropped, but the deputy pulled up his gun. "You stay put," he said.

In two minutes Sheriff Beal and Ernie, both out of breath, came into the room. There was a look of triumph on Beal's face as he marched over to Carol and shoved the envelope at her. "Is that your writing?" he asked, half panting.

Carol looked at it, and her heart sank. She couldn't lie, not with their box number on the back of the envelope and a sample of her writing in Ernie See's hands. She said weakly, "Yes."

"So you wrote him, did you?" Beal said. He wheeled to face McFee. "Where do you get your mail in Wagon Mound?"

"Why—box seventy-three, the post office."

"Ah," Beal said. He held the envelope in both hands for the puzzled McFee to look at. "So you didn't arrange to meet Dave Coyle here and plan that kidnaping? There's the evidence, in you own daughter's handwriting. She's admitted it! What do you say to that?"

McFee looked bleakly at Carol, and Carol ran into his arms. "Oh, Dad, I wrote him! I'm sorry! I—I hoped you wouldn't find out!"

McFee put his arms around her and stroked her hair while she sobbed on his chest.

"What have you got to say, McFee?" Beal drawled. On his rosy innocent face was the look of a schoolboy who had just found a quarter.

"Nothing," McFee said calmly. He looked bewildered, crushed.

"Then I'll have to jail you," Beal said calmly. "And if Judge Warburton gives you bond on this evidence, you can bet it will be so high that you can't meet it. Because, Mr. McFee," Sheriff Beal said angrily, "I think Sholto has been murdered by your outlaw friend and you paid him to do it."

VII

CAROL AND MAITLAND stayed with McFee until nine o'clock, and all the while the town buzzed with excitement. Judge Warburton, who could set McFee's bail if he was to get bail, was out of town for two days, but already a messenger had been sent to fetch him back. That was Senator Maitland's work, and he had argued half the evening with Sheriff Beal to effect it.

Carol sat in her father's cell, listening to the life of the town. Bruce McFee was still stunned by the news. He had refused to eat or even talk, and now Carol was worried. A week of jail would kill him, she knew, crush his spirit, take all the fight out of him and whip him for good. But what was even worse, her father was gentle with her. Instead of raving and storming around in his anger, he was quiet and subdued. Ever since childhood she had been sure of one thing: her father's anger with her worked in inverse proportion to the gravity of her crime. Let her dirty her dress, and her father roared and threatened until finally they both laughed. But let her lie to him, even a small lie, and he was quiet, like he was now.

She sat beside him on the cot in his cell, and she could hear Senator Maitland's patient voice arguing with Sheriff Beal in the office up front. The Yellow Jacket jail was a spacious six-cell affair, brand new and built of stone. In the narrow sheriff's office was a door to the right of the desk. This opened onto a dark corridor, off which opened Ernie See's tiny sleeping quarters. The door at the other end of the corridor opened on to the cell block, and both these corridor doors were ajar now, so that Maitland's voice, continually harried by Tate Wallace's and Sheriff Beal's, came dimly to them.

Carol looked at her father to see if he was listening, and he was not. He had his elbows on his knees and was staring at the floor. Carol wanted to humble herself, to beg his forgiveness, to do anything that would change that look of misery on his face.

"Dad," she said suddenly, "why can't I be arrested? You didn't write the letter, didn't even know I'd written it! I can make them believe it!"

"Don't talk nonsense," McFee said wearily. "They'll believe what they want to believe."

Then Carol said humbly, "Dad, I didn't know it would do this."

43

"Of course you didn't," McFee said in a patient voice. "You just didn't think."

"But—I was desperate," Carol said bitterly. "I would have asked anybody for help!"

McFee turned his head to look at her, pain in his eyes. "But why, Carol, why did you choose Dave Coyle to ask for help? That's what I can't understand."

"He"—Carol paused—"he isn't as bad as you think."

McFee laughed bitterly. "My dear, every sheriff in every county in this territory knows Dave Coyle. So does the U.S. commissioner. So does the Governor. Are you putting your judgment of men up against theirs? Carol, you're a pretty girl. Even the dogs like pretty girls. Coyle was nice to you because you were pretty. But cross him, and he'd cut your throat." He clenched his fists and looked at the floor. "That's why I helped with that reward for him. I don't want a dog like that even speaking to you!"

"But he was trying to help you, Dad!"

"Hah!" McFee said shortly. His neck was getting red. "This is the way he helped me. I'm accused of hiring him, when I never saw him and would shoot him on sight if I did." He shook his head. "No, that little killer saw a chance to make some ransom money. He didn't want to help you and he didn't want to help me. He wanted to help himself."

Carol didn't speak for a moment. Maybe her father was right. But there was something else. She said quietly, "Has anyone told you what he said to Wallace in the baggage car?"

"Yes," McFee said indifferently.

"Dad, how much land does the Three Rivers outfit own?"

"Oh, fifty thousand acres or so. I don't know," McFee said impatiently.

"And how many cattle?"

"Ten thousand or so. Their range is overstocked. Why?"

"Dave Coyle knew Wallace. It couldn't have been more than three years ago that Dave met Tate Wallace, or Wallace Tate, in Dodge City." She looked at her father. "Isn't it strange that a crooked tinhorn gambler who couldn't even pay his debts three years ago is running an outfit like the Three Rivers?"

"Maybe he doesn't own it."

"Who does? Has he ever said?"

McFee shook his head and looked at Carol, a flicker of interest in his eyes. "It's nobody's business but his."

"It might be ours."

McFee looked at his daughter. There was an urgency in her deep brown eyes that McFee didn't miss, but he was puzzled. "How?"

"Three years ago Wallace was a tinhorn, gambling under a fake name. Today, and for two years, he's been the manager of a big cattle company."

"What's that got to do with us?"

"He's not a cowman! He didn't earn his job! He was put here to fight and steal from us. Who put him here?"

"Why, any damn money-hungry crook could have!"

"But it was a money-hungry crook who knew your hand was hurt and that your signature was changed! It was a money-hungry crook who knew Sam could be bribed! It was a money-hungry crook who knew all about us, Dad!"

McFee said bluntly, "Nonsense! I——"

He was interrupted by the entrance of Sheriff Beal and Senator Maitland. Maitland looked tired as he stood aside and let Beal open the cell door.

"They've sent for Warburton, Bruce," Maitland said, and he added to Carol, "You'll have to go now, Carol."

Carol kissed her father good night and went out with Maitland. On the way back to the hotel she said, "Senator, what chance has Dad to get out of this?"

Maitland shook his head. "They can keep him locked up a long time on suspicion of complicity in murder, Carol," Maitland said. "It's bad."

"And I'm to blame," Carol said bitterly.

"The young do foolish things," Maitland said quietly, smiling gently. "Your foolish thing just happened to take a serious turn, my dear."

Carol didn't say anything, only nodded glumly.

"You must promise you won't get in touch with Dave Coyle again," Maitland said gravely. "Once more, and they'll probably try to hang your father."

"I've learned my lesson," Carol said bitterly.

At the hotel she and Maitland parted at the head of the stairs, and Carol went into the sitting room of their suite. The lamp wasn't lighted, and she started through the room in the dark. But halfway to the door she knew she wasn't sleepy and that she couldn't sleep for hours.

She went across to the table, fumbled with a match, struck it, and lighted the lamp.

Then she turned and hauled up short, a stifled cry escaping her.

"Dave Coyle!" she breathed.

"Pull down the shades," Dave said curtly. He stood there, a dark beard stubble on his face that softened the sharp planes of it. He looked hungry and mad and tired, and he was all of them.

"I will not," Carol said hotly. "Get out of here!"

"Where's Wallace?"

"Get out of here, I said!"

"I heard you. Where's Wallace?"

"If you don't get out of here I'll scream!"

"Go ahead."

The muscles in Carol's neck grew taut, and she opened her mouth to scream. Dave lunged for her and clapped a hand over her face, stifling the scream. Carol fought and kicked, but Dave held her tightly. When she ceased struggling he said, "I'll let you loose if you shut up. Will you?"

Carol was mad. She shook her head in negation.

Dave said, "I can wait as long as you can."

He pulled her over to a chair, sat down, pulled her down in his lap, and held her there. They sat that way for a full minute, Carol tugging at his hand and not succeeding in pulling it from her mouth.

Presently Dave said, "Changed your mind?"

This time Carol nodded, and Dave freed her. She came to her feet, her face crimson, her eyes blazing. "You—you——"

"Pull down the shades," Dave said coldly.

Carol stamped her foot in anger. She would have screamed, but she had given her word she wouldn't. She glared at Dave for a long moment, and he only stared back at her, his gray eyes steady, a sneer on his face. She began to understand now why people hated him. So did she—almost. But if she was to get rid of him, she might as well do what he said. She went to the big front windows and yanked down the shades, then turned defiantly on Dave.

"Where's Wallace?" he asked.

Carol said passionately, "Haven't you done enough harm already, without doing more?"

Dave regarded her coldly. "The trial has been postponed, hasn't it? What more do you want?"

"I want my father out of jail!" Carol cried.

Dave said blankly, "Jail?"

"They've arrested him!" Carol said hotly. "They found the envelope to my letter that you left in your room! That's all the proof they needed that Dad had thrown in with you and was in on the kidnaping!"

Dave rubbed his hand slowly along his jaw, frowning. "What charge?"

"Complicity in murder! They think you killed Sholto for him." She paused. "Did you?"

Dave's eyes turned hard. "Sure. I ate one of his drumsticks."

Carol flushed, but her gaze was steady. "Now you see what you've done? If you'd gone away when I told you to and left us alone this wouldn't have happened!"

Dave walked over to her and faced her and said coldly, "Sit down."

Carol was afraid of him then, afraid of the look in his eyes. She backed up, and a chair caught her under the knees, and she plopped into it.

Dave stood above her, his eyes musing. "Shut up and talk sense. Are they going to set bail?"

"I don't know," Carol said, her voice still indignant. "Senator Maitland says if they do they'll wait a long while to do it. I told you, they think Dad paid you to kidnap and kill Sholto."

"I heard you too," Dave said dryly. He kept looking at her, but his mind wasn't on her. He was thinking of Sholto out there with Will Usher and of what Wallace would do, now that McFee was in jail. He thought he knew. He said, "They won't set any bail. And your dad won't get out."

"How do you know?" Carol said. It seemed the truth now that he had said it.

"I know."

He stood stock-still, staring over Carol's head. Then he took a deep breath and started for the door.

"Where are you going?" Carol said swiftly.

"To jail."

"To rescue Dad? But you can't! They'll——"

"No. I'm goin' to jail," Dave said slowly.

For a long moment Carol only stared at him, and then she said weakly, "Oh, you mean give yourself up?"

Dave nodded.

"But they'll hang you!"

"What do you care?"

"I—I don't," Carol said and added weakly, "but it seems so stupid. What will it get you?"

"I'm goin' to talk to your dad," Dave said dryly. "It's the only place he'll listen to me, I reckon, and that's only because he can't help it. When I've made him see he's walked into a frame-up that will let him rot in jail, then I'll take him with me."

Carol's lips formed the words, "Take him with you?" and then she said, "Take him with you where? You'll be in jail."

"No. I'll be out."

"But—how will you do that?"

A look of annoyance crossed Dave's face. He said sharply, "Lady, I don't know. I never know what I'm goin' to do until I have to, and then I do it. I've never stayed in a jail yet."

"But—but I don't understand. Do you mean you'll break jail?"

"That's an idea. Yes. I'll break jail," Dave said dryly.

He started for the door again. Carol closed her mouth, which had been opened in surprise, and said, "You can't go out there! They'll kill you."

Dave turned and regarded her with a fast-vanishing patience. "For about fifteen years, lady, I been wipin' my own nose. I still can."

He opened the door, stepped out into the corridor, and paused at the head of the stairs. Then a wry smile crossed his face, vanished, and he tramped down the stairs.

Old Bitterman at the desk looked up from his newspaper, saw a man's back as he went toward the lobby door, and settled again to his reading.

Dave hit the boardwalk, swung under the tie rail, crossed the road, and pulled up in front of the sheriff's office. The door was closed, the shade of the only window pulled down. He regarded the place a moment, letting a pair of punchers walk past him. Then he crossed the boardwalk and tried the door. It was locked. He knocked.

A voice called through the door, "We're busy. Come back later."

Dave grinned at that. With a posse just come from hunting him, with seven thousand dollars' reward on his head, he had to break into the sheriff's office to get himself arrested.

He went out to the edge of the boardwalk and searched the road. He saw a rock in the road, swung under the tie rail, picked it up, and threw it through the window of the sheriff's office. The glass jangled to the boardwalk, and there was an uproar inside the office.

The door swung open and Ernie See, with Sheriff Beal just behind him, stepped out.

"Who did that?" Ernie asked.

Dave stood just beyond the tie rail, his hands on his hips, legs spread a little. "I did," he said. "I'm Dave Coyle."

Ernie peered through the half-darkness and then said to Beal, "A drunk."

"Listen, son," Beal said patiently, "come back and pay for this tomorrow. Now get along home."

Ernie turned, swearing disgustedly, and went back into the office, while Sheriff Beal still regarded Dave. Dave walked toward him, swung under the tie rail, and came up to him. He reached out, cuffed Sheriff Beal twice in the face with the flat of his hand, yanked his hat down over his eyes, then put his foot in Beal's soft belly and shoved. Beal went over backward through the office door and sprawled on his back. Dave walked in, stepped over him, and said to Ernie See, who was staring in amazement at the sheriff, "What do you have to do around here to get arrested—scalp the sheriff on the church steps?"

Ernie lunged for him then, wrapping both arms around his body and bawling, "Get his gun, Harve! Get his gun!"

Two minutes later Dave was in the cell next to McFee, and half of Yellow Jacket was milling in the cell block, waiting for a chance to see him. Ernie was shouting, shoving them out, cursing them, and pushing them with a harried look on his face. Finally, when they were cleared out, Sheriff Beal and Ernie confronted Dave on the other side of the bars. Dave sat on the cot and yawned.

"All right now, Coyle," Beal said in a businesslike way. "Let's have the story."

"What story?"

"Where's Sholto? Did you kill him? Why you givin' yourself up?"

Dave said mildly, "I come in here to take McFee out."

Ernie looked blankly at Sheriff Beal, and then color started to crawl up his neck. "You mean you're just goin' to walk out with him?" he said.

"That's about it," Dave answered and yawned.

Ernie took a deep breath and said thickly, "Listen, runt, if we have to, we'll hold your trial in that cell and hang you to the ceiling rafter."

"Boo!" Dave said, staring blankly at him.

Ernie's fists gripped the bars until his knuckles were white. "I'm goin' to kick that cocky face of yours in someday!" he raged. "I'm goin' to load a pair of oversize boots with horseshoes and I'm goin' to kick your head till it rings like a church bell!"

"Ernie, Ernie," Beal admonished. Ernie, his face white with rage, got a grip on himself, and then Beal turned to Dave. "All right, Coyle. Talk."

"Tomorrow," Dave said. "I need sleep."

"Why, damn you——" Ernie began. Dave yawned, lay down on the cot, and turned his back to them.

Beal shoved Ernie, who was murmuring inarticulate threats out into the corridor, and closed the door behind him. He was content to let Dave cool off for a while. The jail was new, built of stone, the bars made of the best steel.

When they had gone Dave raised up on the cot and looked in the next cell. McFee, his craggy face white with anger, his eyes full of murder, was standing there looking at him.

"Save it," Dave said. "I'm sleepy."

He turned over and went to sleep, while McFee was still looking at him.

VIII

WHEN TATE WALLACE heard of Dave Coyle's arrest he didn't believe it, but he followed the crowd that stampeded out of the saloon into the cell block. He was shoved out with all the others, but not before he got a glimpse of Dave Coyle, hands on hips, staring insolently and indifferently at the crowd that Ernie See was trying to break up in the cell block.

Wallace went out then and waited on the edge of the boardwalk until Marty Cord, his foreman, drifted out. Wallace nodded his head and Cord came over to him, a puzzled expression on his unshaven face, and together they turned downstreet. Wallace walked with the stiff and lazy stride of a man who has spent many long hours in the saddle. His brain was fogged with weariness, and he was dead for sleep, but more than sleep he needed to think this over.

They shouldered into Tim King's Keno Parlor, a big saloon that ran the full half block to the alley and was two stories high. Wallace shoved his way through the crowd and started back through the gaming tables to the stairs that led up to the gallery. A percentage girl threw her arms around Wallace's neck, but he pushed her away and went on.

They mounted the steps that led to Wallace's room. Although Wallace was general manager of the Three Rivers Cattle Company and had a certain dignity to maintain, he scorned it. Instead of staying at a hotel, he took a dirty room in a noisy saloon, like any saloon bum or a rider of the chuck line. Old habits were ingrained, and this was one of them.

His room fronted the street and contained a paint-peeled iron bed and washstand. He lighted the lamp, waved Marty Cord to a seat, and then sank down on the bed.

"What's wrong with it, Marty?" he growled. "That ain't like Dave Coyle. And where's Sholto?"

Marty Cord was of the same stamp as Wallace, a Texan, maybe forty-five, with a face that contrived to be cunning and brutal and forceful, all at the same time. He wore the rough clothes of a puncher, too, although on this night he was wearing a faded and wrinkled coat over a dirty collarless shirt.

He shifted a wad of tobacco delicately into his opposite cheek and spat in the corner.

"Nothin' looks wrong to me. They got that little hellion at last."

"But it don't——"

Wallace paused as a knock came on the door. He looked at Marty and nodded his head, and Marty came out of his chair, loosening his gun at the same time.

Marty opened the door a few inches and a voice said, "I'm lookin' for Tate Wallace."

"What about?" Marty growled.

There was a pause, then the voice said, "Sholto."

Marty swung the door open, and a stocky rider tramped in. He was anonymous-looking, with his unshaven face, greasy Stetson, and dusty clothes. He might have been any one of a hundred men downstairs in the saloon.

Wallace stood up as he entered and said, "What did you say?"

Marty closed the door and put his back to it.

The man said, "Sholto."

"Where is he?"

"You know, don't you?" the man asked.

Wallace looked at Marty Cord, and Marty stared at him.

Something passed between them then, and Wallace shook his head imperceptibly. He said to the man, "Dave Coyle's got him, ain't he?"

The man grinned. "You don't catch me on that, Wallace. Coyle's in jail; I just heard it. It don't matter who's got Sholto. You want to buy him back?"

Wallace stared at him speculatively, his brain working fast. This was what he had been expecting all day, some word from someone about the ransom money. But the events of the last few minutes had changed that—changed it enormously. For Bruce McFee and Dave Coyle were in jail on suspicion of collaborating in the murder of Sholto. And if Sholto was really found dead, then McFee and Dave Coyle would hang! And McFee's suit against him then would vanish.

Wallace smiled crookedly. "Who said I wanted to buy him back?" he drawled.

The man stared at him blankly. "Hell, he's your witness in court. How you goin' to win the case if you ain't got him?"

"Did you ever hear of two witnesses?" Wallace lied.

For a long moment they looked at each other. The disbelief on the man's face turned to blank amazement. "Two witnesses?" He grinned suddenly. "You're runnin' a sandy, Wallace. You're tryin' to beat the price down."

"Ask me how much I'll offer you for Sholto," Wallace asked softly.

"Well, how much will you?"

"Nothin'—not even the price of a drink."

The man laughed. "It won't do you no good to bluff us, Wallace. You need Sholto."

"That's my offer, mister," Wallace said. He smiled crookedly. "Keep him. Stuff him and mount him. See if I care."

The puncher regarded him carefully, then looked at Marty. "He drunk?"

"Stone sober," Marty drawled. "You drunk? If you ain't, and you can understand American, get the hell out of here. We can't do business with you. Can't you understand that?" He opened the door and stood aside.

The man looked perplexed. Will Usher hadn't made any provision for this kind of retort, and the messenger didn't know what to do. Finally he shook his head. "I'll be back," he said. "I'll be back when you git some sense, Wallace."

"Don't bother," Wallace said.

The man went out, and Wallace leaped for the door and closed it. Then he whirled on Marty. "Follow that bird,

Marty! Find out where he's goin'. He'll take you to Sholto! Then come back and let me know!"

"I don't get it," Marty said.

"You damn fool. I don't want Sholto!" Wallace said swiftly. "McFee and Coyle are in jail on suspicion of his murder. If we can get to Sholto and murder him and put it on Coyle, then him and McFee will hang. And I can take over the whole damn McFee range! Now git!"

He pulled the door open, and Marty stepped out. The messenger was just going down the stairs, and Marty started after him. Wallace stood there in the doorway, watching Marty leave, a smile on his face.

He would have been surprised to learn that what he had just done was approximately what Dave Coyle had expected him to do. Dave had guessed everything, except the time and the place.

IX

WHEN DAVE wakened next morning it was to find Ernie See and Sheriff Beal waiting with his breakfast. While Ernie held a gun on Dave, Sheriff Beal put the tray in his cell. They did the same to McFee, who didn't even get up to receive his food. The sheriff and Ernie went out then.

Dave wolfed his food down in silence, afterward rolling and lighting a smoke. He looked over at McFee, who was sitting listlessly on his cot.

"You better eat," Dave said. "You'll need it."

McFee didn't even answer him, didn't even look at him.

"You and me are breakin' out of here, so you better eat," Dave repeated.

McFee slowly turned his head to regard Dave. His eyes were bitter, disillusioned, past anger. "If I could get out of here," McFee said, "I'd get a greener and blow a hole a foot wide in your belly."

Dave said, "You'll get the chance, because we're leavin'."

"Are we?" McFee asked with savage sarcasm. "What are you waitin' on? There's nobody here to see you. Walk out!"

"I'm waitin' on you to find out for yourself they won't let you out of here in six months."

McFee laughed bitterly, getting angry now. "They'd let me out of here if you'd tell them where Sholto is!"

Dave shrugged, stood up, and bawled, "Sheriff! Sheriff Beal!"

Ernie See and Beal strolled in a minute later. Dave looked at McFee and then said to Beal, "I kidnaped Sholto for the ransom money. Me and Will Usher throwed in together. Will arranged for me to get on the train in the coffin. He had the horses planted there at the top of the grade. I took Sholto up to the old Lazy K Knife line camp, aimin' to hold him there until Will Usher got the ransom money from Wallace. But Usher crossed me up. He was waitin' at the line camp. He throwed down on me and was goin' to kill me, collect my bounty and Sholto's ransom. I broke away. Usher's got Sholto." He had been talking easily, insolently. Now he looked back at McFee. "Now listen to what they say, McFee." He turned his head to regard them again.

Ernie See sneered. He said mockingly, "And the Princess married the young King, and they lived happily ever and ever after." He made a rude and unprintable noise with his lips.

Dave grinned and looked at McFee. "See?"

"All right, Coyle," Sheriff Beal said. "Now let's have the real story."

"You got it," Dave said.

Beal smiled faintly and shook his head. "What did McFee pay you to kidnap Sholto and get him out of the way?"

Dave looked at McFee. "Are you listenin'?"

Sheriff Beal said testily, "We know Miss McFee wrote you on her dad's orders! We know you came to Yellow Jacket to talk to him! We know you were in Sabinal and we saw you kidnap Sholto!" He shook his head. "Two and two make four, even in this county, Coyle. We think you killed Sholto for McFee. Now do you aim to talk?"

McFee said hotly, "Anybody that says I paid Coyle a cent or that I even talked to him is a liar!"

Ernie See said sarcastically, "Man alive, but I'm a liar. And I like it, and I think I'll stay that way."

McFee looked angry and helpless. He glanced over at Dave, who was leaning against the bars watching him. Dave had a faint smile of cynical amusement on his lips, and McFee looked even angrier when he saw it.

Beal said, "McFee, I've already advised your lawyer what to do. I've told him to tell you to plead guilty. Now that we've got Coyle, I advise it even more. You'll get off with a couple of years' sentence. Coyle, of course, will be tried on other charges that carry a longer sentence. We can't try you on murder charges, McFee, because we haven't found Sholto's body. If and when we do find it you'll be tried for murder too. So I'd advise you to plead guilty to kidnaping a witness and get a light sentence just as quickly as you can."

McFee, hands gripping the bars, stared at him as if he were a lunatic.

He bawled angrily, "But you just heard Coyle say Sholto was alive, you damn jug head!"

"McFee," Beal said caustically, "I'm fifty years old. I been sheriff of this county for ten-fifteen years. In that time I've learned to eat without being fed, to read, to write, to talk. In other words, maybe I'm as smart as the average twelve-year-old kid. And a twelve-year-old kid wouldn't believe Dave Coyle or you. A six-year-old kid wouldn't. Hell, nobody would." He glared at McFee. "The trouble with you is you been the Big Augur in this county too long. And when somebody like Wallace drifts in and settles here you try and clean 'em out like a tinhorn in a gold camp. You ain't bright, that's all."

McFee was speechless. He heard Dave's soft laugh, and it maddened him and at the same time impressed him. Dave Coyle was showing him just how useless it was to argue with the law when you got in bad with it. For the first time since his arrest he was scared. A cold panic gripped his belly, and he thought his knees were going to cave in. He said hoarsely, "You mean you're goin' to keep me in jail?"

"Look," Ernie See said harshly. "Who the hell do you think you are, McFee? You may be a tin saint to your Bib M outfit, but to us you're just another moneybags that's got too big for his pants. Stay in jail? Hell, yes, you'll stay in jail till we find Sholto's body. The next time you see open sky after that will be on the way to your trial. The next time after that will be a couple of years away!"

McFee felt sick. He left the bars and walked back to sit on his cot. Dave watched him, his eyes impersonal.

Then Beal said to Dave, "Want to talk to me now, Coyle?"

"I'd as soon poke a skunk with a stick," Dave murmured.

Beal's face smiled, but his eyes didn't. He said slowly, "There's a lot of sheriffs would like to be in my shoes right now, Coyle. I know a dozen of 'em that would give a hundred dollars to have you in their jail, just to beat it out of you. Me, I'll see you later."

Dave said, "Better make it fast, Sheriff."

"Why?" Ernie asked.

"Because I'm goin' to break out of here."

Beal, cursing him, walked out, taking Ernie with him. Dave dropped his cigarette, stepped on it, then looked over at Mc-Fee. He was sitting on the cot, face in hands, utterly still.

"I told the truth," Dave said.

McFee's hands fell away. He said, "I know you did. I don't know how I know, but I feel you did."

"You're in here till you rot."

"Nonsense!" McFee said sharply. "If you didn't kill Sholto and Will Usher took him from you, then Usher will get the ransom money from Wallace. Wallace will buy him back."

Dave didn't say anything for a moment, then he came over to the connecting bars of their two cells and looked pityingly at McFee.

"Beal was right about you, I reckon," he drawled insolently.

McFee looked up. "Right in what way?"

"You ain't got the brains of a six-year-old."

McFee looked blankly at him, too surprised to be angry.

"Listen, McFee," Dave said savagely. "Where are you now?"

"Where am I now? Why, in jail, of course!"

"Who stands to gain most if you stay here on the charge you're being held on?"

McFee thought a moment, then said, "Wallace."

Dave said jeeringly, "Then don't tell me you think Wallace is going to buy Sholto back, so you can go free of a murder charge."

McFee wasn't slow now. He bounded up off the cot and faced Dave. "What did you say?"

"I didn't say it, but I will now," Dave murmured coldly. "Wallace don't want Sholto back. He'll kill him before he'll let him come back!"

The two men stood there, staring at each other between the bars. On Dave's face was a look of alert arrogance. On Mc-Fee's face was a look of consternation, of the earth dropping out from under his feet. He said in a sick way, "Let me alone," and walked back to his cot. Dave went over to his cot, sat on it, drew up his knees, leaned against the wall, and watched McFee.

For fifteen minutes the older man sat there staring at the floor, clasping and unclasping his hands.

Then McFee looked up and his eyes were bleak. He said bitterly, "You started this, Coyle. I hope they hang you."

Dave said, "When was your lawsuit supposed to begin in Santa Fe?"

"Today."

"It ain't goin' on, is it?" he said arrogantly, triumphantly.

"No. Because I'm in jail, because I'll stay here!"

"Not unless you want to," Dave said. He came off his cot and went up to the bars. "McFee, you ain't a fighter, that's all. Not the kind of a fighter I am, anyways. What's a jail? The jail hasn't been built that will hold me. You think I give myself up last night because I was sorry for you?"

"Why did you?"

"To get you out of here, if you got the guts to come!"

For a moment neither of them spoke. There was a challenge in Dave's eyes, and in McFee's was a moment of wild speculation. Dave seized on that and said wickedly, "You're an old man. Maybe you can't stand the ridin', the sleepin' every two days, the fightin', the bein' hunted."

McFee said swiftly, "I can stand anything a runt like you can!"

"Then maybe you're scared of bein' named an outlaw," Dave jeered. "Nice people won't speak to you."

"I can take that too!"

Dave shrugged. "Then I reckon you just don't give a damn about your spread, what you leave your girl, or what happens to you."

McFee's face looked grim as death. He came off the cot slowly and said, just as slowly, "Coyle, I don't like you. Next to Wallace, I'd rather look at you swingin' from a cottonwood tree than anybody I know. But you're shrewd. I'll give you credit for that. You've got gall—enough for a hundred men. And you've got a queer kind of reckless guts that I don't rightly understand. Someday when this is over I hope I get the chance to even up with you for getting me in this. But right now I need you. I'll go with you."

"McFee," Dave said gently, "I don't like you either. You're a hardheaded Scotchman without anything but money and a temper. Somewhere along the line you wrote your own Bible, and I reckon you live up to it. You're not as shrewd as I am. You're dumb. You're bull-headed and you're tough. But you're the wrong kind of tough, McFee. You're tough on the little people—the people that can't help themselves, like Lacey Thornton. I'll throw in with you too. Not because I need you. I'll throw in with you and help you because your girl is human, and she's in trouble, and you're too damn dumb to get her out of it!"

"If you ever touch that girl of mine I'll kill you!" McFee said softly.

"I wouldn't try," Dave said tonelessly. "She's too good for me, and I know it." He looked wickedly at McFee. "She's too good for you too."

"I know it."

They glared at each other a moment, hating each other, and then McFee said grimly, "If we do get out—and I said 'if'— what can we do outside of hide? It won't help Carol if I live in a cave in the Corazon."

"I said you were dumb," Dave jeered.

"I'm askin' you," McFee said stubbornly. "What can we do?"

"The first thing we can do is get Sholto's wife and hide her," Dave said calmly. "Then we take Sholto away from Usher."

"But I don't want Sholto!" McFee burst out.

"You do! You got to prove you didn't kill him! And after we've got him safe, then we're goin' to find out who's behind Wallace!"

McFee started. He said slowly, "Have you talked to Carol?"

"Lots of times," Dave said, puzzled.

"I mean about who's behind Wallace. She thinks someone is too."

"You think there ain't anyone?" Dave said dryly. "And him a tinhorn gambler three years ago?"

"I don't know."

"I do," Dave said. "When we find out who it is, then we'll put Wallace away and him away." He smiled faintly. "Then you can go back to your spread and put another three thousand reward on my head."

McFee smiled too. "I reckon I will," he said grimly. "But right now we might as well shake hands, hadn't we?"

"No. Just keep your mouth shut and let me think."

He walked back to his cot and lay down, his hands under his head. Sooner than McFee expected Dave said, "Is Carol comin' to see you this mornin'?"

"She's Miss McFee to a saddle bum like you!" McFee said shortly.

"Is she?" Dave asked, ignoring him.

"Yes. Pretty soon."

"You and me will stage a fist fight through the bars when she gets here," Dave said quietly. "Make it good, but don't bloody my nose. I'll save that till later. You got that?"

"I don't see——"

"Nobody asked you to," Dave said shortly. "I'm bossin' this."

He turned over and went to sleep, and McFee nursed his anger in silence.

A little after nine o'clock Carol, wearing a dark maroon dress, and Senator Maitland were shown into the cell block. Ernie See led the way, and he was carrying two chairs. He set them down in the corridor, motioned Carol and Maitland toward them, and said, "Nobody gets in that cell. Also, I'm goin' to watch you from the end of the corridor."

Carol sat down, glancing swiftly at Dave, who was sleeping. Then she asked her father how he was, and they began to talk. Presently Dave raised up on his cot, and talk ceased. All three of them looked at him.

Dave's face was cross. "You got the whole outdoors to jabber in," he said sourly. "I got a six-by-six cell. I'm tryin' to sleep. Shut up, will you?"

McFee said automatically, sternly, "Nobody talks to my daughter that way!"

"I did, didn't I?" Dave said truculently. He sat up and said to Carol, "Shut up, I said! I want to sleep." He looked at McFee. "How do you like that?"

McFee was genuinely angry. He had forgotten Dave's instructions, and that made it all the more convincing. He came over to the adjoining bars and said, "When I get out of here I'll kick your pants clear up into your throat."

"Listen to Grandpa," Dave jeered.

Carol rose and said indignantly, "Stop that, Dave Coyle!"

Senator Maitland said gently, "Here, here!"

Dave said jeeringly to McFee, "You couldn't kick a mushroom over, Grandpa. Don't brag."

"Step over here and see if I can't!" McFee cried.

Dave stepped over to him and grabbed his nose and twisted it. McFee yelled and lashed out at him through the bars. Dave ducked and came up and put his hand through the bars, the flat of his palm against McFee's face. He pushed. McFee backed across the cell and sat down. Carol screamed. McFee growled in his throat and rushed at Dave, who hit him.

McFee kicked him, and then grabbed Dave's shirt and ripped it. Dave slugged him in the stomach, and McFee clouted Dave alongside the ear.

All that happened before Ernie See arrived. He shoved Carol out of the way, unlocked the door, grabbed McFee by the collar of his shirt, and yanked him away from Dave.

"Boys, boys," Ernie said mockingly. He was enjoying this; Dave could tell.

"Take him away from me," Dave said coldly. "I'll unscrew his head."

Carol said hotly to Dave, "You—you bully, you beast!"

Dave looked at her. "Shut up, sister, or I'll spank you."

Carol was so mad she couldn't speak. Senator Maitland's kindly face was distressed. "Please," he pleaded. "Let's act like human beings and not dogs."

Ernie See let go of McFee's shirt and said, "Keep away from him."

"Take him out of there," Dave repeated. "I don't want him around me."

"That's just too bad," Ernie drawled ominously. "We always aim to please our customers, but I'm a little deaf. But I got a nice drafty cell over there by the window that's empty. One more ruckus like this and you'll go over there, mister."

Dave only sneered at him and went back to his cot. Ernie See said to Carol, "You better go, miss. I may have to work him over to show him some sense."

"I hope you do!" Carol said indignantly, her eyes flashing. "He's—he's insufferable!"

She and Senator Maitland went out, and Ernie stood there in the cell block, watching Dave. "Tell me, sonny," he drawled. "You still goin' to break jail?"

"I'll break jail and your head and McFee's head," Dave said arrogantly. He turned over on his cot, his back to Ernie. Ernie laughed and went out.

When he was gone Dave sat up. McFee was rubbing his nose, and his eyes were angry. "You didn't have to insult Carol," he said.

"It looked good, didn't it?" Dave challenged, grinning.

"Yes," McFee said reluctantly. "I still don't see what you aim to do, though."

Dave didn't say anything. He turned to his cot, a canvas-covered one on a wooden frame. He jumped on one side with both feet, and the frame broke. He pulled the canvas away, took the broken frame, and twisted it free of the end. What he held in his hand was a wooden club some three feet long and two inches thick. He hefted it, judged its weight, and then looked at McFee.

"I think we better stick together when we get out of here," he said quietly. "You'd get caught if we split up and met."

McFee looked curiously at him. "But we aren't out."

"When we get out," Dave went on patiently, "I want you to stick with me. Understand?"

McFee, baffled, only nodded.

Dave gave him the club in his hand. "When I give the word we'll start yellin' and cussin'. That will bring Ernie and maybe Sheriff Beal here. When they come in I'll be lyin' on the floor, my nose bleedin', and I'll be unconscious. They'll ask you what happened. Tell them we got to fightin' and that I broke the cot, grabbed a club, and started after you through the bars. Tell them you took the club away from me and let me have it alongside the head. Ask 'em if I'm dead and cuss me out. Make it look good. You got that?"

McFee nodded slowly, a scowl on his face. "But I don't understand——"

Dave cut in on him. "Hit me in the nose."

"What?"

"Hit me in the nose."

McFee fisted his hands, looked down at them, then up at Dave, and smiled. "I couldn't do that, not when——"

Dave drove a blow into McFee's face. The older man's head snapped back, and for one second there was a look of astonishment on his face, and then he lashed out at Dave through the bars. When it was done Dave had a bloody nose. His eyes were watering with the pain. He stood there a moment, letting the blood drip on his shirt. He said, "Muss your hair. Tear your shirt."

While McFee was doing it Dave went over and jumped on the cot, and it collapsed with a crash. Then Dave began to curse aloud, motioning McFee to join in. McFee did, and they yelled a torrent of abuse at each other.

In approximately a quarter of a minute the first corridor door swung open, and then Dave heard the pounding of feet in the corridor.

He lay down on the floor, sprawled on his face, and looked up at McFee. McFee nodded grimly, and then Dave closed his eyes.

He heard the boots close now and then Ernie See's hard voice: "Put that thing down, McFee!"

Dave heard a clatter of wood on the floor, and McFee, panting, said, "Damn right I will! I'm through with it!"

"What happened?"

McFee said grimly, "Take a look at him! He started to argue with me and then slugged me, and then he broke the cot, hauled out a hunk of wood, and hit me!"

"But you got it now," Sheriff Beal's voice said.

"Damn right I have!" McFee bellowed. "I took it away from him and laid it across his head."

"Pull your gun, Ernie. Let's take a look at Coyle," Beal said.

There was the sound of the door unlocking, and then they stood over Dave. Beal rolled him over roughly and looked at him. He shuttered up his eyelid, and Dave lay limp as a rag.

"Where'd you hit him?" Beal asked McFee.

"The head, I told you! I hope to hell it killed him!"

"So do I," Ernie said. He knelt by Dave and felt his skull and said, "Well, he ain't got a cracked head."

McFee was making a good job of it; Dave could hear him still panting.

"He will have the next time," McFee said.

Beal said angrily, "There ain't goin' to be no next time, McFee. Personally, I wouldn't care if you knocked his head into the next room, but he's goin' to stand trial. And we're goin' to separate you two."

McFee didn't say anything. Ernie said with bitter relish, "I got just the place for Coyle, Harve. Let's give him the 'icebox.'"

"He's liable to get sick," Beal said. "It's cold there in that cell in front of the window."

"Maybe it'll take some of the salt out of him," Ernie said. Dave heard him tramp down the cell block and unlock the door to the end cell, the "icebox." He came back and Beal said dubiously, "I dunno. It's cold there."

"Hell, Sholto's cold too—if he bothered to bury him!"

"All right, Sholto," Beal said grimly. "Take his arms. I'll take his feet."

Dave was picked up. He opened his eyes a little to see how Beal was holding his legs. Beal faced him and grabbed his feet at the ankles and lifted. Ernie held him under the arms, so that his hands almost dragged the floor. Beal was too busy to watch him as he maneuvered out through the cell door and into the corridor. This wasn't so good, Dave reflected swiftly. Ernie was the strongest, the fastest thinker, and he had hold of his arms. But he would have to go through with it anyway.

They stumbled down the corridor with him, and then Beal backed around into the open door of the cell. Dave did two things at once then. His arms, which were hanging down to the floor, suddenly went stiff as he grabbed Ernie's boots. And with his feet he kicked savagely at Sheriff Beal's belly.

Ernie, with his legs pinioned, was driven off balance by the kick, and he fell backward, taking Dave with him. And Beal, kicked in the belly, also fell backward.

Ernie let go one hand to break his fall, and Dave twisted. He landed on top of Ernie, squirmed over, and with one vicious bat with his hand drove Ernie's head into the stone floor. Ernie slacked, unconscious, under him, and still lying on him, Dave grabbed his gun and rolled over beside him and looked up at Beal.

Beal was gagging for breath, sitting up, but he had stubbornly gone for his gun. Dave swiveled his up and said, "Want a shoot-out, Beal?"

Beal was a courageous man. But right now, coming half erect, he was sick and gagging for breath. It took some swift thinking to do what he did then. He dropped his gun as if it were hot and fell to his knees, his arms around his belly. Dave vaulted into the cell and shoved him over on his back. Beal was making queer sucking sounds, like a fish that is out of water, his mouth working spasmodically. Dave ripped off Beal's belt, laid it out on the floor, then rolled Sheriff Beal over on it, face down. He yanked the belt up tight, pinning Sheriff Beal's arms to his sides.

Leaving him, Dave stepped out into the hall and dragged Ernie in beside Beal. Ernie was limp as a sack, so that it was hard to get his shirt off him. Dave succeeded, however, and then put on Ernie's shirt, shedding his own torn and bloody one. Then he trussed up Ernie the same way he had trussed Beal.

When he was finished Beal had quit gagging. He was looking at Dave through sick eyes as if he would like to murder him. Dave ripped his old shirt in half, balled it up in his right hand, straddled Beal, and leveled his gun at him.

"I'm goin' to ask you just this once," Dave said. "Are you goin' to open your mouth and let me gag you, or am I goin' to have to clout you over the head?"

Beal opened his mouth, and Dave rammed the shirt into it.

Afterward he did the same with Ernie, then he stepped out, shut the door, locked it, and took the keys.

He went down the corridor to McFee's cell, unlocked it, and McFee stepped out.

"Quit shakin'," Dave said coldly.

"Goddlemighty!" McFee whispered. "I wouldn't of done that for a thousand dollars."

"Nobody asked you to," Dave sneered. He handed him Sheriff Beal's gun and shell belt. "Put these on. We're goin' out now. I want you to stand in the door of the sheriff's office and take a look at the horses in sight. Pick a fast one. I'll do the same. Get on your horse and walk him, don't run him, out of town. Look like you belonged there, understand? Don't get panicked."

McFee licked his lips. "All right," he said. "But give me time. This is comin' pretty fast."

Dave rammed Ernie's gun in his waistband and led the way out into the office. Beal had been in the midst of writing a letter when he was interrupted by the fight. The paper, a broken line of writing across it, was lying beside an open ink bottle and the pen.

Dave walked into the open door and stood there, McFee beside him. "How about that black?" Dave asked, looking downstreet.

"Good," McFee said shakily.

"Take him. I'll take that chestnut down the tie rail a ways." He looked scornfully at McFee. "Quit shakin'."

"I can't help it," McFee said softly. "Hell, I'm scared."

Dave dropped McFee off at the black horse and went by him. They passed a couple of punchers, and Dave said, "Howdy," and received a pleasant reply.

Dave sneered and set off downstreet, McFee behind on. The chestnut didn't look so good at close range. He passed him up and took a bay next to him. He mounted, pulled aside for a buckboard and team that was just swinging into the tie rail, and then put his horse into the street to wait for McFee.

McFee came up. He was glancing from side to side, and his mouth was grim. He was sweating, Dave could see.

Dave waited until McFee was even with him, and then they walked their horses down the street. People looked at them and glanced away, incurious. One or two people looked for quite a long moment, then went about their business, thinking they were mistaken. They rode peacefully out of town.

X

For its headquarters the Three Rivers Cattle Company had taken over an old homesteader's stone house on one of the long benches that jutted out from the foothills of the Corazon's west slope. A log wing had been added to the three stone rooms, a porch flanking the whole of the south side, and a bunkhouse had been built. It squatted there on the flats amid a tangle of pole corrals and outbuildings, unlovely, bleak, and treeless. On the east side of the log wing there was a small rectangle of flower garden which was filled with blooms, a chicken-wire fence around it. That, however, was the only touch of color or neatness in the whole place. Bottles, tobacco tins, cans, and pieces of worn-out gear littered the yard around the house and bunkhouse. It was as slovenly as an unmade bed.

Wallace, because he had got in late the night before, had slept through the early-morning hours, and now his crew, numbering fifteen men, were loafing around the horse corral, awaiting orders. Marty Cord, who usually gave out the morning's work, had not returned yet. There was no *segundo*, for Wallace trusted no man other than Cord. And to disturb Wallace for any reason whatsoever was to invite being fired, the men had long since learned.

Long after nine o'clock Wallace came to the door of the main house in his sock feet, his pale hair rumpled, sleep still heavy in his eyes. He saw the men clotted in the shade of the barn and corral, and he cursed softly. Cord hadn't come home last night either. He went back into the house, got his boots and hat, and started out across the yard. His face was ugly with temper this morning. It was yesterday that Dave Coyle and McFee had walked out of the county jail, leaving Sheriff Beal and Ernie See tied and gagged in a locked cell. He had had them both in the palm of his hand, as neatly framed as two men could be, and then that blundering Beal had let them slip through his hands. Yesterday Wallace had wanted to kill Beal. He still wanted to today. There was only one cause for cheer in the whole picture, and that was that Beal and Ernie and the whole town and county believed McFee and Coyle were guilty of Sholto's murder. McFee had damned himself by this escape. Now all that remained to do was take care of Sholto. And where the hell was Cord?

At the corral Wallace cursed his men out for loafing and sent them about their business away from the ranch. They were a hardcase crew, used to cursing and needing it. Afterward he came back to the log wing, his face sullen and ugly, and went into the kitchen.

Two women, one an elderly, placid-looking woman, the other young and pretty, were busy in the kitchen. Wallace threw his hat on the table in the center of the room, sank into a chair, and said, "Gimme some breakfast."

The older woman watched him speak, then began bustling about. The breakfast, or that part of it that would keep, was in the oven. She set about frying eggs, while Wallace swilled a cup of hot coffee. The younger woman was kneading bread, and she paid him no attention.

Wallace watched her a moment, his pale eyes speculative, and then he said, "They're tellin' in Yellow Jacket that Coyle killed your husband," he drawled.

The girl whirled to face him, dismay and fear in her face. She looked at Wallace, and then her expression changed. She was a pretty woman with warm dark brown hair and eyes almost the same shade. Relaxed, her face might have been serene and placid, but not now. There was a tension there, and it had been there for a long time, so that her expression was worried and almost sullen.

She said levelly, "You lie."

Wallace grinned crookedly. "I'm only tellin' you what they say."

"Let them say it. Dave Coyle never killed a helpless man."

"But Dave Coyle ain't got him," Wallace said, watching her.

She seemed puzzled, and he went on, "Dave was in jail in Yellow Jacket. He broke loose yesterday. He claims not to know anything about Sholto at all. Don't that prove to you that he killed him?"

"No."

"Then where is he?"

"He—he escaped," the woman said.

"Then why ain't he come back here to you?"

"He'll be back," the girl said stanchly.

"Me, I think he's dead," Wallace said. Sholto's wife didn't; he could see that. And now there was no fun in ragging her, so he ate his breakfast in surly silence.

He was almost finished when Sholto's wife said, "There's a strange rider just come in."

"Alone?" Wallace asked quickly.

"Yes."

Wallace left his breakfast, grabbed his hat, and went out. Lily Sholto watched him through the window, her face twisted with hatred. Then she felt a hand on her arm and turned to face the older woman. Mrs. Babson looked at the girl and shook her head, and Lily sighed, then smiled. Mrs. Babson couldn't talk, for she was mute. And she couldn't hear, for she was deaf. She was just another precaution that Wallace had taken, so that nothing that went on here would be repeated outside.

Wallace, glancing around as he walked toward the corral and the strange rider, saw one of the crew shoeing a horse at the blacksmith shop. He whistled, then beckoned the rider, and went on his way, feeling more comfortable. He was a little edgy with strangers now that Marty Cord was gone.

But it turned out that the man wasn't a stranger. He was the same man who had demanded the ransom for Sholto in Yellow Jacket. Then where was Marty? Wallace felt a cold suspicion, mingled with anger, as he approached him.

"Don't worry none," the rider said without preliminary. "Your rider that followed me is safe enough, for all of me. I shook him."

"What rider?" Wallace asked coldly.

The rider shrugged. He glanced at the man walking over to them and said, "You couldn't be spooky, could you?"

"About what?"

"Dave Coyle, I reckon."

"Listen," Wallace said meagerly. "Light a shuck out of here. I ain't goin' to buy Sholto back from you, so that's over."

The man grinned. "Buy him back?" he echoed, and then he laughed shortly. "Mebbe not. But do you know what you're goin' to do?" He paused, letting Wallace savor the question, and then he said, "You're goin' to pay us fifty thousand dollars not to bring him back."

Wallace just stared at him, scowling. "Say that again."

"I said you're goin' to pay us fifty thousand dollars to keep Sholto hid. Is it worth it?"

"You're loco," Wallace said angrily.

The man shrugged. "Suit yourself. Sholto's murder is hung on McFee and Coyle, and they've escaped. That means a price on their heads, and sooner or later someone will gun 'em." He grinned. "You'd look damn silly, now that you've got McFee outlawed and a murder hung on him, if Sholto was to show up. Of course, with Sholto, you could likely win your court fight. But with him murdered, you already got it won. McFee will hang or get killed. Now do you savvy?"

"I savvy," Wallace said slowly. The Three Rivers rider was standing just a little behind him, listening.

"If I don't aim to pay you off to keep Sholto hid, what will you do?"

"Turn him over to Sheriff Beal. Beal will send the word out that McFee ain't wanted. Then you'll have to go on with your court fight."

Wallace regarded him with a queer smile playing on the corner of his thin lips. "And if I pay you, what do you do?"

"Whatever you say. We'll keep Sholto hid, if you say the word. We'll turn him over to you to keep hid, if you want."

"Will you—get him out of the way for good?"

The man stared at him, understanding him well enough. He said quietly, "Not for that price. Do your own killin', Wallace."

"Who's got him?" Wallace said abruptly.

The man shook his head. "Now I don't aim to tell you that."

"Where is he?"

"Nor that neither."

Wallace's hands had been hanging at his sides. Now he raised his right hand in one fluid motion, and when it came to rest hip high there was a Colt .44 in it, cocked, leveled at the rider. Wallace said, "This time I'll find him myself."

The rider didn't even seem surprised. "I don't reckon you will."

Wallace said, "Joe, take his rope and tie him."

The Three Rivers man did Wallace's bidding. Afterward Wallace led the way over to the blacksmith shop, his rider leading the hog-tied messenger. In the blacksmith shop Wallace pointed to the big anvil and said, "Tie him over that, face up."

The messenger was ordered down on his knees, his back to the anvil. He said with just a suggestion of alarm in his voice, "What are you aimin' to do to me?"

Wallace only smiled and told his rider to get on with the job. The messenger was bent over backward and lashed to the anvil, the rope running under his arms. Then Wallace went over to the forge, blew the coals there into a glowing heat, took a branding iron from the rack, and laid it on the coals.

The messenger, who was watching him carefully, saw him

and said, "I don't know nothin' about it, I tell you! I was only sent here!"

Wallace turned to him and only smiled faintly. He picked up the iron by its long handle and came over to the messenger. Smiling crookedly, he held it close to the messenger's cheek. The man shrank away from it as far as he could, the sweat standing out on his forehead.

"Now," Wallace said thinly, "I'm goin' to shove this square in your face unless you talk. I'm goin' to give you one chance —one, you understand!"

The messenger nodded.

Wallace said, "Who's got Sholto?"

The messenger said earnestly, "Wallace, I'm only a nester over on Blue Crick! I was paid fifty dollars by Turkey Gordon to come to you with this word! That's all I know, and you can kill me and I can't tell you more, because that's all I know!"

"You don't know who's got Sholto?"

"Somebody Turk's workin' for, and that's God's own truth!"

Wallace didn't want to believe him. With the iron still inches from the man's face, Wallace asked savagely, "Then how in hell was you to deliver the money?"

"I was told to ride up the long grade before you get in Wagon Mound. Beginnin' at the turnoff to the old mill, I was to start whistlin' 'O Susanna' over and over, and I'd git picked up pretty quick."

Wallace cursed him then and raised the iron, ready to stamp it in the man's face. The man moaned and turned his head away, and just as the iron reached its peak, ready to descend, a sharp voice said:

"Put that down, Wallace!"

Wallace's hand paused. He turned his head. There, standing in the doorway, was Dave Coyle.

Wallace saw Dave didn't have a gun in his hand, and in that second he acted.

He threw the iron at Dave, and his hand streaked for his gun. Dave ducked the iron, and then from his hip a flash of orange fire blossomed. Wallace's Stetson went sailing off behind him. Wallace's hand quickly fell away from his gun butt.

And then the rider, who had been to one side of Dave, unseen, dived at him and they went down. McFee suddenly stepped out from behind the door, a gun in his hand. He said swiftly, "Keep your hands away from that, Wallace." Wallace, who had started for his gun again, paused once more, then raised his hands. The Three Rivers hand had piled into Dave, and now they were down together. Dave was on the bottom, and the puncher was slugging wildly at him. Dave saw the sizzling iron lying only three feet from his head. He raised a leg to brace himself, then suddenly wrapped his arms around the puncher, and rolled him over.

The puncher's side hit the ground, and Dave rolled him over on his back.

The puncher screamed. Dave had rolled him over on the hot iron. Dave got off him. The puncher scrambled away from the iron and lay there moaning.

Dave said meagerly to him, "You come off lucky."

He glanced up at Wallace. "You hadn't ought to do that to me, fella. It'll get you hurt sometime."

He kicked the puncher to his feet, then said, "Get in there with your boss."

When the puncher and Wallace were standing together Dave looked at the messenger, still bound to the anvil. He said to Wallace, "Untie him."

Wallace did. Dave said then, "Now you three jaspers just sit down on the floor with your backs to that anvil."

They sat down sullenly, the puncher still moaning with pain. Dave bound them to the stump on which the heavy anvil sat. Its weight would hold them there, and if they succeeded in crawling to their knees it would topple over on one of them.

Dave stepped back and said, "I don't figure you'll need a gag, Wallace. Your crew's rode out for the day. I heard you send 'em, because we were hidin' in the loft. That only leaves two women, don't it? Well, one of 'em's deaf, McFee says, and the other won't be here." He raised his hand in mock salute. "McFee will keep you quiet, I reckon, while I do a little business."

He said to McFee, "Try and hold your temper and don't shoot Wallace unless you have to."

He grinned at Wallace and walked around to the side where the messenger was tied. He said, "You said 'O Susanna,' didn't you?"

The messenger nodded, and Dave went out and up to the house. He knocked on the door through which Wallace had entered that morning.

It was opened by a pretty girl who started a little at sight of him. Dave took off his Stetson.

"Mrs. Sholto? I'm Dave Coyle."

"I—guessed you were," she said, bewilderment in her voice.

"Wallace has likely told you I killed your husband. Do you believe it?"

"I don't believe anything he says," Lily Sholto said bitterly.

"You want to see Jim Sholto again?"

"Then you've got him?"

"I haven't, but if you come with me I will have."

She regarded him with puzzlement in her eyes. Dave smiled a little and said, "Look, Mrs. Sholto. Nobody's told me anything; I've just guessed. Your husband got in a jam of some sort. That's what Wallace held over him to make him witness that fake deed. And to make sure that your husband didn't run out on him he's holdin' you here. Is that right?"

The girl stared at him a long moment, then moved her head slightly in assent.

"Then once you're out of Wallace's hands it means your husband can break loose, don't it?"

"Why—yes."

"Then you better come with me," Dave said gently.

"But Wallace will turn over the—the information to the sheriff," Lily said slowly. "Jim will be outlawed."

"That's right," Dave said. "You reckon you'd rather have him work for Wallace than be an outlaw, Mrs. Sholto?"

Sudden decision came to Lily Sholto's eyes. She said quietly, "I know I wouldn't." She started to turn away, and Dave said, "Don't say anything to that woman in there. Just walk out."

Lily hesitated, looked long at Dave, then, as if her mind was made up, took her apron off and stepped out the door. "I trust you, you see," she said quietly.

Dave only nodded, and they walked out to the blacksmith shop. When Lily Sholto saw Wallace tied to the anvil her eyes widened, and she looked sharply at McFee and Dave. Then they saddled three horses and rode off. Already the messenger and the Three Rivers rider were yelling for help. Wallace wasn't, because he knew it was no use.

XI

CAROL WAITED one miserable day and a half until the last member of the second and larger posse hunting her father and Dave straggled into Yellow Jacket. There was no sign of Dave Coyle and McFee, the sheriff's office reported. It was believed that they were heading into the desert country to the east, although all sign of them had been lost before they reached Sabinal. Sheriff Beal was raging like a madman. When Carol went to bed that night Beal had already laid before the county commissioners a suggestion for an emergency appropriation for a permanent dozen deputies, the best trackers and shots in the county. They were to be paid to systematically hunt down and kill Dave Coyle and McFee.

Carol awakened late the next morning, knowing that she couldn't stand this any longer. To sit here almost within sight of the sheriff's office, knowing that over there men were planning to hunt down her father and kill him, like they would hunt down a mad dog, was intolerable.

She sent word to Senator Maitland, asking him if he would drive her back to the Bib M. When she got his answer that he would have the buckboard at the hotel in fifteen minutes she felt a relief that was hard to put into words. What had happened these last few days was bewildering. Her father had turned from a sane man into a maniac. He had hated Dave Coyle enough to put a reward on his head and fist-fight him in jail, yet he had escaped with Coyle. And she had started out by liking Dave Coyle, and now she hated him. Everything was changed, so that she didn't know what to believe or whom to believe.

When she went down into the lobby, Bitterman carrying her bag, Ernie See rose from a lobby chair and came over to her. "Mind stoppin' in at the sheriff's office before you go, Miss McFee?"

"How did you know I was going?" Carol asked sharply.

"Saw the senator hitchin' up. He's over at the office. Would you like to come?"

"I wouldn't like to, but I will," Carol said tartly and added, "What for, so you can show me how you plan to kill my father?"

Ernie didn't say anything, only held open the lobby door. He and Carol walked downstreet to the sheriff's office without exchanging a word. Sheriff Beal rose at her entrance, and Senator Maitland, his face troubled, smiled and spoke to her.

"This'll only take a minute, Miss McFee," Beal said coldly. "I only wanted to show you some things. They ought to convince you, I reckon, that you ought to make your dad give himself up."

"How could I?" Carol asked impatiently. "I don't know where he is."

"He'll turn up," Beal said grimly. "A bad penny."

He unfolded a newspaper and laid it on the desk. A story on the front page in bold type was circled with a blue pencil mark. "I just got this by the Sabinal stage," he said slowly. "You might have heard about me askin' the county for money to hunt your dad down?"

"I did!" Carol said angrily.

"Well, I got it, and not from the county. Here. Read this." He shoved the paper at her.

Carol saw it was the Sabinal weekly *Clarion*. In a boxed message on the front page was this story:

This office has received anonymously the sum of five thousand dollars. The sender specifies that it is to be offered as a reward for the capture, alive or dead, of Bruce McFee, Yellow Jacket County rancher, guilty of paying for the murder of a witness who was to appear against him in court of law. The money has been forwarded this day to Sheriff Harvey Beal, and with it goes the heartiest approbation of all decent-thinking folks in this county.

Carol's face was crimson with anger as she finished. She threw the paper on the desk and said, "That's a cheap trick of Lacey Thornton's to get even with Dad!"

Beal held out a bank draft and said, "What's cheap about five thousand dollars?"

Carol could only glare at him, speechless with anger.

"There's that," Beal said, "and then there's this. It come on the Sabinal stage today too. Open the envelope."

Carol did, and a shower of crisp new bank notes fell to the desk. Inside was a note. She read: "This is reward for the capture, dead or alive, of Bruce McFee. (Signed) A Friend of Law and Order."

Beal looked at her and said gently, "If there's ten thousand dollars' reward for the capture, alive or dead, of your dad, do you see, Miss McFee, what I'm tryin' to tell you? Your dad will have a bigger price on his head than Dave Coyle. Why, there's hundreds of men in this county and surroundin' counties that will give up their jobs, oil up their guns, and spend years huntin' for your dad. He can't win."

Carol's face was pale, and her lips trembled with indignation. "Oh, it—it's rotten!" she said passionately. "It's beastly! I can't believe that people feel that way about Dad! It's just that—that two men have seen a chance to get Dad murdered, and they're willing to pay cheap bounty hunters like you to do it for them! Can't you see? It's just another way of assassinating an innocent man!"

Ernie See said, "Innocent of what? He escaped, didn't he?"

"One moment," Senator Maitland said. "You're overstepping your authority, Beal, and you know it as well as I do. You haven't proof that Sholto is dead! You haven't any right or authority to offer an 'alive-or-dead' reward for Bruce McFee. 'Capture and conviction,' yes, but 'alive or dead,' no. And I'll fight you from hell to breakfast to prove it in court!" His kindly face was stern-looking, unrelenting, Carol had never seen him so angry.

"You got ahead of me, Senator," Sheriff Beal said dryly. "I said, 'If there's a ten-thousand alive-or-dead reward.' I was tryin' to show Miss McFee what's liable to happen." He looked at Carol now. "Your dad is runnin' with Dave Coyle. If anybody tries to capture them there'll be shootin and killin'. And the minute anyone is killed tryin' to capture them, Miss McFee, the court will give me permission to add 'alive or dead' to the reward. And I want him to give himself up before that happens. I want you to tell him, too, that travelin' with Dave Coyle will get him hanged—and damn quick!"

"I'll tell him!" Carol said angrily. There wasn't any more to say to these two men, so she turned to Maitland and said, "Come on, Senator," and went out. Maitland, his kindly face grim, followed her.

Carol didn't say anything while her bags were loaded into the buckboard at the hotel, and she didn't speak until they were out of town.

Senator Maitland kept looking at her, and finally he took her hand in his. "Don't worry, my dear. It'll work out some way," he said gruffly.

"But, Uncle Dan, how can it?" Carol cried. She hadn't called him Uncle Dan since she was a child, and it seemed to touch him. He squeezed her hand and said, "Wait. Time settles a lot of things."

Carol got a grip on herself and looked around her. They were going across the long sage flats west of town, angling toward Wagon Mound, the third town of the county that lay twenty miles west and near the Corazon. It was a crisp fall day, but out in the sun now it was almost hot. This was the time of year she loved, when the chamiso blossomed a gaudy yellow and laid its sharp and pleasant odor over the country. Now and then, off near the creek bottoms, she saw the yellow banners of the cottonwoods touched by frost, and below them the crimson splendor of the wild-plum thickets. The air was limpid, pulling the Corazon to the north miles closer, and the sky was cloudless with the high cold.

She said quietly, "Uncle Dan, who sent that money to Beal?"

Maitland roused himself and said, "I don't know, child. It's hard to tell."

"I think Lacey Thornton sent the first five thousand. He's hated Dad ever since he left the Bib M. He'd pay to see him hang!"

"Possibly," Maitland said. "He's a better hater than he is an editor."

"But who sent the other five thousand?"

"I don't know. One of your father's enemies, perhaps." He smiled and shook his head. "When a man rises to the top he's bound to step on toes. Maybe your father didn't know it, but he probably stepped on many toes."

Carol said slowly, looking at the road beyond the horse's ears, "It's the same man who is behind Wallace."

Maitland looked swiftly at her, surprised. "Behind Wallace? What are you talking about?"

"Hasn't it seemed queer to you, Uncle Dan, that Wallace tried this steal when Dad's hand was crippled and his signature didn't mean a thing? Hasn't it seemed queer to you, too, that Wallace was a tinhorn gambler two years ago and that he's boss of one of the biggest cattle companies in the territory today?"

"I hadn't thought of it," Maitland said slowly. "Yes, it does seem queer. What do you deduce from that?"

"That there's somebody else's money and brains directing Wallace. And that man, whoever he is, is a friend of Dad's. Look, Dad doesn't sign his name ten times a year. Who else but a friend would know about Dad's signature being as shaky as it is? Who else would know Sam, our old foreman, well enough to know he'd take a bribe and then bribe him? No, it's a friend of Dad's who's doing it, or somebody that knows him well. And my guess is that man sent that last five thousand reward money too," she finished bitterly.

Maitland shook his head. "That's an awful thought, my girl, a terrible thought."

"Terrible or not, it's true!"

Maitland was silent a moment, and then he said, "You have a logical right to suspect me."

"Oh, Uncle Dan!" Carol cried. "How can you say that?"

Senator Maitland smiled. "I didn't say you did, my dear. I said you have a right to. There's Doc Mosher and Josh Bitterman, your dad's best and oldest friends. And the Governor. Would you say Doc would do it?"

"No," Carol said quickly. "He's been loyal to Dad for years! He's understood his hardness and forgiven him and tried to soften him. No."

"Josh Bitterman?"

Carol smiled. "No, certainly not. He's as cantankerous and hardheaded as Dad. He's independent, and he doesn't envy any man alive. Besides, he hasn't the brains."

"That leaves me and the Governor. He'd hardly do it."

"Don't be ridiculous, Uncle Dan," Carol said shortly. She looked at him. "I've hurt you."

"Nonsense," Maitland said and smiled faintly. "But I insist I get either a clean slate or that I'm suspected." He frowned. "If it's a friend of Bruce's that's doing it he would have to have several things. First, brains."

"You've got the brains," Carol said, laughing.

"Second, ambition."

"Well, a man doesn't get to be a senator without having ambition," Carol teased him.

"Third, he'd have to have money to buy the Three Rivers outfit."

Carol sighed mockingly. "And you haven't any money, have you, Uncle Dan?"

Maitland laughed gently. "Hardly. If I'd stuck to my law business I might have made some. But I'm too fiddle-footed. I'm a politician."

"That lets you out."

Maitland said dryly, "At least it lets me out as far as mailing five thousand dollars in bank notes to Sheriff Beal. Whoever this man is, he must have money. Lots of it."

"Of course."

Maitland shook his head. "I think you're wrong, Carol. Three Rivers could be backed by a syndicate of gamblers, bent on crooked work. Wallace could have been put in there to run it for them, being one of their kind. And as for getting information about your dad, you've forgotten Sam, your old foreman."

"What about him?"

"If he could be bribed to disappear, certainly he could have been bribed to give Wallace all the information about your dad that was needed. Isn't that right?"

"Yes," Carol said slowly. "That's right."

"So your case has been picked to pieces by a jackleg lawyer," Maitland drawled and laughed at her.

"But I still think I'm right," Carol said stubbornly.

They were silent a long time, each thinking of the matter. Finally Maitland said, "This is an interesting suspicion, Carol. Does your dad share it?"

"I've told him. But he was too worried."

"And young Dave Coyle?"

"I don't think he does," Carol murmured and added bitterly, "I hope not, anyway, or he'd interfere again."

Maitland shook his head. "A dangerous and disagreeable young man, your Dave Coyle. But his crimes will catch up with him, and soon, I believe."

The ride was a long and dreary one. They paused in Wagon Mound, a straggling frontier town of a dozen false-front stores and a tangle of stock pens squatting along the railroad. After supper they headed on out to the Bib M, McFee's spread. It was six miles from town and middle evening before they reached it.

McFee had sent their housekeeper back to her people when they had left for Santa Fe, and Carol wondered what she would do alone in the big and silent house.

But as they rounded the butte that headed the valley where the home ranch lay they saw lights ahead. Carol said swiftly, "Could it be Dad?"

"I hope not," Maitland said, concern in his voice. "He'd be a fool to hide out here."

"Hurry, Uncle Dan!"

The road sloped down into a pleasant sheltered valley. Against the north slope, where a stand of cottonwoods pointed down to the grassy valley floor, the house stood. It was a two-story affair of the stone of the country, with a gallery running along its front. Considering the country, it was an old place, mellowed by a decade of living. The outbuildings were dark, the stone bunkhouse deserted, for Tate Wallace's land steal had left Bruce McFee a piddling thousand acres of desert range without water or grass. The Bib M riders had been paid off, with the right to return if the court fight against Wallace was won.

Maitland drove into the yard, dismounted, and tied the

team to the small tie rail in front of the house. Carol, however did not wait for him. She ran up the walk under the gallery and tried the front door. It was locked, and she yanked the bellpull impatiently.

Maitland was standing beside her when Lily Sholto, in the dark dress and white apron of a servant, opened the door.

Carol stood there, surprise making her speechless, when Lily said, "Miss Carol, I'm the new housekeeper."

Carol walked in, unable to take her eyes off this pretty girl. "But—who hired you?"

"Your father," Lily said.

"Dad! Has he been here!"

Lily nodded. "With Dave Coyle. They've left." She closed the door behind her and took an envelope out of her apron pocket. "This is for you."

Carol took the envelope and ripped it open and was ready to draw out the letter when a thundering knock sounded on the door.

The three of them stood there staring at each other, and then Carol said faintly, "Answer it, please."

When Carol and Senator Maitland had left the sheriff's office the corridor door opened and Lacey Thornton stepped out. He'd been hiding in the corridor, where he could hear every word that was said. He looked a little less red-faced then he looked that day at Sabinal, but not much. A lifetime of hard drinking had flushed his tight little monkey's face until it was a uniform brick red and held the stamp of perpetual anger.

He scratched his fringe of copper hair and looked at Beal. "Well, it didn't work. Maitland gummed it up."

"She's scared, I think," Ernie See said. He shook his head. "But I shouldn't have brought Maitland over. If he hadn't been here we'd have made her believe that reward was 'dead or alive' right now. She'd have led us to McFee then, all right."

"Maybe she will now," Thornton said.

"She ain't scared enough," Beal said. "She's just mad."

"You know what I think?" Lacey Thornton said. "I think he's at the Bib M."

"At his spread? Hell, he'd be a fool to do that," Beal said. "Why?"

"It's the first place we'd look for him."

"Have you looked?" Thornton asked dryly.

Beal looked at Ernie and grinned sheepishly.

"There you are," Thornton said. "McFee's travelin' with Dave Coyle, and I keep rememberin' that time Coyle ate in the commissioner's kitchen when that reward was put on him. Coyle's that way. He does what you don't figure he'll do and hasn't got the nerve to do. It's like him to convince McFee the safest place for them to hide is right at the Bib M, the last place you'd think of lookin'.'"

Beal said bluntly, "You're right." He said to Ernie, "Let's head for the Bib M. We'll get there about dark and hole up until Carol McFee and Maitland get there, then bust in on them and search the place."

"It's worth a try," Ernie agreed.

The three of them left the office, locked it, and after Beal had deposited the money in the bank, got their horses and rode out across the flats toward Wagon Mound and the Bib M. Ernie See seemed preoccupied during the first half-hour, and Beal and Thornton did most of the talking. But in one of the silences Ernie said to Thornton, "You hear what Miss McFee had to say about you, Thornton?"

"I heard her," Thornton said grimly. "She thinks I put up the money."

"Did you?"

"No!" Thornton yelled. "I wish I'd thought of it, though!"

"Funny," Ernie said mildly. "Why'd they send it to you instead of to us?"

"I don't know. Maybe they wanted it printed in the Clarion."

"We'd have told the Clarion," Ernie said stubbornly.

Thornton turned on him, his red face glowing. "Why ask me? I tell you I didn't put up the money. But I think it's a good idea. I thought it was so good that I rode over on the stage to show it to you. But that's all I did!"

"Sure, sure," Ernie said gently. But he wasn't convinced. Hadn't Thornton, in public and out of it, cursed Bruce McFee and threatened him and fought him? He had. And now Thornton had appeared with the money and the proposition of trying to scare Carol with the reward threat until she led them to McFee. No, it was more than coincidence. There was nothing unlawful about it, but why hadn't Thornton come out with it and been aboveboard? Ernie thought he knew. Thornton hated Bruce McFee so much he was ashamed of it himself. It was hardly within the dignity of a country editor to offer money for, as Carol McFee had put it, the assassination of an enemy, so Thornton had given it anonymously. Ernie didn't like McFee much better than Thornton did, but somehow that stuck in his craw. He was already ashamed of trying to scare Carol, but he put it down as necessity. Any means justified the ends, if Dave Coyle and McFee were trapped.

It was well after dark when they arrived at the Bib M. They left their horses tied to the fence in the horse pasture and quietly made their way up to the buildings. There was a light in the house, but the other buildings were deserted. Ernie first conducted a search of the barns and outbuildings. A couple of horses had come in from pasture to drink at the tank, but that meant nothing. They could be Coyle's and McFee's or they could be ranch horses. But one thing he was sure of; there were no horses saddled for a quick getaway.

The three of them squatted behind the bunkhouse to await the arrival of Carol and Maitland.

They had waited an hour, when they heard the buckboard pull into the place and stop at the tie rail by the house. Guns drawn, they walked softly toward the house, seeing Carol pull the bell rope and Maitland join her. When they were let into the house Beal said, "Wait a minute. Give McFee time to find out who it is and come out."

They counted thirty seconds, and then Beal got impatient. "Come on!" he said.

They went up to the door, and Beal kicked it in his anxiety to get inside.

It was opened by the maid, and Beal stepped in, gun drawn, followed by Ernie and Thornton.

Carol, an envelope in her hand, stood in the hallway, Maitland beside her. Carol had a startled expression on her face as she saw Beal.

"What are you doing here?" she asked angrily.

"We aim to search the house," Beal said grimly. "Don't you scream or raise a fuss, Miss McFee."

Carol's heart sank. Hadn't this new girl said her father had gone? She was sure she had. She looked at Lily, and Lily's face seemed serene. Assured by it, Carol's panic vanished, and in its place came anger. What right had they to hound her even to her own house? And with Lacey Thornton too.

Maitland said sharply, "Let's see your warrant, Beal."

Beal's innocent-looking face got a little hard. "My face is my warrant, Maitland. If it don't suit you, sue me." He looked at Carol. "You take me upstairs, Miss McFee. Have your girl take Ernie through the lower rooms. And you just walk ahead, please, in case your dad wants to act salty with a gun."

"I won't!" Carol said.

"You better," Beal said gently. "I've never locked up a woman yet, but there's a first time for everything."

Carol, uncertain and angry and a little afraid, looked to Maitland for help.

"You don't have to do it, Carol, but you'll probably keep them from looting the place if you stay by them."

Beal flushed. "That's somethin' I'm not liable to forget next election, Senator."

"Which reminds me that you have an election coming up also," Maitland said with gentle irony. "Even Stephen, eh?"

Beal grunted and waved Carol on. She put the letter down on the table, then said to Lily, "Show them the downstairs, Lily," and went ahead of Beal up the stairs.

Lily said to Ernie, "If you'll come this way I'll show you."

Ernie had been looking at her for a long time, wondering where he had seen her before. Then he said abruptly, "I know you. You're the girl that asked me in town when Wallace was goin' out to his place."

Lily's face was impassive. "Yes. You didn't tell me."

"Changed jobs?" Ernie asked curiously.

Lily only nodded and said, "Do you want to come along?"

Ernie could take a hint. She didn't want to talk about herself. He said, "Sure," and followed her. He liked her looks this time even better than he had last time, but that wedding ring troubled him. He wished vaguely she wasn't wearing it. Maitland and Lacey Thornton tagged behind as he went into the living room and began to look around.

For a half-hour after that there followed a systematic search of the house from basement to attic, Thornton helping, Maitland watching. There was a confusion of doors slamming, of walls being tapped, of furniture moved, of beds poked under and barrels upended. At the end of the search they met in the hall again.

"I hope you're satisfied," Carol said hotly.

Ernie flushed uncomfortably. "Well, we got to look at it from the side of the law."

"The next time you come," Maitland said grimly, "you'd better have a warrant, my friends. Because even lawmen are fair game for a shotgun, if they haven't got a warrant."

Carol looked at Lacey Thornton and her lip curled in contempt. "And since when have you been a lawman?" she asked.

"I deputized him," Beal put in uncomfortably.

"Is that in return for the favor of putting up five thousand dollars for the capture of my father?" Carol asked.

Beal squirmed. "All right. We're doin' our best."

"Then get out of this house!" Carol cried. "If I ever see any of you around here again I'll take down Dad's shotgun. And you, Lacey Thornton! I'll have Dad horsewhip you in public the next time you see him!"

"That'll be pretty hard to do if he's in a coffin," Ernie said angrily.

The three of them stalked out, and Lily Sholto, who had remained silent all through this, closed the door after them.

Carol sank into the nearest chair and looked at Maitland for a long moment. Then she said miserably, "Isn't there any way to stop this, Uncle Dan?"

Maitland smiled his tired smile. "This is just the beginning, Carol. Try and be calm."

Carol did. She leaned back in the chair and closed her eyes and relaxed. Forget them, she thought. Be thankful Dad wasn't here when they came. What had she been doing before they came? Oh, the letter, of course.

She opened her eyes and looked at the table where she had put the letter.

It wasn't there!

For one short second she stared at the table, then jumped up.

"The letter!" she cried. She looked at Lily. "Have you got it?"

Lily looked startled. "You put it on the table, miss."

"But it's gone!" Carol cried. She looked in consternation at Maitland, who was staring goggle-eyed at the table. "You left it there?" he asked blankly.

"Yes! And they took it!"

She ran for the door, threw it open, and went out into the night. She couldn't see or hear anything. It was too late!

She came back in the house and said swiftly to Lily, "Do you know what was in it?"

"No, miss," Lily said. "Mr. Coyle told me not to tell you anything or talk about myself. The letter would tell you all you should know."

Carol looked bleakly at Maitland. "Oh, Uncle Dan! What if Dad told where he was hiding?" She was near tears.

Maitland came over and took her in his arms, and Carol sobbed wildly on his chest. Maitland stroked her hair and said softly, "Don't look at the dark side so much, my dear. There, there."

XII

IT LACKED an hour of dawn when McFee and Dave approached the spot where the sawmill road joined the Wagon Mound road. McFee was dog-tired and sleepy and hungry and saddle-stiff, and he wished Dave would stop that gentle off-key whistling. During that day and night they had scrapped with Wallace, delivered Lily Sholto at the home ranch, and then had ridden on here. More than anything else, McFee wanted a bed, some hot food, and some quiet. Dave Coyle seemed to want nothing.

"All right," Dave said, turning in the saddle. "You know 'O Susanna'? Ride up the road whistlin' it."

"Me?" McFee said and added hastily, "Oh no. I'm no good at foolin' anybody."

"Who said you had to?" Dave asked coldly.

"But if they see it's me and not the messenger they'll hit for the brush!"

Dave said patiently, "When they stop you tell them you want to ransom Sholto yourself and take him in to Sheriff Beal."

"But they'll want to know how I found out about this whistlin' business," McFee objected.

"Sure they will. They'll want to know so bad they'll take you to Usher so he can beat it out of you."

McFee didn't say anything for a moment. "What'll you do?"

"I'll follow you," Dave said, still patiently.

McFee said suddenly, "Coyle, I don't like this. We're walkin' into a bunch of killers. We can't hope to get out of there alive with Sholto."

Dave said jeeringly, "All right. Let's ride in to Wagon Mound and get a posse up."

McFee said stubbornly, "But this is suicide!"

Dave shifted faintly in his saddle, his arrogant gaze on Mc-

Fee in the dark. "I dunno why I bother with you," he said softly. "I don't reckon I will any longer." He pulled his horse around, as if to ride away.

"Wait a minute," McFee said hastily. Dave stopped, watching him. McFee rubbed his face with the palm of his hand. "I'm tired," he said quietly.

"Sure you are," Dave jeered. "You got a price on your head by now, I reckon. Nobody'll let you rest. You eat on the run and sleep on your gun and you'll wear out a saddle before it's over. But it's what I been doin' for years. Remember that the next time you raise the ante on me by three thousand dollars."

McFee said wearily, "Quit it."

"You're yellow," Dave said calmly. "Take that bank account and that spread away from you and you're an ordinary old cow poke—only not so good."

McFee's chin came up. "You're a liar!"

"Then what are you waitin' for?" Dave countered.

McFee picked up the reins off the horn and looked through the darkness at Dave, his eyes savage and harried and beaten.

"One more day," he said, "and then this will be over. I told Carol in that note I left that we'd have Sholto into Yellow Jacket tonight." He smiled wickedly. "Just picture me tonight, Coyle. I'll sleep in a bed. I'll eat a good dinner. I'll have a cigar and a paper to read. And you—you'll be hidin' out in the brush, jumpin' every time a rat steps on a leaf. You'll be eatin' jerky and ridin' all day and wonderin' when somebody will cut down on you from the next ridge. And don't you worry. I'll have an extra three thousand on your head, just to keep you movin'."

Dave smiled faintly. "It scares me to death. Are you goin' out there, or am I goin' to ride off?"

"I'll go," McFee gibed wearily. "I'm the one that takes all the risks, while you, the brave gunman, stays hid."

"That's right. Only when we get in the tight spot there at Usher's camp, remember who gets you out."

McFee didn't say anything, only pulled his horse out of the trees onto the road and vanished into the darkness. Dave slipped out of the saddle and tied his horse. He set out on foot now in the darkness, listening for the sound of McFee up ahead.

Presently, as McFee passed the sawmill road, he began to whistle. It was a thin, flat, woebegone whistle, but the tune was recognizable. Dave let him get a ways ahead, and then he followed him, walking in the deep noise-muffling dust of the road.

Suddenly he heard a man's voice call out, and McFee's whistling stopped.

Dave froze, listening.

"Bart?" the sleepy voice called.

"It's Bruce McFee," McFee answered. "I want to buy Sholto back."

There was a long wait, and then a voice said sharply, "Stick 'em up, McFee. There's three of us here!"

"All right." At least McFee's voice didn't sound panicky, and Dave thought maybe the older man would carry it through.

"Now what do you want?" a rough voice said.

"I told you. I want to pay Sholto's ransom and take him back to Beal, so I can get out from under this murder charge."

"Who told you to whistle that tune?"

"What does it matter?"

"Plenty, mister. Where's your little playmate?"

"I shook him," McFee said dryly. "No, not exactly that. He just rode off and let me get myself out of this jam the best way I could."

There was a long silence, and then a voice said, "You'll come with us."

There was a sound of horses approaching him, and Dave faded back into the timber, thinking the riders would turn off on the old mill road. But they passed the turnoff, and Dave was suddenly aware that they were coming toward him, heading up into the mountains above Wagon Mound. Remembering his horse across the road and the likelihood of it whickering when it smelled these horses, Dave crouched low in the road and ran across it and moved swiftly toward his horse. He reached it, clapped a hand over its nose, and then listened while the riders passed him.

So Will Usher wasn't hiding out close to here, then? Will was too smart and wary to risk holding Sholto close to these pickup men for Wallace to surround with his crew. If Dave knew him Usher would be hidden many miles from here.

He squatted on the ground now, shivering a little in the coming dawn, wondering if McFee would be tough enough to hold out under Will Usher's questioning until he got there. Dave thought he would because he had so much at stake. He rolled a cigarette, went out to the road, listened, heard nothing, then lighted his cigarette, held the lighted match low, squatted, and studied the tracks in the road. The twenty minutes he had spent at the Bib M putting a double cleat on a shoe of McFee's horse had been worth it, for the print was plain enough to anyone looking for it. McFee hadn't even known he did it, so there was no chance of his giving it away.

When in half an hour or so it became light enough to track, Dave set out after them, heading toward the mountains. In an hour he picked up a road. As the day grew brighter he looked around him uneasily. He was heading into a narrow canyon whose sides were steep, and he knew this road. It led into a dead-end box canyon in a deep fold of the mountain where the Southern Belle mine was located.

He pulled up and looked ahead, puzzled. There was no turnoff on this road, so Will would have to be at the Southern Belle. It was a small mine, with a reduction mill and shack on the valley floor. The mine itself was behind the reduction mill far up on an almost vertical slope. The ore was sent to the reduction mill below in buckets on a cable.

But the Southern Belle was supposed to be working now! Yet it couldn't be, if Will Usher was hidden out there. He had picked a perfect spot to hide, where nobody except the mine crew went. And the valley was so narrow, its sides so steep, that nobody could get in without being seen.

So this was where Sholto was, Dave thought bitterly. He might as well have been locked in a safe. It might have been possible to try the road at night, but in the daytime it was impossible. One lookout could keep an army from coming in.

Dave looked at the road again and made certain that the tracks of McFee's horse led into canyon. Then he dismounted and looked about him. The rough shoulders of the mountains reared up on either side of the road, bleak and forbidding. The mine lay two miles up the road, as he remembered it.

For a long moment he stood there looking at it, baffled. And then, his mind made up as to what he had to do, he turned to his horse and went through the old ritual. He loosened the cinch, slipped the bit, tied up the stirrups, and then, before he drove the horse off, untied the lariat and looped it over his shoulder.

Afterward he left the road and started toward the mountains. In half boots it was cruel punishment to climb these rocks, but he set about it grimly, making his slow way up the face of the mountain. Soon the morning sun started to beat down on the rocks and the steep slope was an inferno. Sweat soaked his shirt and rolled off his face, and still he climbed, pausing only when he was gagging for breath. His main worry now was that McFee, seeing how hopeless it was for anyone to follow him, would quit on him and fail to play out his bluff. Time was slipping by, and each minute made it harder for McFee to string out his story. Dave thought of Will Usher's gunnies, tough, hard, and skeptical. If they doubted McFee they would beat him up on suspicion.

Dave climbed for another hour and knew he was to the south of the deep canyon. He started working north now, still climbing, and presently to his left he saw the land fall away abruptly. This was the canyon, and he could see the opposite wall close now. He knew that a few hundred yards ahead and upward he would come to the head of the canyon.

When he did he was in the treacherous shale, and he paused. Behind him the country lay flat as a table, baking in the sun. He got his breath and then looked above him. There, far above the strip of shale in the living rock, the bucket cable was anchored. Dave achieved it, and then looked down. He could see nothing, except a section of the valley floor far below just being touched by the late-morning sun. A giant iron cleat was anchored in the rock, and the single rope of cable ran through it and down to the lip of the canyon, where a thick iron roller protected it from the sawing edge of the rock. Gingerly, clinging to the cable, Dave inched his way down to the lip and looked over. He drew back almost at once, a sick feeling in the pit of his stomach.

Ahead of him and far, far below lay the reduction mill, its roof looking the size of a postage stamp from this height. He could pick out several things that looked like ants lining one section of the canyon wall. These were the horses, he supposed. And still smaller spots crossing between the two buildings were probably the men.

The cable itself swooped sickeningly toward the canyon floor, looking frailer than a spider web. At regular intervals the ore buckets connected by a smaller cable hung immobile by the pulleys on the big cable, showing the mine was not at work.

And to get to the canyon floor hundreds of feet below he must go down that cable. The thought of it chilled him. And then he thought of McFee, and thinking of him and hating him, he thought of Carol. If he could get Sholto back McFee would go free, and Carol would be happy. At least he would have made up for the blunders he had already committed. Sudden decision took hold of him, and he cast about for some way to get down. He couldn't ride the buckets, for they weren't working, nor climb down hand over hand, for it was too far.

And then he thought of his lariat. The cable, of course, would eat into it if he slid down on it, but if he tripled the rope, wouldn't it be possible to reach the first bucket, change the rope to a fresh hold, slide to the second bucket, and so on?

He didn't know, but he did know one thing. If the cable bit through the rope too fast he had a drop that would break every bone in his body. They could bury him in a fry pan.

Thoughtfully he looked at his lariat, shook his head, then set about making three equal lengths of it. He twisted this about one of the cables, grabbed it with both hands, then, taking a deep breath, he swung off into space. The cable gave a little with his weight, started to sway, and then he picked up speed with the sickening force of gravity. He was swooping down on the ore bucket with the speed of lightning, it seemed. It was only a matter of seconds, and he slammed into the ore bucket, breaking the force of the blow with his feet. He put a foot over the side of the heavy bucket, pulled himself inside, and rested, his hands shaking. Then he looked at the rope. The slide had eaten almost through the three strands, and he shuddered a little when he saw the frayed ends. Three thicknesses wouldn't do. He'd have to take six.

He looked about him. He was hanging out in space right at the shaft mouth. It seemed solid and safe in there, but the feeling was unfounded. He had to go down now. There was no other way out. This time, with six thicknesses of rope, he swung out again and again he shot down the cable with dizzy speed. He hit the second bucket with the force of a pile driver, knocking the wind out of him. But he crawled inside and again got his breath. He was more than halfway down. There was one more bucket and then the yawning mouth of the ore hopper atop the mill. The cable ran on down to be anchored in the canyon floor in front of the mill.

Buildings were closer now, but he was still far above them. Nobody was in sight, and again, after laying six thicknesses of rope across the cable, he swung out.

When he achieved the third bucket he looked at his rope and saw that it was used up. The trip from this bucket to the roof would have to be made hand over hand, without the rope.

He left the rope in the bucket, gripped the cable, and began to lower himself down it. It took an eternity, but finally he was on the lip of the big ore hopper. He rested there, listening. One of the horses below had seen him, and now he eyed him with faint interest.

Dave swung down from the hopper to the roof and, crouching by it, eyed the shack across the canyon floor. It seemed empty, and yet he couldn't be sure. He waited a full ten minutes and saw nothing and concluded that Will was in the building beneath him.

Dave tiptoed up to the edge of the roof and peered over. Two men were standing about thirty feet from the door, their backs to him, talking.

Dave reached up for the cable over his head, crawled hand over hand down it, and then dropped the six feet to the men. He landed astride the shoulders of both men, knocking them to the ground. One man yelled as he fell. Dave whipped out his gun and brought it down on the man's head with a savage force. The other man had been knocked out by the fall. Dave picked up one of their rifles and ran the thirty feet to the door. He flattened against the side of the building just as he heard a table overturn inside and the heavy tramping of feet. The door was yanked open, and at the same time Dave swung the rifle, butt foremost. It caught one of Will Usher's gunnies full in the belly and doubled him over like a jackknife. Dave grabbed him before he fell, held him up with one hand, palmed his gun up with the other, and, using the man as a shield, stepped into the room.

He had a fleeting glimpse of the room before it exploded into action. Will Usher, his gun half out, was lunging for shelter behind Sholto, who was sitting motionless in a chair by the overturned table. McFee was standing against the wall, his hands raised over his head. And in that split second Dave caught sight of the man flattened against the wall inside the door. He wheeled away and back just as the man's gun exploded. The man Dave was holding jarred with the impact of the slug. Dave stuck his gun in, turned it at right angles, and fired just as a window crashed somewhere. The man fell. Then he lunged inside the room over the two bodies on the floor. A gun boomed from the rear of the room, the slug slapping against the wall behind him.

McFee yelled: "Be careful!" as Dave swung up his gun and sent a shot toward the rear of the place. A door slammed; a body fell heavily, and then it was still.

Dave said swiftly, "Where's Usher?"

"Out the window!" McFee said.

Dave ran for the shattered window, stuck his head out and saw nothing, then turned and lunged out the door. Usher had just dived behind the horses. Dave was out the door, running toward him, when Usher shot over the rump of a horse. The slug whistled by Dave's ear, and he dived for the protection of the two unconscious men in the yard. Usher shot again, this time over his head. Dave grabbed the rifle of one of the men, propped him on his side, laid the rifle across him, and then called, "Come on out, Will. You can't make the break."

"Damn you! Come and get me! I'll kill every horse here if you do." He sent another shot at Dave that went over his head.

There was a long silence. Dave couldn't shoot for fear of hitting the horses, which they needed. And Will Usher knew it.

Suddenly Will bawled, "I'll make a deal, Dave! Give me a horse and let me out of here and I won't shoot the horses."

McFee yelled from the house, "Take him up on it, Dave! There's a man guardin' the canyon below! We can't get out afoot!"

Dave said, "Nothin' doin', Will. I wouldn't trust you. You'd fort up out there and send that man for a posse in Wagon Mound." He paused. "I'm comin' over, Will."

"Wait a minute!" Will cried, real terror in his voice. "I'll ride out with you, Dave! I'll pull that man away and take him with me!"

"I'm comin' after you, Will!"

"Dave! Dave! Listen, you need the horses, and I'll kill 'em all if you start over here! Listen to me! I'll give myself up if you'll give me your word you'll turn me loose at the mouth of the canyon. I'll get you by my man!"

McFee bawled, "Dave, you fool! Take him up!"

Dave cursed bitterly. There was McFee howling like an old woman because he was afraid to be afoot in a country where a posse was likely to ride him down. And now Will Usher, because McFee was afraid, would go free. For one stubborn moment Dave told himself McFee could be damned, but he knew he couldn't let Will kill the horses. What was he doing this for? To get Sholto back and McFee free of his charges. Will Usher would have to wait.

Usher bawled, "Give me your word, Davey, and I'll take you out of here!"

Dave dropped his rifle in disgust. This was twice he'd missed Will Usher. He said shortly, "Come on out. You've got it."

XIII

WILL USHER walked out from behind the horses, smiling broadly. He had no fear of being killed now, for Dave Coyle's word, to lawman or outlaw, was never broken. He walked over to Dave, his handsome face smiling. Somewhere in the turmoil he had lost his hat, but he was still wearing his dusty frock coat and his soiled gloves.

"Well, well, Davey," he said wryly. "I thought I had a place here that was Coyle-proof."

"You'll never have one, Will," Dave said. "When I get through with this business I'm goin' to spend a little time on you."

They looked at each other a moment, Will Usher's face troubled, his eyes angry. He looked like a gambler who had tried to fill a bobtail straight and was both surprised and angry that he hadn't. Dave Coyle looked disappointed too—and grim.

McFee, now that the shooting was over, tramped out of the mill shed, Sholto behind him. Dave looked at McFee and, remembering that McFee, instead of warning him of the man inside the shack waiting for him, had stood there with his hands in the air, said sardonically, "I don't know what I'd do without a fightin' partner like you, McFee."

McFee's face was a brick red. "I'm not a gun-fightin' man," he said.

"Why mention gun fightin'?" Dave sneered. "Here." He handed McFee his gun. "If he says boo just hold tight and maybe it won't fall out of your hand."

Dave went back into the mill shed. The man behind the door had shot his partner, and they were both lying dead across the sill. Dave went on through the office to a smaller one and found what he was looking for. The watchman had been bound and gagged and was lying on the floor. Dave untied him.

Afterward he went out to the horses. Usher and McFee mounted first, and Dave swung up alongside of Sholto's horse.

"I've got your wife safe," Dave said to Sholto. "You don't

have to go back to Wallace now. We're showin' you to Beal so he'll free McFee, and then you can ride out."

Sholto's eyes lighted up with a faint hope, and he said, "Thanks."

"You let me get past you that night at the line camp. I pay back my debts."

They rode out of the canyon. Will Usher called down his guard, who was forted up on the canyon slope, and Dave disarmed him and gave him the extra horse.

At the mouth of the canyon Will Usher said, "I'll leave you here, Davey boy," and grinned at him.

Dave shifted in his saddle and regarded Usher with speculation in his eyes. "Aim to high-tail it, Will?"

Usher laughed. "I don't reckon. You know why, Davey? Because I think they'll nail your hide to the wall before you're through here. I aim to help 'em."

Dave nodded agreeably. "Stick around. It'll save me trouble huntin' you."

Usher laughed, waved agreeably, and headed down the road toward Wagon Mound. Dave and McFee and Sholto cut through the timber, rounding the base of the Corazon, and headed for Yellow Jacket.

It was a long ride and a hard one, and Dave hurried. He wanted more than anything else at this moment to get McFee off his hands. Once that was done, once it was proved to Carol that he was willing to help her father, he would be free to work on what was important. Sholto, after all, was a minor matter, a nuisance, a by-product of the court fight. What was important was the identity of the man behind Tate Wallace.

Darkness caught them far out on the flats west of Yellow Jacket. A chill night wind riding the earth bit into them and gave its warning of winter soon to come. It seemed to Dave, looking over at Sholto and McFee with their shoulders hunched against the cold, that all of them would be glad to part company. McFee was sulky, not even cheered by the prospect of his freedom. Sholto was more quiet than any man Dave had seen. He seemed to be considering something, keeping his own counsel. The three of them were like strangers, not even wanting to speak to each other.

When they were finally in sight of the lights of Yellow Jacket, Dave said grimly, "Well, we'll part company pretty quick. What do you aim to do then, McFee?"

"Take up the fight where you interrupted it," McFee said bitterly. "That is, if Sholto goes back to Wallace and intends to swear he was witness to the deed."

Dave said to Sholto, "Will you?"

"I don't know," Sholto said. "I got to think."

They picked up the road south of town, and now the lights of the town were distinct up ahead. They passed the first houses on the outskirts of town, and Dave peered through the darkness at Sholto. Would he show himself to Beal, then vanish? Or would he hunt up Wallace again? Dave didn't know and didn't care. But he did know that if he were in McFee's boots he would be talking, pleading, threatening, or buying him off. Instead McFee was sulkily watching Sholto.

They passed into the business section now, and ahead were the lights of the saloons. The sheriff's office was lighted also, Dave saw. When he came to the middle block of the town, where old Badey's store threw out its light into the street, he reined up.

"This is as far as I go," he murmured. "I'll wait and see if they free you, McFee." He looked at the tie rail in front of Tim King's Keno Parlor. It was jammed with horses. Through the big front window he could see a section of the bar. And there, back to the window, was Tate Wallace. Dave looked at Sholto. Sholto had seen Wallace, too, and his face was a little pale.

McFee said impatiently, "Let's go, Sholto."

Sholto put his horse in motion and rode beside McFee up the street. He was watching Wallace through the saloon window. They were just angling across the street to the sheriff's office when Sholto reined up.

"I'm not goin' in, McFee," he said stubbornly.

"Not going——" McFee's voice died, then he said, "But dammit, man, you've got to! I'll hang for your murder if you don't!"

"No," Sholto said shortly. "It's either you or me that will hang. It might as well be you."

"What do you——?"

"I mean Wallace is in town now," Sholto said swiftly. "He blackmailed me into witnessin' that deed. He was holdin' my wife a prisoner there at the Three Rivers to make sure I didn't run out on him. But Coyle has got my wife hid. Wallace ain't got anything to make me come back, so he'll tell."

"Tell what?"

"That he saw me kill a man," Sholto said evenly. "I killed

him, all right. I was drunk and mad and I shot him, and they can hang me for it. And Wallace has told Beal."

"How do you know?"

"He didn't come after me when Usher had me, did he? No. He knows now that if he can't hold Lily any more I'll light a shuck the first chance I get. So he'll tell Beal. He's told him. He's here. And I'll stand trial." He pulled his horse around. "Sorry, McFee, but I got my own hide to think of."

"Wait a minute!" McFee ordered. Clumsily, then, he pulled out a gun and leveled it at Sholto. "I'm not hanging for any man, not even——"

Crash!

A six-gun bellowed from somewhere, and Sholto was driven over the saddle horn and fell into the road on his face, his shirt in back welling crimson blood.

XIV

ON THE heel of the report McFee's horse began to pitch. In terror it arched its back and started to buck in a circle. Men began to pour out of King's Keno Parlor.

About the tumult Dave yelled: "Run for it, McFee!"

Then someone opened up with a six-gun from the opposite sidewalk, someone who had recognized Dave's voice. Another shot hammered out. Dave yanked his horse around, leaned over its neck, and roweled him savagely, heading out of town. What had happened? Somebody planted up on the roof of Badey's store had shot Sholto! Dave had seen the gun flash. And there was McFee, a gun in his hand, threatening Sholto, who seemed as if he was aiming to ride off. McFee was in for it now. And all Dave could do was run to keep from getting the same thing. Already he heard horses pounding down the road behind him.

Back in town Ernie See and Sheriff Beal had been the first out the door of the sheriff's office. Ernie took the scene in at a glance as he vaulted the tie rail. McFee's terrified horse went into a savage sunfish, and McFee flew out of the saddle. He landed on his shoulder, and Ernie dived on top of him. He wrestled the gun out of his hand, and when he stood up Beal was leaning over Sholto. Men were running toward them from the saloons, and still others were swinging into the saddle and heading out of town.

Beal looked up from Sholto and said to Ernie, "He's dead!"

Slowly McFee hauled himself to his feet, looking dazed. Beal said wickedly, "That hangs you, McFee—hangs you higher'n any kite ever flown!"

"But I didn't shoot him!" McFee cried.

Beal said, "Give me that gun you took from him, Ernie." Ernie gave it to him, and Beal spun the cylinder. There was one cartridge shot. Beal smelled the barrel and said evenly, "One empty, and there's a powder smell. How about that, McFee?"

There was a murmuring of the men surrounding them, and McFee looked helplessly at them. "But I didn't do it, I tell you! I only had a gun in my hand! He wouldn't come in!"

"By God, we ought to string him up!" one man in the crowd said.

Ernie said to McFee, "If you're smart you'll keep your mouth shut!"

"Get him inside," Beal ordered.

Ernie, his hand on McFee's arm, broke the crowd and took McFee into the sheriff's office, through it, and into the cell block and the cell. Beal, with a half-dozen select citizens, followed.

McFee looked dazed. It had all happened too fast.

Beal, from the other side of the door, said, "What happened?"

"I was bringin' Sholto in here to prove to you I never killed him—me and Dave Coyle, that is. Dave stayed downstreet and left me to bring him in. Sholto balked just in front of the office. I pulled a gun on him and told him to come along. Then come a shot, and my horse started to pitch. That's all I know."

Beal said sarcastically, "Beautiful. A good little Injun spirit aimed the gun and pulled the trigger, I suppose."

"But I didn't kill him!"

"Who did? Dave Coyle? Sholto's back was to both of you," Beal said slyly.

McFee stared at him, his hard dislike for Dave forming into suspicion and then into certainty. He hadn't shot Sholto himself. There was nobody else on the street except Dave. The shot had come from somewhere down there. Dave had given him that gun, taken from a dead guard at the mine. Dave hated him and had said so. Suddenly it came to him, clear as crystal. Before, when they were in jail, Dave was accused of killing Sholto at McFee's orders. But by getting Sholto safe, then planting him with McFee in front of the sheriff's office, and then shooting him, the blame for Sholto's murder would be settled for once and all—on McFee's head. It was that easy, that cynical, that slick. McFee's eyes focused on Beal, and he was not even clever enough to dissimulate.

"Yes!" he bawled. "Coyle shot him! He was the only one who would shoot him!"

Ernie said in angry and withering disgust, "How I'd love you for a pardner, McFee."

McFee was excited now. The truth had fully dawned on him, and he set out to spread it with a bullheaded passion.

"But I tell you, Coyle's framin' me! He killed Sholto! He put Sholto up to stallin' at the last minute so's I'd draw a gun! I tell you, Coyle did it!"

Ernie See was really angry. He hated Dave Coyle with a hatred that was all-consuming, but he hated a disloyal man more. But above and beyond that, he was puzzled. This didn't make sense. Why would McFee bring Sholto, on whose recognition he would go free, up to the very doorstep of the sheriff's office and then shoot him? The answer was he wouldn't. No sane man would. And the story of Dave Coyle shooting him was too farfetched to be worth any consideration. McFee had jumped at Beal's bait like the simple fool he was. But that left the question unanswered. Who shot Sholto?

Beal was saying heatedly, "If you ask me, McFee, it was somethin' you and that damn hellion planned beforehand! That's his idea of fun, and yours, too, I reckon. If your horse hadn't pitched you'd be ridin' off with Coyle now and laughin' at what you'd done! Damn you!" he added with savage anger. "You ain't even fit to stretch a rope!"

Beal turned then and said to the others, "Get me ten men that'll make good deputies to guard him. I'm goin' to sleep them right here in the cell block. This time he won't get away."

He named four men to watch McFee, then tramped out into the office, Ernie behind him. Beal yanked down a rifle from the wall rack and then he looked at Ernie, anger and bewilderment in his face.

"What's this country comin' to?" he asked seriously. "When that can happen things is pretty bad."

Ernie said quietly, "McFee didn't shoot Sholto."

Beal's movement in taking the gun down was arrested. He was immobile a second, then he said, "You think Coyle did?"

"I don't think either of 'em did," Ernie said bluntly.

Beal just stared at him in voiceless amazement.

"Harve, when I took that gun from McFee it was cold. It hadn't been shot."

"It was warm when you give it to me," Beal countered angrily.

"I held it by the barrel."

They glared at each other, and Beal said, "You sayin' Coyle shot him?"

"No."

"And McFee didn't either?"

"McFee didn't shoot him, and Coyle didn't either," Ernie said stubbornly.

Beal's mouth formed a grim line. He went over to the desk and laid the gun on it and put his hands on his hips. "Ernie," he began quietly, "it ain't no secret to me that you're a bull-headed, openhanded gent. But by God, when you try to tell me that a man dies of spontaneous combustion or somethin', you're also crazy as hell! You're crazier than hell!" He ran a hand through his hair and made a hopeless, angry gesture. "Goddlemighty, I think I'm goin' crazy myself!"

One of McFee's guards opened the corridor door then and said, "McFee says if you want to catch Coyle go out to his place, the Bib M. He's sure Coyle will head for there."

Beal said crisply, "Get goin', Ernie. He'll have shook that gang by now in the dark. Pick 'em up and ride hell for leather for the Bib M."

Ernie tramped out, his face sullen and angry—and baffled.

XV

IT WAS not hard to shake the posse. Dave cut off to the west, once he was out of town, rode a quarter of a mile, cut back toward town, and rode completely around it, coming up so close to the rear of the posse he could hear them arguing. They were on the ground, lighting matches, trying to pick his tracks out of a tangle of others on the flats.

Dave made a wide circle of them then and headed west. He didn't know why he was going this way, except that it led to the Corazon and safety.

All this had stunned him, and for a moment he reined up, wondering if he should go back to town and hunt down the bushwacker. But how could he? All he had had to do was climb down off Badey's roof and mingle with the crowd. He urged his horse on and tried to think.

Whoever shot Sholto knew that Sholto was being brought in. The only people who knew that were Will Usher, who could have guessed it, and Carol, who was told it in McFee's note to her. Whom had Carol told? Until he knew he was at sea, just guessing. Will Usher might have killed Sholto, but what would he gain? Nothing, no money, no prestige, no pardon, nothing. The secret lay with the note to Carol and whom she had told. Dave put the spurs to his horse then, realizing that McFee would depend on him to learn this from Carol. He didn't know how long it would take Sheriff Beal to worm this from McFee and head for the Bib M himself, but he guessed it wouldn't take long.

It was a long ride, and he was dog-tired. His horse was tired, too, but this was one time he couldn't spare the leather. He took off across country, taking his direction from the high cold stars. He had never felt lonelier, more puzzled, more defeated in his life. And more stubborn. For it was plain to him that this would be a fight to the finish now. Whoever risked that shot was willing to risk his life to win. And what puzzled him more than all else was that Wallace, the man who would be most interested in seeing McFee saddled with a murder, was visible through the window of King's Keno Parlor when the shooting occurred. It didn't make sense, but it did make an airtight, sealed, and delivered frame-up for Bruce McFee.

The Bib M was dark when he rode into the valley before it, and he drew a deep breath of relief. He rode into the yard, was about to tie his horse at the tie rail, and then thought better of it. He led the horse around to the woodshed in back and tied it there, then came around to the front door and knocked and tugged at the bell rope.

A lamp was lighted upstairs, and he heard soft footsteps on the gallery above him.

"Who is it?" Carol asked softly.

"Me."

"Dave Coyle? What do you want?" There was an undercurrent of hostility and anxiety in her voice already.

Dave said, "Come down here."

Carol went inside and came downstairs and opened the door. She faced him in a gray wrapper bound about her, and her hair was braided in two long ropes down her back. Her face was soft and pink, sleep still in it.

She said immediately, "Where's Dad?"

"In jail."

Carol took that without a word, but she was hating him when she looked at him. "And you're free," she said angrily. "I guess I should have expected that. How did they catch him?"

Dave told her about the happenings in town. When he told her of Sholto a look of pain supplanted the anger in her face, but she said nothing. When he was finished he waited for her to ask questions, but she only said softly, "Poor Lily."

"Your dad never killed him," Dave said. "He didn't shoot."

Carol said scathingly, "Do you think I have to be told that? What's more to the point is did you kill him?"

Dave said patiently, "No."

"Then I guess that's all I want to know about it," Carol said bitterly. "I'm glad you've come. I have a proposition to make to you."

Dave didn't say anything, only watched her, the lamplight making his cheekbones seem flat and high, his eyes deep.

"I'll sign over half my inheritance to you if you'll leave the country," Carol said wearily. "Once upon a time, before you came here, we only had a simple court fight to win. Now Dad has to face a murder trial." She made a grimace of disgust. "Oh, can't you see that we don't want you, that you can't help us, that we hate you! Leave us alone! Why do we have to suffer you too? On account of a foolish girl's mistake in writing you?"

Two spots of color burned deeply in Dave's cheekbones. She had a right to say that, only he hated her for saying it. At that moment he hated the whole McFee family, and only his stubbornness kept him from walking out into the night.

He put a hand flat on the hallway wall, leaned on it, cuffed his Stetson back off his black hair. In his eyes were tiny pin points of anger. He said with savage anger, "Listen, I don't want anything out of you McFees—not even a kind word. Did you ever hear me say I'd help you?"

"Why—no," Carol said truthfully.

"I kidnaped Sholto because I saw a chance to make a piece of money, not to help you! I got your dad out of jail because Beal figured wrong and thought we'd throwed in with each other. All I got out of it was a cussin' out from your

dad and a cussin' out from you. I expected that, I reckon.
You're trash, the lot of you!"

Carol winced under the slow, measured whiplash of his
words, but she kept looking at him.

"Another thing," Dave went on, his spare, quiet words coming in a level monotone. "I'd hate to have you think I ever
done anything for you. I've known honky-tonk girls I'd sooner
help than you. I'd sooner help Lily Sholto than you, and I
saw her just once in my life! So don't get any wrong ideas
about me."

"I never have had," Carol said with quiet contempt. "You're
utterly selfish, a cheap little killer."

"That's right," Dave said levelly. "So don't expect me to
make a hero out of myself just because you spoke to me once.
I want you to get this through your thick McFee skull: *I'm
in this because somebody is tryin' to make a sucker out of me,
not to help you.*"

Carol said presently, "I don't understand that."

"That's because you've got McFee blood in you," Dave
gibed. "The McFees don't understand anything. But I'll tell
you. When I make plans I like to see them work. I planned
to get Sholto and take him and your dad back to Beal, so
your dad would go free. But somebody shot Sholto. My plans
were spoiled. I don't like it."

"My, my," Carol said in vicious mockery. "Did someone
cross our nasty little bad man?"

"They tried to," Dave said arrogantly. "They won't get away
with it. Not if you tell me something, that is. Lord knows, I
don't like to ask you. In the first place, you probably couldn't
remember. In the second place, even if it means your dad
gets out of jail, you wouldn't tell me. You'd——"

"Will it get him out of jail?" Carol said swiftly, her anger
forgotten.

"Yes."

"Then ask me."

"Who read that note your dad sent you besides you?"

"I didn't even have time to read it myself," Carol said
quickly. "It was stolen from that table while they searched
the house for you."

"Who's they?"

"Sheriff Beal, Ernie See, and Lacey Thornton. They followed me home and came in right away. Senator Maitland
and Lily and I showed them through the house. When we
came back to the door here the note Lily gave me and I'd

put on the table was gone." She hesitated. "How will it get him out of jail?"

"Because it told you that we were bringin' Sholto in to-night. Whoever stole it killed Sholto."

"Then it was Thornton!"

"If you believe that all lawmen are honest and that all lawyers are nice old men."

Carol took a moment to understand this, and then her lip curled in contempt. "That's so typical of you that——"

Carol took a moment to understand this, and then her lip as if listening to something. "What is it?" she asked.

Dave didn't answer for a long moment, then he backed away from the door. "Lots of riders," he said tonelessly.

"After you?"

"I reckon."

Carol said slowly, viciously, "I won't hide you."

"Then you better get a mop and a bucket, because this'll turn into a pretty messy place."

Carol said wickedly, "Let's see how the bad man gets out of this! I'm going to tell them you're here!"

"I know you will," Dave sneered. He turned and ran up the stairs, then looked around him. He could see down the upstairs hall to a glass-paned door that let out onto the gallery. He hurried down the hall, softly opened the door, and listened. Someone was knocking below. He crawled out to the railing of the gallery and, lying on his stomach, he could see a dark tangle of men below. They were splitting up to surround the house.

The knock sounded again and the door opened, and Ernie See's voice came plainly. "Where's Dave Coyle, Miss McFee?"

"Why—what are you talking about?" Carol asked calmly.

So she hadn't given him away after all! Dave didn't know why, but he was glad she hadn't. His anger with her melted away.

Ernie was saying patiently, "We found his horse out back. It's three o'clock in the mornin', Miss McFee. You got the lamps lit. You're out of bed. You see, it's no use makin' a bluff. And this time I have a warrant."

Carol said nothing.

Ernie went on patiently. "The place is surrounded, so he can't get away." Suddenly he shot at her, "Your dad's in jail for murder!"

"He isn't!" Carol cried. It sounded as if she were really surprised.

"Yes'm," Ernie said. "And Sheriff Beal thinks if we get Coyle we'll have the man who really did the murder. Your dad will go free. Now will you let us in?"

Carol said quietly, "And you, Mr. See? You believe Coyle is guilty of the murder?"

Ernie's answer was a long time in coming, and then it was spoken with an undertone of savage forbearance. "No! I don't think either of them killed this man! But I'm the sheriff's deputy, and he believes it, so I guess I got to search the house whether you like it or not. Do you aim to let us in?"

"There's not much I can do to stop you," Carol said.

Dave heard the posse tramping into the house. He inched back from the railing and lay there, his mind working quickly and futilely. He couldn't let them take him. He had to be free to work at this.

He stepped back into the hallway and saw the moving light of a lamp somebody was bringing up the stairs. In pure desperation he ducked into the room at his right, walked through it to the side window, and looked out. He could see the figures of men standing out there, waiting for the posse to flush him out into their guns. Now there was the sound of someone in the next room. He could hear doors being opened, wardrobes being searched. Across the stairway other men were searching the opposite room. It was a matter of minutes before they reached here.

A slow angry resentment burned within him and then died. He'd have to fight his way out this time. He went swiftly to the window that opened onto the gallery and softly opened it. He crawled through it and went over to the railing. Two men were in conversation there below under the big spreading cottonwood whose farthest feathery branches touched the gallery railing. Dave knew he couldn't shin down the pillars, or they would pick him off before he was halfway down. Fifteen feet was too far to jump. And he wouldn't, couldn't, shoot them.

And then he heard the door open in the room beyond him and knew he must act at once.

He climbed up on the railing, looking out into the tangle of foliage ahead of him, drew a deep breath, and jumped out, his arms spread wide. Crashing into the thin branches, he brought his arms together, hugging everything to him. He didn't get any big branches, but he got one reasonably thick one. And as he fell, then, he hugged it tighter. His drop was checked a little, and then he heard the branch snap, followed by the crackling sound of the smaller ones.

Then he heard the sharp dry rip of bark peeling off, and he fell downward and outward in a pendulum swing. But the bark was peeling off more slowly than his fall, and it was checking his fall. When he felt himself at the bottom of the arc he let go. He sailed out into space, then landed jarringly on his side. He felt his gun slide out of its holster, heard it slide off in the leaves. Then a burst of gunfire from the ground and from the gallery opened up on him.

He came to his feet, looking for his gun and not finding it and knowing bitterly that he couldn't wait to search. He ran, zigzag fashion, toward the corrals, until he was out of the light, then paused and listened. Men were shouting all around him, and he could hear them pounding down the stairs and out the door. He lay down where he was, hoping against hope that they wouldn't find his gun. Already men were running out toward the corral, passing him in the dark. They were shooting now, shooting at shadows and the night and everything they thought might be the seven thousand dollars that his carcass represented.

Carol came to the door with a lamp. Ernie came out after her, took the lamp, and went over to the place Dave had fallen. He stooped, picked up a gun, then turned and yelled: "Get some lamps and lanterns! He lost his gun!"

A half-dozen lamps and lanterns were commandeered, and then the posse spread out in a wide half circle and started toward the corrals.

Softly, cursing bitterly, Dave began to crawl toward the corrals, taking advantage of all the cover he could. They knew he was unarmed, and they'd shoot him down in a second now if they saw him. They could afford to be brave. He heard one man on the other side of the horse corral call, "I got this side covered, Ernie!"

Dave rolled under the bottom rail of the horse corral and then, bending over, crossed it. Beyond, two men were talking. Dave crawled over in the shadow of the big tank and considered his position. They would soon close in on him, joining up with the men on the other side of the corrals who had rushed ahead. If he ever got out of this he'd need his luck to do it. There was just no way out.

In one long bleak moment Dave considered this. He was going to have to surrender. He raised his hand to the edge of the trough, ready to hoist himself up and surrender. Bitterness was hard in his throat. And then his hand touched the water. The big round tank was almost full of water. A rim of ice was forming at the edges.

Suddenly he paused and knew he was going to do it. He crawled over the edge of the tank and put his feet inside. The water clawed at him like hot iron, but he lowered himself in it clear to his neck. He couldn't breathe, and the cold was like an iron band around his chest. But he remembered to take off his hat and kneel on it so it wouldn't float. He hoped bitterly that nobody would notice that the water level was above the rim of ice. He found a cleat near the bottom of the tank, and holding onto it in readiness, he looked over the rim and watched.

The men with lanterns were coming closer, the first one almost at the corral. They were shouting back and forth now on both sides. Suddenly Ernie See stepped into the corral and Dave heard him say, "If he ain't here he's in the barn."

Dave waited until Ernie was halfway across the corral, and then he took a deep breath and gently pulled himself underwater, using the cleat to hold himself there. He tried to hold still, but he knew he was shivering. How long could he stand it? He was sure that with the light from the lantern reflected in the water it would look only black and deep to a man investigating. Unless they looked carefully, he would be invisible under the water's surface.

He tried to count, but even before he got to ten his lungs started to ache. Then the pain and the torture came, and he held out doggedly.

When he was certain that he couldn't live if he didn't get air right away, he slowly let himself up, careful again not to disturb the water. He came up, his eyes open—to find himself staring at the broad back of Ernie See, not six inches away from him.

Ernie was sitting on the edge of the trough!

With exquisite agony Dave slowly drew in his breath. Ernie was talking to a man sitting beside him, saying, "We'll work over the barn now. Flush him into the corral here."

Dave couldn't smother the chatter of his teeth; he couldn't stand the agony of this ice water another moment. Already his muscles were balled into vicious cramps that ached like a throbbing tooth. With a hand that was numb he gently reached out for the gun in Ernie's holster. His hand was shaking so the gun seemed to hammer on the leather of the holster as he slipped it out.

When it was free he rammed it savagely into Ernie's back, came to his feet, and wrapped a wet arm about Ernie's neck.

"You there," he said to the man beside Ernie, "throw your gun away and hurry it!"

The man did and then raised his hands to the night sky. Dave shoved Ernie off the trough and clambered out.

"You and me are goin' to walk over to a horse, Ernie," Dave said, his teeth chattering. "You better figure out how and make it quick!"

Ernie said thickly, "The hell I will!" He looked around him for the others, but there was only the dim light of a lamp from behind the barn.

"*Bueno*," Dave said harshly. "I didn't have a gun tonight, but I got one now! Watch me!"

He cocked the gun, and there was something in his manner that was deadly and final.

Ernie backed off and said, "Hold it!"

"I can't much longer; I'm cold."

"Then follow me."

Ernie walked toward the corral gate. When he got there he yelled to the man with the lantern in front of the barn, "Go help 'em, Russ. I'll watch this side."

"What about the corral?"

"Mickey's here and two others."

The man went into the barn. Dave prodded the two of them out the gate, and they walked swiftly toward the house. They could hear the shouts of the men inside the barn. A horse was tied to one of the cottonwoods near the house. Dave mounted it and without a word galloped out into the valley.

Ernie See's voice raised in a savage bawl: "Get your horses! He's gone!"

Dave smiled at that. He was cold, almost frozen, but he knew he was free. He knew something beyond that too.

One of five men—Sheriff Beal, Ernie See, Lacey Thornton, Senator Maitland, and Will Usher—was Sholto's killer and Wallace's backer.

XVI

The approach to the Three Rivers spread did not appeal to the aesthetics in Will Usher's nature. He was a man who liked fine things, and although that liking had got him into much trouble, through the short cuts he took to get fine things, it still didn't cure him. He didn't like Three Rivers. There were no trees, and the whole place looked as if a Fourth of July picnic had just pulled off the grounds. But Will was in no position to appear critical right now. Or was he? He didn't know what attitude to take with Tate Wallace—the superior or the inferior—and he decided to let events shape his course.

Before he had pulled into the yard proper an unshaven hardcase strolled out from the shade of the barn, where he left two of his companions.

"What do you want?" the puncher asked. Will looked at him and decided he was dirty and offensive and needed taking down.

"I know one thing I *don't* want," Will said equably, "and that's any of your lip, my man."

He ignored the man's surliness and looked at the buildings with contempt mounting in his eyes. "Wallace around?"

"Not to you, he ain't."

"Tell him I'm the gent that tried to make him pay for Sholto," Will said. "I want to talk to him."

The calm brassiness of Will Usher impressed the puncher. He growled something and set off across the yard to the house. Will followed him and dismounted at the porch. He sat down on its edge and wiped the sweat from his hatband, then looked the place over. No, it wasn't much, he decided. If he owned the place and the money that was behind it he'd turn this over to rats and mice and build down near the junction of the three rivers, off the bench.

Will contemplated it for a long time and finally grew impatient. What had happened to that puncher sent to get Wallace? Will reached in his coat for a cigarette making, and his elbow bumped something. He glanced around and saw a pair of boots and, looking higher, saw a man standing there watching him. It was Wallace, all right, he knew, but he didn't know how he'd got there.

Will very calmly looked away, rolled a cigarette, and lighted it.

Wallace said quietly, "So you're the ranahan that wanted fifty thousand from me, are you?"

"That's right," Will said, looking off across the flats.

"How'd you like to get kicked as far as the drift fence you passed a couple miles back?"

Will said calmly, "I wouldn't like it. You won't do it, either."

"Oh, won't I?" Wallace taunted. He stepped off the porch, heading for the crew by the barn.

Will said softly, "Think a minute, mister. You'll see how you can use me."

Wallace's step lagged and then paused. He turned around slowly, and now his face was curious, alert. Slowly he walked back to confront Will.

"What did you say?"

"I say you can use me. Remember, I'm the lad that helped Dave Coyle kidnap Sholto in the first place."

"That'll mean you'll get kicked three miles," Wallace said.

"You're still dumb," Will said pleasantly. "I know Dave." He looked up at Wallace and said, "You want him, don't you?"

"Dave Coyle? Hell, he don't worry me."

"He's goin' to."

They watched each other carefully a few seconds, and then Wallace came over and sat down beside him. Wallace looked obliquely at him, studying him a moment, then said, "How's Dave Coyle goin' to worry me?"

"He's helpin' McFee, I heard him say he was and I saw him do it."

Wallace laughed. "Nobody can help McFee now."

"Except Coyle."

"How?"

"They were both in jail once, weren't they? They both broke out, didn't they? And Sholto, your witness, is dead."

"Sure he is," Wallace agreed. "I don't need him any more, though. McFee killed him."

"Not McFee."

Wallace looked at him sharply. "Who says he didn't?"

"I do. I didn't see it, but they told me about it in Yellow Jacket."

"Did they tell you either McFee or Coyle or both together didn't do it?"

"They told me they *did* do it. I say they didn't. And I know."

Wallace smiled thinly, carefully. "Go on."

"McFee didn't kill him, because Sholto was McFee's only alibi—the alibi he needed to go free. Coyle didn't do it because he was Sholto's friend. Sholto let him escape from me."

"Then who did kill Sholto?" Wallace asked.

Will grinned. It was a flashing smile, wise and disarming. "You think I'm going to accuse you of it? Far from it, my friend. You had an alibi. So did your men. I took the trouble to learn that."

"Then who did?"

"The man backing this outfit here."

Wallace kept the faint smile on his face. His eyes gave away nothing, not even his temper. Will didn't even bother to look at him, and for some reason that annoyed Wallace more than the accusation.

"Now that's somethin' to chew on," Wallace said dryly. "It's news to me, but how did you figure it out?"

"It's pretty simple," Will said calmly. He picked up a handful of dust and sifted it through his fingers, watching it idly. He spoke casually. "Start with Miss Carol McFee. She sent me a letter written to Dave Coyle but mailed it in an envelope addressed to me. She verified something that I'd suspected for a long time. That deed you have from McFee is phony, of course."

"The court ain't said so."

"Exactly. You were out to sink McFee, ruin him, grab his land and his property. The whole swindle depended on Sholto, your witness. But Sholto is kidnaped, believed murdered, and McFee is arrested for that murder. That takes care of McFee nicer than any lawsuit. First, it makes it seem that he's killed your witness to protect himself. Second, it hangs him and ends the lawsuit. If his daughter brings it up again there's always the memory of her father killing your witness. No jury in the world would find for her, in that case. Am I right so far?"

"It sounds convincin'," Wallace admitted dryly.

"Good. To go on. You have McFee in jail. Presto, he's out! And presto again, he's back with the witness and is in the clear. Almost! For on the doorstep of the sheriff's office Sholto is killed. McFee and Coyle are guilty. And there's your lawsuit won again, hands down."

"I did get lucky, didn't I?" Wallace murmured, watching Will.

"Certainly. Especially since you didn't kill him."

"That's right, I didn't. So where are you?"

"So I'm just where it begins to get interesting," Will murmured. He looked at Wallace now. "You're the man who stands to win a hundred thousand dollars by the hanging of McFee for the killin' of Sholto. You didn't kill him, and your men didn't, but somebody did it for you." He spread his hands. "So I'm forced to believe that you aren't alone in this business."

Wallace laughed softly. "Who's in with me, if that's so?"

Will shrugged. "I don't know. I don't care. All I'm interested in is helping you to keep what you've gained. I'll do it for—say twenty-five thousand."

"Do what?"

"Get rid of Dave Coyle for you," Will said mildly.

Wallace studied his handsome face. He could see the strength in the man and the cunning. But the gall of him made him mad.

"Hell, I can shoot," Wallace said irritably.

"So can he." Casually first. "But where is he?"

Wallace said wryly, "I dunno. He may be in my barn out there, for all I know."

"Exactly. You can't find him, and you can't kill him if you do."

"But why should I want to?" Wallace asked sharply. "He can't hurt me."

"He can get McFee out of jail. He has once already. And he can again."

"That makes McFee all the more guilty."

"It also earns you a slug in the back," Will said gently, promptly.

Wallace didn't say anything for a long moment, and then he said, "So you think Coyle will break McFee out and McFee will kill me?"

"He'll either kill you, or he'll turn up proof of your swindle."

Wallace glanced abruptly at Will, who was smiling faintly, triumphantly.

Will got up then, pulled his gloves tight, and said, "Well, since you're not interested, I'll move on."

"Wait a minute," Wallace said slowly. "Come back here."

Will came back and faced him.

"Just to play safe, suppose I make the deal. You get Coyle out of the way. Can you do it?"

"Don't pay me unless I do," Will said promptly. "I'm a businessman, and I believe in cash on delivery."

"Understand," Wallace said flatly, "I haven't admitted anything you say is right. I'm just willin' to put up the money for you to kill an outlaw."

"Naturally, naturally," Will said smoothly, and he grinned his disarming smile. "I think you've needed me for a long time, Wallace.

XVII

IT WAS afternoon when Ernie, with five of his posse, returned to the Bib M. The chase after Dave Coyle had been a fruitless one. Just after they had left the valley, riding hell for leather after Coyle, they had flushed a rider and chased him until two hours past dawn, finally cornering him in a series of wind-eroded clay dunes southwest of Wagon Mound. The stuff had bogged down his horse, and Ernie's crew had surrounded him, and the man had surrendered. He turned out to be some chuckline rider who had built up a stake in a poker game in Yellow Jacket earlier in the evening. He'd run, he said, because he thought he was being held up.

Ernie had been too disgusted to swear. Coyle, of course, was free as a bird, miles away. But Ernie kept remembering those wet clothes and the misery of them. Wouldn't Dave want to shuck them and get warm? And what was easier than circling back to the Bib M, getting a change, and going to bed? It was something that Coyle would pull, confident that he wouldn't be suspected. This thought kept nagging Ernie until he named off five men to ride back with him to the Bib M and sent the others home.

Approaching the Bib M from the north, keeping the barns and outbuildings between them and the house, he searched the outbuildings and especially the barn loft. Afterward he scattered his men through the stand of cottonwoods and half-heartedly approached the house. He was a little sorry for Carol McFee, and he felt sheepish about bothering her. But duty was duty.

He yanked the bellpull and waited, a stubborn-faced, tired-looking man at the fag end of his patience.

The door was opened by Lily Sholto. She was pale, and there were dark circles under her eyes, and her face was so sad that Ernie felt a pity for her without knowing why he did.

"Mornin'," he said, grinning a little. "I'm back again. Is Miss McFee home?"

"She's gone to town to be with her father."

Ernie frowned. "And she's left you here all alone?"

"No, she's bringing the body back here, and then I'll go back to town with her, because we'll be moving out."

Ernie looked at her blankly, alarm in his eyes. "Body? Is McFee dead?"

"The body of Jim Sholto."

"Oh," Ernie said. He was about to add, "I see," but he didn't see at all. He said, "Miss McFee is buryin' him here?"

"Yes."

"Did she—was she—is she just doin' it——" He said awkwardly and bluntly, finally, "Why is she bringin' the body here to bury it?"

Lily said softly, "Because she's so kind, I think. Is there anything wrong with that?"

"No, no," Ernie said hastily. Then he said stubbornly, "Look, did she know Sholto? I mean, why don't his kin bury him?"

"I'm his kin," Lily said quietly. "I'm his wife. Didn't you know?"

Ernie looked as if he had been hit. There was anger and pity and shame in his face as he took off his hat.

"I'm—I'm plumb sorry, Mrs. Sholto. No, I didn't know."

Lily didn't say anything, only waited courteously for Ernie to go. Ernie understood that she didn't want him around, that she wanted to be alone. But there was something else he could do. He said, "Where are you buryin' him, ma'am?"

"Out at the edge of the cottonwoods to the south, there on that rise."

"Good day, ma'am," Ernie said then.

He rounded up his men, and when they saw him his eyes had turned bleak and his jaw was set. He said, "There ought to be shovels out in the shed. We're goin' to dig a grave."

They worked at it for two hours, and Ernie never gave up his shovel. A lot of things were simmering in his mind while he worked in the hot sun. Before today Sholto had just been a man who had the bad luck to be killed. Today it was different. He had been this girl's husband, and he'd been bushwhacked. Ernie wasn't a man of many words or many thoughts, but that afternoon he pledged to himself that he'd see Sholto's murder avenged or turn in his badge and move out of the country.

They finished in late afternoon and set out for Yellow Jacket. The lot of them were tired and hungry, and Ernie the most tired of all. It was late in the evening when they arrived in town. Only the saloons were lighted, and Ernie dropped his crew off at King's Keno Parlor for a nightcap and went on to the sheriff's office. The place was dark, and after putting up his horse downstreet at the feed corral Ernie let himself in with the key and went back to the cell block.

McFee's guards were playing poker, and McFee was asleep. Ernie tramped back to his room off the corridor and let himself in. There was the smell of tobacco smoke in the room, and he supposed these guards had been in bed. He struck a match, lighted the lamp, then turned around to throw his hat on the cot.

Dave Coyle was sitting there, watching him.

For two long seconds, his hand extended with the hat in it, Ernie stared at Dave Coyle. He was so weary that it took that long to be sure that he wasn't lightheaded and just seeing things.

Then Dave spoke, and he was sure he wasn't.

"I haven't got a gun. I want to talk to you."

Ernie looked down at his waist. Sure enough, he didn't have a gun in sight, but he could be sitting on one. Some inner caution told Ernie that he'd better keep his mouth shut and not yell and play this cagey. His hat fell to the floor, and he licked his lips. He was afraid and ashamed of being so, so he said dryly, "We've been wantin' to talk to you too. Hadn't you heard?"

"You and Beal? Well, I don't want Beal. I want to talk to you. Alone. Private. Like we are now. Don't call anyone or you'll be sorry."

"You might be sorry too," Ernie said tonelessly. "There's bars on that window."

"I didn't mean that kind of sorry. I mean you'll be sorry afterward if you don't listen."

Ernie looked at him carefully, quizzically, his fear slowly fading. Then he shook his head. "Man, I give up," he said softly. "Why in hell didn't you surrender last night and save us the trouble of chasin' you instead of comin' here and doin' it?"

"I ain't surrenderin'," Dave said quietly. "After we talk you'll know why."

Ernie slowly, experimentally drew his gun. Nothing happened. He pulled a chair toward him, locked the door, then sat down, his glance never leaving Dave. Ernie thought: This is it. I wonder if I'll get him when it breaks.

Ernie said with a confidence he didn't feel, "It better be good. Start off."

"I was lyin' on that gallery last night when you come to the Bib M," Dave said slowly. "I heard you say to Miss Mc-Fee that you didn't reckon I shot Sholto."

"I don't," Ernie said. He was interested now.

"And you don't reckon McFee did, either."

"No. It don't hold water, not a drop."

"You're right," Dave said, watching him. "We didn't. I saw the shot. It come from the roof of Badey's store."

Ernie forgot his fear now, forgot who he was talking to. He said, "I knew it! See who it was?"

"No. If I had of I'd of killed him," Dave said quietly. "I left town with a posse on my neck. You know that."

"And you want me to work on that?" Ernie said cautiously. "Hell, man, it could be anyone in town."

"It could be five men," Dave said. "Just five men."

Ernie came up straight in his chair, suddenly alert. "How do you figure that?"

"Remember when you and Thornton and Beal followed Carol McFee out to the Bib M, hopin' to trap us?" Ernie nodded, and he went on: "Remember, she was just openin' a letter when you broke in?"

Ernie scowled and shook his head. "No."

"She was. She hadn't read it. She laid it on the table and took you around the house. After you'd gone she looked for the letter. It was gone, stole."

"What was in it?" Ernie asked swiftly.

"That letter," Dave said slowly, "was from McFee. We'd been there earlier and left it with Lily Sholto." He paused, watching Ernie. "It said that we'd bring Sholto in to the sheriff's office the night after next. Last night, that was. We did. And Sholto was shot."

Ernie was listening carefully, hanging on every word. Dave raised his left hand, spread the fingers, then started ticking off each finger as he said, "There was you, Beal, Lacey Thornton, and Maitland. Four men. One of you killed Sholto."

Ernie said swiftly, "You think I did. That's why you come."

"I know you didn't. That's why I'm here."

Ernie felt a sudden flush of pleasure, but his face didn't show it. He scowled and rubbed his jaw. "Then it was a grudge killin' against Sholto. It had nothin' to do with the Three Rivers outfit, because Wallace has an alibi."

Dave smiled thinly. "Whoever killed Sholto is the Three Rivers outfit."

Ernie stared at him blankly, then shook his head. "No. Wallace is Three Rivers."

Dave, talking in a steady voice, told Ernie some things then that was like lighting a lamp in a dark room. He started out with his conversation with Carol, with the supposition that the deed was forged. Then he skipped to Wallace and told of what he knew of him. Then he explained the kidnaping of Sholto and how Wallace refused to buy Sholto back, once McFee was in jail on suspicion of Sholto's murder. Slowly, point by point, he built up the case against Wallace, finally proving that Wallace was the only one who stood to gain by Sholto's death. And then, he said, the night Sholto was killed Wallace and his crew had an alibi. Someone unknown, the man behind Three Rivers, was the killer. Nobody else could have been.

He paused a moment, letting that sink in. Presently Ernie said, "It holds water. It makes sense. But have you got proof?"

"No, but I'll get it."

"How?"

Dave said quietly, arrogantly, "I'll have your killer, the man behind Wallace, in a week. I'll have him in jail for you."

This was too much for Ernie. He sneered openly. "You've made brags in your life, Coyle. Some you've backed up. You can't back that one up."

"Not alone," Dave said quietly. "I can if you'll help me."

"Me?" Ernie said blankly. "But hell, I'm a deputy s'posed to be huntin' you!"

"You're also sworn to uphold the law," Dave pointed out. "Or are you scared of me?"

"I'm talkin' to you, ain't I?" Ernie said hotly.

Dave nodded. "You are. You're talkin' to me without shoutin', without threatenin' me, without braggin', and without pokin' a gun in my face. Maybe it's because we both hate murder that you're listenin'. But now I'm wonderin' somethin'."

"What?" Ernie asked belligerently.

"If you don't love a tin badge more'n you hate murder."

Ernie felt himself getting mad, but when he looked at Dave Coyle, at that quiet alert face, not jeering, he paused. And slowly a feeling of shame came over him. Dave Coyle had touched him where it hurt. He had told what seemed to be the truth, but it was not the truth. To prove that to himself

Ernie only had to think of Lily Sholto. He'd sell his badge for a drink if he could get Sholto's killer.

He said quietly, "I'm going to prove you a liar."

"You'll help me? Even if it means breakin' the law?"

Ernie's honest face was sober now. "I will. I'll do anything short of murder."

"You're passin' up seven thousands dollars' reward."

"I ain't a bounty hunter," Ernie said grimly. "You prove to me you're more'n a cheap outlaw, and I'll forget that."

They didn't shake hands on it because they didn't need to. Dave's doubt of Ernie was far more binding than a mere handshake, and Ernie's skepticism of Dave was equally binding. Their pride had done that.

Ernie put down his gun on the table as a token of his honesty, tilted his chair back, and said, "Since we're partners, let's have it. What do you aim to do first?"

Dave leaned back against the wall, his forehead creased in a scowl. "See if I figure right, Ernie. The way I look at it, here's the way it stands. Wallace—and whoever's behind him —don't have to make another move. They're set. All they got to do is let the law take care of McFee. That right?"

Ernie nodded.

"Then it's up to us to make 'em move."

Ernie grunted. "How?"

"Steal the forged deed."

Ernie's head yanked up, and his tired eyes opened wide. He didn't say anything for a long moment, and then he murmured, "That'll make 'em move, all right. But how——" His voice died. He was looking at Dave.

Dave's head had slowly turned toward the window, as if he were listening. There was a faint, unnoticeable rustling of brush outside the window, and then Dave exploded. His hand had been near Ernie's hat. He picked it up, and in one fluid motion he threw it at the lamp, at the same time rolling off the cot onto the floor.

The lamp winked out; he hit the floor, and on the heel of his fall came the blasting, deafening roar of a shotgun through the window, then a swift pounding of feet toward the alley.

Even as the buckshot was still rolling about the room, the plaster above the bed still sifting down, Dave had come over to Ernie, who had reared out of his chair.

"You hurt, Ernie?"

"N-no."

"Listen. Make it quick. Lead that gang in the cell block

outside before they come in here! Find out which of those four men is in town. Meet me at the feed stable!"

There was the pounding of feet behind the door, and Dave dodged against the wall. Ernie yanked the door open and faced the excited guards.

"Outside!" Ernie bawled. "Somebody took a greener to me! Split up and head for the alley!"

He led the way, pounding out of the sheriff's office. The five guards beat their way back between the buildings. Dave followed on their heels and then walked swiftly and unconcernedly down the street toward the darkened feed stable.

Back in the alley both groups met, and then Ernie began to swear blisteringly. It was as black as the bottom of a well, and the bushwhacker was gone.

"What happened, Ernie?" one man asked.

"Happened?" Ernie raged. "Why, I was lyin' on the cot, too damn tired to go to bed. I heard somethin' outside, reared up, saw somethin' move behind them bars, threw my hat at the lamp, and ducked. Then this greener cut loose through the window!"

"Dave Coyle," one of the guards said bitterly. "That sounds like him."

Ernie was about to protest, and then he thought he'd better start allaying suspicions right now. "It's likely," he growled. "That damn little whelp!"

He judged he had given Dave enough time to get out now, so after futilely beating the alley for five minutes he ordered the guards back to the cell block. What few people were still up were collected in front of the jail, but he ordered them home. Beal, he thought, would be down soon, and he didn't want to listen to him any more. He remembered what Dave had told him, so he dragged his weary bones out in the street again.

At the hotel he found that Senator Maitland was registered. He asked if Lacey Thornton was in town, and Bitterman said he wasn't here. Beal was here, of course, and so was he, the fourth man.

But Ernie didn't want to pass up any chances. He started the rounds of the three saloons still open, idly inquiring if Lacey Thornton was upstairs anywhere. Two of them said no.

At King's Keno Parlor the first sight that met his eyes was Wallace standing at the bar drinking with a handsome frock-coated man who wore buckskin gloves. With a new suspicion simmering inside him, Ernie walked up to the bar and said bluntly, "I'm gettin' an alibi from everybody in town, Wallace. Where was you when that greener went off?"

Wallace grinned and looked at the barkeep. "Where was I, Tim?"

"Right here," Tim King said. "Him and his friend, both."

"Gimme a drink," Ernie said in disgust.

Wallace's companion came over on Ernie's other side. "Has it occurred to you that Dave Coyle might be the man you're lookin' for?" he asked pleasantly.

Ernie's face showed only a weary disinterest. "Hell, yes, it's occurred to me. I suppose it was."

He let it ride that way, wondering who the man was, and drank his drink. When he was finished Wallace said, "Well, Ernie, I'm movin' in on the Bib M tomorrow. You might's well tell Beal."

"You are?" Ernie asked, surprise in his voice.

"I've got the legal right," Wallace said calmly. "I've waited two weeks longer than the deed called for. McFee's case against me is finished, I think, since he tried to kill my witness and will hang for it. Any reason I have to wait?"

"Why—don't reckon," Ernie admitted.

"Well, I want to make it legal. Tell Beal for me. You can tell Miss McFee too."

"Sure." Ernie said good night, went back to the gambling tables and heard other alibis, and then went out, heading for the feed stable. The news from Wallace wasn't so good. He wondered what Dave would say to that.

He came up the alley to the corral behind the feed barn and was walking toward the driveway when a voice said beside him, "Well?"

It was Dave. Ernie said, "Beal's in town; Maitland's at the hotel; I'm in town—and Wallace was talking with a stranger when it happened."

"What stranger?"

"Good-lookin', frock coat, yaller gloves, very fancy. Told me you likely did it."

That would be Will Usher, Dave thought. So Will had thrown in with Wallace now, had he? Dave smiled faintly in the dark. Leave it to Will to smell money and rub elbows with it.

Ernie said wearily, "That mean anything to you? Three of the four was here."

"I dunno," Dave said.

"Then does this mean anything to you?" Ernie asked

gloomily. "Wallace is movin' into the Bib M tomorrow."

For a moment there was silence. Ernie heard what sounded to him like the soft, noiseless laugh of his companion.

"What's funny?" he asked.

"Why, nothin'," Dave said. "Only that deed is as good as stole right now. Listen." And he began to talk, and Ernie listened—listened long and carefully—and was dumfounded at what he heard.

XVIII

SHERIFF BEAL came into the office next morning brisk and beaming, his cherub's face still pink from his morning's shave. He found Ernie in the swivel chair, feet cocked on the desk, hands behind his head.

"Well, well," Beal said briskly. "They tell me you were shot at last night, Ernie."

"Yeah," Ernie said sourly. "It ain't any fun. Where was you?"

"In bed."

"So you don't come down to see about it unless I'm dead, eh?"

Beal looked carefully at him. "Boy, you got up on the wrong side of the bed this mornin'."

"Sure I did—and stepped right into a pound of buckshot and plaster," Ernie said sourly. He had made no move to get out of Beal's chair, in itself a sign of revolt. Beal sensed something and leaned on the desk.

"What's the matter with you, Ernie?"

"I'm fed up," Ernie said grimly. "I been chasin' that damn Coyle from hell to breakfast, and all I got out of it was dust in my eyes. I get laughed at and cussed at, just because I don't believe fairy stories about who killed Sholto. Then I git shot at." He looked at Beal. "And you ask me what's the matter. Ain't it enough?"

Beal laughed and said, "Boy, our job's done. In a week Mc-Fee's trial will be over, and we'll be rid of this mess."

Ernie grunted sourly. "Wallace says to tell you he's movin' on the Bib M today."

Beal frowned a little, and Ernie went on, still sourly, "Says it's legal enough, so he's movin' in."

"Well, I guess it is," Beal said, nodding. Beal was in a

cheerful mood that nothing could destroy this morning, but Ernie was determined.

He said, "I just been down to get Sholto's stuff from the coroner. Lookit what I found." He pulled out a drawer. In the bottom of it were some coins, some dirty matches, a stockman's knife, a sack of tobacco, and a worn and dog-eared letter.

Beal looked at them without interest and said, "We'll give them to Wallace."

"I wouldn't," Ernie said slowly.

Something in his voice made Beal look at him. "Why not?"

Ernie picked up the envelope, held it in his hand, and said, "Read what's inside."

Beal did. It was a note on a dirty piece of paper. It said, "I'm all right. I'll see you soon. (Signed) Jim." Beal read it and said, "He was likely goin' to send it to his wife before McFee killed him."

Ernie grunted. "Don't you notice anything funny?"

Beal looked at the letter again, turned it over, studied it, then said, "Why, no."

Ernie said with seeming irrelevance, "Remember when you and me rode out to the Three Rivers to take a look at Wallace's deed that McFee give him?"

"Of course. Why?"

"Remember Sholto's signature?"

"Sure. It was on the deed as a witness."

Ernie pulled his feet down, stretched, yawned, cuffed his hat to the back of his head, then said casually, "There was a signature on the deed all right. It said 'Jim Sholto.' But it wasn't that writin'."

Beal came to his feet, his good humor suddenly evaporated. Ernie concluded that his little job of writing the note last night and dirtying it and sleeping on it made it look convincing enough.

Beal suddenly groaned softly and stared at Ernie. "You sure?"

"You saw the deed," Ernie said. "Remember, that writin' of Sholto's was round and kind of shaky-like, like he was drawin' a picture? Well, this ain't like that."

"But my God!" Beal burst out. "Do you realize what this means?"

"Sure I do," Ernie said. "It means Wallace has got to prove that the signature on his deed is really Sholto's."

"But—but dammit, he's movin' today! He'll fight! Why—

we'll be in one hell of a mess, twice the mess we've been in."
Beal's face was a picture of panic and dismay. He groaned
again and said, "What'll we do?"

Ernie shrugged. "You got me," he said, immediately cheerful.

"Look," Beal said. "I got to be here today when McFee's
arraigned. You go out and take a look at that deed."

"Nothin' doin'," Ernie said flatly.

Beal's face hardened. "You want to keep your job, Ernie?"

"Not that bad," Ernie said cheerfully. "Hell, I ain't goin'
to start another damn war in this county. I'll quit first." He
grinned at Beal. "Then where'll you be, Harve? You start
gettin' tough with Wallace and you won't be able to hire a
deputy. No man wants to commit suicide."

Beal only glared at him. Ernie scratched his head and went
on, "I got a way, I think. I been studyin' on it, and I can't
see what's wrong with it. It wouldn't make Wallace sore, and
you could still find out if Sholto's signature is a phony."

"How?"

"Send a man out with word to Wallace to bring the deed
with him when he moves in to the Bib M today. Tell him
it's just protection for the sheriff's office. He takes possession,
and you want to be sure it's legal. Tell him you want a look
at it, just to protect yourself."

"What if it ain't legal?"

Ernie spread his hands, palms out, and said, "Turn it over
to the U.S. commissioner's office and let them sweat."

Beal thought a moment and said, "Yeah, that'd be all right.
We could look at it without makin' him suspicious."

"Sure."

"I'll send a man," Beal said.

The office door opened just then, and a mild-looking townsman walked in. After the greetings he said, "Harve, someone
busted in the office last night."

Beal frowned. "What would anybody want in the county
recorder's office? Is anything missin'?"

"Not that I can find. Books is all in order. Stamps are all
there. But still the lock was busted."

Beal said to Ernie, "Go over and take a look, Ernie."

Ernie hoisted himself to his feet and followed the man out.
The county of Yellow Jacket did not have a courthouse. Its
business offices were in the front of the second story of Badey's
store. The courtroom was in the rear. Both were approached
by a wooden stairs on the outside of the store. Ernie fol-

lowed the county clerk up to the top of the steps, investigated the lock, and scratched his head. "It's busted all right. But since nothin's gone, what's the difference?"

The clerk laughed. "I guess there isn't any."

"I'll get a new lock," Ernie said. He went down the stairs, and this time there was a smile on his face. Dave had made a neat enough job of breaking in, and he hadn't left a trace of what he was after. Considering that Sheriff Beal had also fallen for the deed fraud and had ordered Wallace to have the deed at the Bib M that afternoon, Ernie concluded that he and Dave made a good pair.

But he wished, almost wistfully, that his conscience didn't hurt him the little it did. But when he remembered last night, the deafening blast from the shotgun, his conscience evaporated.

The only thing left was speculation as to who shot through the window. Beal, Maitland, Lacey Thornton—or somebody Wallace sent?

He didn't know, and he wished savagely that he did, for whoever it was knew that he'd been talking with Dave.

When Dave saw the first pennant of smoke rise from the chimney of the Bib M after dawn he waited long enough to give Lily Sholto time to dress and then knocked at the kitchen door.

Lily answered and let him in. She even smiled a little as she shut the door behind her.

Dave said quietly, "It was pretty lonely last night, wasn't it?"

"I've got over it, Dave," Lilly said. "I thought all last night about it, and I know something now. Jim was lucky to be killed."

Dave didn't say anything, and Lily went on, "I suppose you guessed that Wallace had something on Jim."

"I figured he did."

"Well, it was murder," Lily said. "Plain, inexcusable murder. Jim killed a man once, a good man, when he was mad. Wallace saw him do it. He held that over Jim for three years and brought Jim here from Texas when he came. Every waking hour of Jim's life he thought of that murder. It was never away from him. It rode him and sucked the very life out of him. I tried to help him, but I couldn't." She shrugged. "Don't you think he's better off now?"

Dave nodded again, admiring this girl's sense.

Lily shuddered a little, as if shaking off the memory. "That's why I'm not very sad about it. I'll miss him, but he's through with all that—through with it." She smiled again and said. "You'll want breakfast."

"I could use some," Dave said. "I'm goin' to look through the house."

He disappeared in the front part of the house, and Lily set about getting breakfast. She liked Dave Coyle. Carol McFee could hate him and like him by turns, but there was none of that uncertainty in Lily. For Dave Coyle, outlaw or no outlaw, was the only man she could remember who had tried to help Jim, to be a friend to him. It was Dave Coyle who had taken her from Wallace's place, where every drunken puncher annoyed her, where Wallace taunted her daily, where her life had been lived in constant fear that Wallace, when he couldn't use Sholto, would toss him to the wolves without a quiver of conscience. He had tried to help them. That alone was a passport to Lily's liking.

When breakfast was ready Dave appeared and sat down.

He said, "Ernie said the funeral is today."

Lily nodded, a look of puzzlement in her face. "Isn't Ernie See the deputy sheriff?"

Dave grinned faintly. "Why am I talkin' with him? Well, there's goin' to be a lot of things you won't understand, Lily. But don't wonder out loud. You'll know soon."

"Are you—going to get the man that killed Jim?"

Dave's gray eyes looked steadily at her. "I am," he said.

"Then don't worry about me," Lily said. "I won't ask questions."

Dave pointed to the door to the front part of the house. "When I walk through that door," he said, "you forget I've been here. Don't think about me. Don't look for me. Do everything like you usually do. Wallace is movin' in today. Miss McFee will tell you when she comes out. I reckon you'll move some furniture and such. Don't act nervous and don't look for me. Forget me."

"Then you'll be in the house?"

Dave nodded and went on eating. Presently Lily said quietly, "Dave."

He looked up.

"When this is over, what are you going to do?"

Dave looked puzzled. "What I always did, I reckon. Just knock around."

"And leave Carol here?"

Dave looked blank. "Where would I take her?"

"Where does any man take his wife?"

Dave stared at her a long moment, and then he felt his neck begin to get hot, his face too. He looked down at his plate and shook his head. "I'm an outlaw, Lily. It can't happen."

"Jim was a murderer," Lily said. "It can happen."

"She wouldn't have me."

"She cried the other night when she thought they were going to get you."

"She was crying over Jim bein' shot, I reckon."

"Not all of it, Dave. She was crying like her heart was going to break."

Dave said miserably, "Quit it, Lily. Quit it."

"All right," Lily said wisely. "But just remember it."

Dave got up, his face bleak, and went into the front of the house. There was a noise somewhere up there, and then it was silent. Lily finished her work, then went through the rooms. She was looking for him, like she was told she mustn't. And he was gone, vanished, and yet she knew he was there somewhere.

XIX

JUST AT dusk Ernie, Beal, and Senator Maitland had helped Lily and Carol load the next to the last trunk into the buckboard. It was then that Lily said, "There's someone coming into the valley."

Ernie looked. A canvas-covered spring wagon had just topped the ridge, with flanking riders on each side. It was Wallace, all right, moving in. A dozen more riders trailed out behind the wagon.

Ernie looked at Carol and Carol said, "If you'll bring that last bag, please, we'll go."

Senator Maitland got it from the front door. Beal helped Lily and Carol into the seat, and Ernie loaded the bag while Maitland climbed in and took the reins. Carol handed Maitland something, and Maitland gave it to Beal.

"The key," he said dryly. "Miss McFee has given him everything else; he might as well have that."

Beal flushed a little under the gibe and said, "All you got to do is give the word, Miss McFee, and I'll make Wallace wait until the furniture is moved out."

"Where would I move it?" Carol said dully. "No, he might as well have everything—lock, stock, and barrel.

"I'll see he takes good care of it," Beal said.

"Why shouldn't he? It's his, isn't it?" Maitland said grimly. He slapped the reins down on the horses, and the buckboard moved off. Beal came back to the porch and sat on its edge with Ernie. Beal watched the two wagons pass in the middle of the valley, neither Wallace nor Carol giving any sign of recognition. Afterward he drew out his bandanna and wiped his face with it. Ernie looked sleepily at him and said:

"Cheer up, Harve. It ain't no worse than a toothache."

Beal swore. "What if he won't show it?"

"Tell him you'll kick him off then. You act tough if he does. Act plumb pretty if he does."

Beal said frantically, "Lemme look at that letter of Sholto's again."

Ernie handed it to him, and Beal studied it as if he was trying to memorize it. Then he handed it back, and they got up to meet Wallace and his crew. A sour-faced cook was in the wagon, Marty Cord driving it. Wallace and Will Usher were riding on either side, and the rest of the Three Rivers crew was strung out in the rear.

Beal came out to the tie rail, Ernie loafing behind him. Marty Cord was going to drive the wagon around in the rear, but Wallace stopped him.

Wallace was clean-shaven today, wearing a black suit, and his boots were polished. Ernie studied him covertly, trying to get a hint of his temper.

Wallace swung down, grinned, and said, "Didn't have any trouble movin' them out, did you, Sheriff?"

Beal saw that Wallace was agreeable and he breathed a deep sigh of relief. This didn't look as if there were going to be any argument.

"No trouble. They left a houseful of furniture for you." He cleared his throat and said confidently, "All you got to do to take possession is give me a look at that deed."

"Yeah," Wallace said carelessly. "I got your message. Seems kind of queer, but then you're welcome to look at it again."

"I'm playin' safe," Beal said, with what he hoped was a grim tone. "I don't want McFee claimin' I took your word for the deed. I want to see it."

"Sure, sure. Hand down that iron box, Marty."

Marty Cord reached into the load and lifted down a heavy metal box. Wallace put it on the ground, separated a key from the others he carried in his pocket on the end of a chain, then knelt and unlocked the box. Will Usher watched him with apparent indifference as he handed Beal the deed.

Beal unfolded it, and Ernie came over and looked over his shoulder. Beal read the deed, turned it over, and looked at the signatures.

Ernie said suddenly, "That's funny."

"What is?" Wallace asked, suspicion in his voice.

Beal rammed his elbow in Ernie's stomach, but Ernie went on blandly, "I seen Sholto's writin' once. It didn't look like that."

Beal turned on him, his eyes imploring. But Ernie didn't even look at him. He watched Wallace, whose face had settled into hard, deep lines.

He kept his hot gaze on Ernie and said, "You sayin' Sholto's signature is a forgery?"

"I'm tellin' you what I saw," Ernie said easily.

Beal was too scared to say anything. Wallace suddenly turned and said, "Marty, reach in the barrel where the dishes are. There's a pack of letters on top." He turned to Ernie. "Lily Sholto quit my place so sudden she didn't take her stuff with her. Mrs. Babson sent these letters along."

Marty handed Ernie down a package of letters. "These are from Jim Sholto to his wife," he said meagerly. "Look at the signature."

Beal untied the package, took a letter out, turned it over, and compared its signature with the one on the deed. They matched absolutely.

He said viciously to Ernie, "Take a look, hardhead!"

Ernie did. Then he said innocently, "Why, sure. They're the same."

"Satisfied, Sheriff?" Wallace asked dryly.

"I always was," Beal said bitterly. "It's him that wasn't."

"Oh, I'm satisfied," Ernie said. "Much obliged."

"And I can move in?" Wallace asked Beal.

"Go ahead. The place is yours. Come on, Ernie."

He and Ernie walked over to their horses. Ernie suddenly stopped, snapped his fingers, and said, "I forgot my shell belt." He had taken it off and draped it over a chair back when they were helping load trunks. Whistling, he went back into the house. They heard his whistle fading, then growing stronger. He came out again, strapping on his shell belt. He and Beal got on their horses, waved to the crew, and rode out. As soon as they were out of earshot Beal said bitterly, "What you got to say for yourself?"

"Nothin'," Ernie said blandly.

"What if those signatures hadn't matched?" Beal said, anger in his voice. "We'd of got in one hell of an argument!"

"That's a fact," Ernie agreed. "They did, though. I can't figure it out!"

Beal looked at him a long time, and then he shook his head. "Sometimes I dunno," he murmured glumly. "Sometimes I think I'll put a gun in my mouth and pull the trigger. It's a hell of a lot quicker than lettin' a dumb deputy do it, and it ain't half the worry."

Outwardly Ernie looked injured and remained silent. Inwardly he was laughing. He had given Sheriff Beal one of the most uncomfortable ten minutes of his life. That was just for fun. The other wasn't. Because that deed was at the Bib M now, and somewhere inside the house Dave Coyle said he would be hidden.

Ernie didn't know for sure, but he was willing to bet that Dave was in there.

When Beal and Ernie had ridden away Wallace picked the box up, instructed a rider to drive the wagon around to the rear, told Marty Cord and Usher to follow him, and they went into the house. The cook walked straight through to the kitchen, but the others paused at the door of the living room and looked around them. Wallace, whose idea of elegance was a saloon with a tile floor, looked at the rugs, the furniture, the piano from St. Louis, the heavy pink glass lamps, and the curtains. He whistled in awe and then made a wry face. Marty Cord wasn't impressed. Will Usher was, although his face didn't show it. The three of them looked at all the downstairs rooms, then went upstairs to the bedrooms. When they came to Carol's room Wallace stepped on the threshold and goggled. There was a fluffy counterpane on the bed; the white curtains were starched stiffly, and there was a lingering scent of lavender in the room.

"Well, well," Wallace drawled. He walked over to the bed, picked up the counterpane, looked at it, then ripped it in half and dropped it on the floor. Next he went to the ornate marble-topped dresser. He raised the iron box and crashed it down on the marble, cracking it. Then he threw the box into the big mirror above the dresser. Methodically he went around the room, yanking down the pictures and putting his foot through them. Then he looked up at Will and Marty, and Marty grinned.

"Get this muck out of here," Wallace said. "It looks like a honky-tonk."

"I wish it was," Marty said. He grinned slyly. "You got all the fixin's, boss. Why don't we move some gals out here?"

Wallace laughed. "You like the smell so good, Marty, you can have the place. Me, I'll take somethin' without the perfume. Tell the boys to take over." He looked again at the room. "Anything they don't like they can throw out the window."

He caught Will Usher looking at him with something like dismay in his face. Wallace grinned wolfishly. "You don't like it, dude?"

Will caught himself in time. "I was just wonderin'," Will drawled, grinning, "how we'd get that bed out the window."

Wallace laughed again. This was his hour, and he was in a rare good mood. The Bib M was his, and he set about immediately to pull it down to the level of a cheap hotel lobby. He took McFee's room for himself, the room on a rear corner. It was small, barren of rugs, and a rickety old bed, a heavy dresser, and a chair made up the furniture. He sent Will and Marty up to look over the attic and search the rest of the house, and then he remembered he still carried the iron box.

Suddenly aware that it was heavy, he walked over to the dresser and grabbed the handle of a drawer and pulled. It didn't budge. He set the box on top and tried both hands. Still the drawer wouldn't budge. He kicked it savagely, strode out into the hall, and bawled, "Get that chest up here!"

There was no answer. Marty and Will were on the roof. Swearing, Wallace picked up the box and went downstairs.

The attic, which Marty and Will had searched, was small and empty. A short ladder rose to the trap door in the roof. Will went up, lifted the door, looked at the roof, then stepped down.

Marty was watching him, chewing deliberately and delicately on a cud of tobacco. When Will stepped down off the ladder Marty said, "I ain't had a chance to talk with you alone since you joined up."

"That's right," Will said, wondering what was coming. He didn't like the tough set to Marty's jaw.

"What are you doin' here?" Marty asked.

Will said blandly, "Didn't Tate tell you?"

"So it's 'Tate' now," Marty mocked. "No, he didn't tell me."

"You better ask him."

"I'm askin' you," Marty said slowly, quiet menace in his voice. "I pay off this crew, and so far I ain't had any instructions to pay you off. You look like a joker to me, mister."

Will smiled contemptuously and hooked his thumbs in his belt. "Cord," he drawled, "you're dirty and you're dumb. Maybe Wallace hired me so he'd have someone to talk to besides an ape like you."

Marty flushed and straightened up. "Did he hire you, though?"

Will grinned faintly. "I told you to ask him—or are you afraid you'll get your teeth kicked down your throat?" He paused, amusement in his eyes, as he watched Marty. Then he said, "Before you decide to put a slug in my back, though, you better make sure what it'll get you."

Marty spat without turning his head. The tobacco plopped on Will's boots, but he pretended not to notice it. "Just remember one thing," Marty drawled. "I'm roddin' this spread —both spreads. Tomorrow I aim to have Wallace tell you that."

"Afraid of your job?" Will taunted.

"No, but I reckon you better be afraid of it," Marty said. He turned and went down to the second floor. It was a warning and plain enough, and Will smiled faintly at Marty's back. It was apparent that he wasn't liked here, only tolerated, because Wallace had passed out the word. That was all he wanted, all he needed.

Before the cook called supper the house was overrun with the crew. At first they approached it gingerly, but after supper a poker game started in the living room. Soon there were cigarette butts burning the rugs. Someone had tipped his chair back into a glass-covered bookcase. A vase served as a spittoon, but soon it was abandoned altogether. Bedrolls were thrown on the bedroom floor; riders rested on the beds with their spurs on; rifles were stacked on the hall hatrack, and there was a familiar smell of unwashed bodies, horses, leather, whisky, and tobacco smoke. Wallace took over the dining room for his office, and Bib M had changed hands.

Along toward midnight the crew broke up, and some of the riders drifted off to bed. The droning voices of the two men on watch out by the front tie rail were interrupted by the curses of the men playing poker. Wallace still held a hand in the game, and Will Usher was playing too. The upper story had settled into quiet.

It was then that the heavy dresser in Wallace's room moved out from the wall and Dave crawled stiffly from where he had been hiding all day. The noise Lily Sholto had heard that morning had been Dave carefully kicking out the bottoms of the dresser drawers and the back of the dresser. One stick, nailed to the back of the front panel of all the drawers, insured their being kept closed. Its weight and size insured against its being moved. And in that space Dave had waited, listening, trying to pick up something of what was happening since morning.

He stretched, flexing his muscles, and then went to the open door and looked out in the hall. All the other doors were closed, so the crew could sleep. Softly, then, Dave started down the stairs, wondering if Ernie had failed him. The stairs were carpeted, and he made no noise. The card game went on with desultory talk interrupting the silence. Dave listened until he distinguished Will Usher's voice and Tate Wallace's.

Afterward he moved softly down the dark hall to the door that let on to the kitchen. The door was shut. Dave opened it, then softly struck a match and looked down the hall. The game was going on without interruption. Then Dave set about his business.

When the door was closed there was a space on the jamb to which the hinges were fastened that was hidden. When it was opened this space was suddenly revealed, as when a book is opened. And in this space, just below the hinge, was firmly written in pencil in Ernie's handwriting: "It's in a locked iron box 6 × 9. Will."

Dave blew out the match and pondered. An iron box, six inches by nine inches, contained the deed. That box could be anywhere, buried or hidden, but it was Dave's guess that it was not. He had heard Wallace come in the room where he was hidden, try the dresser drawer, then bawl, "Get that chest up here." It seemed reasonable enough that the iron box was in the chest. Anyway, he was sure of one thing. Two men, directed by Wallace, had delivered something heavy into Wallace's room that evening. Wallace had ordered them out, then had deposited something in the chest.

Dave softly made his way back to the stairs. Still, from the door into the living room, the talk of the card players drifted out. He went back into Wallace's room, closed the door softly, and struck a match. There was Wallace's saddle thrown on the floor against the wall and beside it a stout chest. The match died, and Dave struck another and went over to look at the chest. It was made of oak, ironbound, and its lock was a heavy padlock. Dave's heart sank as he saw it. When the match died he tried to lift one end of the chest. He could move it, but it was heavy.

He sat down on it and thought a moment. If he got the chest to the window and dropped it the noise it would make would wake the dead. Even then the chest wouldn't break and open. That was out. He couldn't burn it, because it would take half the night, and he would be discovered. That was out too. There was only one thing left, and that was to shoot the padlock off. That would bring the whole swarm of them down on his neck. Wallace's crew, Ernie had said, numbered over a dozen. They would cut him to doll rags before he got to the stairs. For the stairs were the only way out. For if he went out the window he would leave unfinished a little piece of business that he was determined to carry out, a piece of business that, if it went right, would straighten accounts with Will Usher for good and all.

For a long moment he sat there in the dark, his face bleak and bitter. For the first time in his life he took into account the possibility of being killed. He wasn't afraid; he just wanted to live to see this thing settled. And then the bitterness passed, and he knew what he was going to do.

His chances would improve a dozenfold if he could keep some of Wallace's men out of the fight, and he thought he could. Remembering Wallace's saddle thrown on the floor, he knelt down and fumbled around. Yes, there was his rope. Dave untied it and took it with him to the door again and glanced out in the hallway. Everything was quiet. A raw snore from one of the rooms across the hall melted in with the slow talk from the card game below.

Dave went into the hall and passed the closed door across the way from Wallace's room. The other two bedroom doors faced each other across the hall. Dave looked at them and noticed that they swung in. The remaining door was the half-glassed one that opened on to the gallery. It swung into the hall, he noticed. That was a weakness, but he'd have to count on the sleepy thickness of these men and their unfamiliarity with the house.

He bolted this gallery door, making a wry face as he did so. All they would have to do would be to climb out of their bedroom windows onto the gallery, break the glass, reach in and unbolt the door, and be on top of him. But he had to take the chance.

Next he took the rope and ran it through the grip on the thumb latch of one bedroom door, then threaded it through the grip on the opposite door. He pulled the rope tight, stretching it across the corridor. Each would be pulling against the other when he tried to open the door. It was a far more effective lock than a bar and bolt.

He came back down the hall then and put his ear to the remaining door. The snores were coming from there—a pair of them. He hoped gloomily that there were only two men there.

Afterward he went back into Wallace's room, lighted the lamp and set it on the floor beside the chest, and drew out one gun. The other was wedged in his levi waistband above his shell belt.

For a moment he just stared at the chest, gauging his chances. He would have to shoot twice. One shot would take care of the outside lock. The second shot would have to be spent on blowing open the small iron chest, for he wouldn't be free to lug that around with him on this night.

A second's doubt assailed him. He wasn't even sure the iron box was in there. He was trying the impossible. His glance raised to the dresser, and along the face of it was the scar of Wallace's spur, where he had kicked it.

To Dave that scar was a symbol. It stood for everything that Wallace believed in—violence and destruction and respect for nothing. And beyond that, it was a symbol of what Wallace and his crew were doing to Carol and her father.

Dave looked down again at the lock. Then coolly, calmly, he raised his gun and shot at the lock. The big padlock spread but did not break. Dave shot again, and this time the lock skittered off across the floor.

Quietly, swiftly, he raised the lid. A litter of papers confronted him, and he threw them aside. Then on the bottom he saw the iron box and lifted it out. He tried not to listen to the other noises from the rooms beyond.

He put his gun barrel to the small padlock, and one shot blew it clear across the room. Opening the lid, he saw the deed there—one lone piece of paper, resting inside the box like a jewel in velvet. Inside it was the receipt. Dave blew the light, folded the papers, buttoned these in his shirt pocket, then came to his feet and moved swiftly toward the door, and opened it a crack.

There was turmoil in the two end rooms, but Dave ignored them. It was the room opposite this that he was watching.

The door suddenly pulled open, and a tousle-headed, bare-foot puncher, holding his pants up with one hand, a gun in the other, ran out. He leaped for the stairhead and ran down, shouting, "Who the hell shot?"

Dave let him pass. He had counted two in that room. Then suddenly, from the open doorway, Marty Cord, with only one boot on, a gun in his hand, lunged for the stairs.

Dave swung the door open, reached out, and wound his arm about Cord's neck, slamming the gun out of his hand with a vicious kick of his boot.

There was turmoil below now, and Dave shoved Cord ahead of him down the stairs, keeping the strangle hold on him. Cord clawed futilely at Dave's arm around his throat, but he was helpless.

Dave rounded the turn in the stairs, took three steps down, and then stopped just as Usher bawled, "Look out!"

Wallace, three punchers, Will Usher, and the barefoot man, all standing in the hall below, swiveled their heads and looked at the stairs. For one utterly silent moment—save for the pounding on the bedroom doors above—nobody moved, nobody spoke, and then Dave said jeeringly, "Will, I reckon it's time to tell Wallace a few things, don't you?" Will, standing just ahead of Wallace, didn't answer.

Wallace had a gun in his hand. He stared at Dave, and with his thumb he cocked his six-gun.

"Wallace, me and Will aimed to steal your deed. I got it in my shirt now. I also broke into the county clerk's office and got the record of it, so you ain't got even a claim to the Bib M." He had relaxed his grip on Marty's throat now, and Marty was silent.

"There's just one thing I want you to know, Wallace, be-fore I walk out of here behind your ramrod. That is, that Will was double-crossin' you all along."

"You're a liar!" Will Usher shouted. He started to turn around to face Wallace, but Wallace was faster. He swung his gun into Will Usher's back, and his face was white with rage.

"You want proof, Wallace?" Dave jeered. "I been hidin' in the house all day. Go look below the top hinge on that door that goes into the kitchen, and you'll see what Will wrote there for me to see while he kept you playin' cards."

Nobody moved. There was pounding on the doors up above, and Dave heard a muted shout.

Marty gasped out, "He's a crook, Tate, Usher is."

"Prince, go look," Wallace said thickly.

"Drop your gun first!" Dave said swiftly.

The tousle-headed puncher dropped his gun, went down the corridor, opened the door, peered in the darkness, fumbled a match out, struck it, and then read aloud, so Wallace could hear: " 'It's in a locked iron box six by nine.' It's signed 'Will'."

He came back down the corridor, and then Usher found his voice. "Damn you, Dave, you lie! I never——"

A muffled shot sounded in the hall. Will Usher's back arched; a surprised expression crossed his handsome face. He tried to scream, took a step forward, fought to raise his gun to shoot Dave, and then every muscle in him collapsed. He fell on his face, his gun kiting across the rug and hitting the bottom step.

Dave said: "Line up against the south wall, and make it quick! I'm goin' out of here!"

On the heel of his speech he heard glass shatter up above, and he knew that he would have to move fast. The crew had discovered the gallery door.

He took a step down the stairs. And then Wallace dodged into the living room. His gun poked around the corner, and Marty Cord, seeing it leveled at him, yelled, "Don't shoot, Tate! Don't——"

Crash!

Dave felt Marty Cord's body jar as if it had been hit with a sledge. For one instant, as Marty's muscles tautened to the breaking point, Dave couldn't believe it. Wallace had shot Cord, his own man, to get at him!

And then Marty sagged. Dave shoved him, vaulted the rail, fell the six feet to the floor, and lunged for the door into the kitchen just as Wallace bawled: "After him!"

A shot slapped into the doorframe, and then Dave was in pitch dark. He lunged for the kitchen door, yanked, but the door didn't give. It was locked. Another shot came down the corridor and slapped into the door ahead of him.

He ducked, turned left, and raced for the end of the dark kitchen. A man pounded into the kitchen from the corridor, and Dave snapped a shot at him. The man tripped and sprawled, and then Dave, remembering from breakfast, lunged through the door from the kitchen into the dining room. It was dark in here, and he flattened against the wall, peering about him in the darkness. He made out a window and ran for it. Halfway there he heard a door slam open, and a shaft of light from the corridor was laid swiftly across the floor. Dave fell and lined his gun at the man in the door and shot. The man, still holding the door handle, fell backward, pulling the door shut.

Dave picked up a chair and threw it through the window, and then three separate shots slammed through the window from outside and bedded in the far well. They had the place surrounded.

Dave ran for the corridor door, then yanked it open, took aim, and shot out the lamp on the corridor table. Now the lower story was half dark, and he stood back against the wall by the open door. Men were still pounding down the stairs, and he could hear them shouting outside. Above the racket was the voice of Wallace in the kitchen: "Try the office!"

Dave stepped out into the dark corridor. Yes, there was one light left, and that was in the living room. He ran for it, saw a man at the open window, facing outside, and then he shot the lamp out.

Now the whole lower story was dark. Dave stood there at the foot of the stairs, listening, beating his mind for some way out of this.

He tiptoed to the front door and opened it. A squeak of the hinge gave it away, and a slug boomed into it the next second. Dave drew back and slowly loaded his guns, listening to the sounds. Someone was moving in the kitchen. A man tripped over the chair in the office. Above, the house was quiet. The man in the living room suddenly kicked the window out and leaped through, and Dave could hear him pounding for the cottonwoods, yelling, "Don't shoot!"

A man in back bawled, "Come give me a lift back here!" And then it was quiet. Men were moving softly outside and in, hoping to avoid drawing fire.

Suddenly a man whispered loudly, "Steve." No answer. "Steve, where are you?"

Dave whispered too. "Here. Who is it?"

"Juke. Where are you?"

"Here. Listen, he's went upstairs," Dave said hoarsely.

"Whyn't you cut down on him?"

"I come off without a gun!" Dave whispered savagely. "You got one?"

There was a movement ahead of him in the dark, and Dave held his breath. Then the man said, "Here!"

Dave reached out and touched a man's shoulder. Quick as

thought he ducked around behind him and rammed his gun in the man's back.

"Don't move! Don't yell!"

He felt the man shaking, and then the rider whispered, "Don't shoot, Coyle."

Dave said softly, "Open that front door and bawl out as loud as you can. Yell, 'Wallace, we got him! He's hangin' out that south window!' You savvy that? Yell it!"

He shoved the man toward the door and yanked it open. A shot hammered out, and a slug whistled over their heads. Dave jammed his gun hard against the puncher's spine, and suddenly the puncher cut loose with a bawl that could be heard for a mile.

"We got him, Wallace! He's hangin' out the south window! We got him!"

Dave kicked the man out into the night, as a babel of voices from all sides of the house welled up. He turned and ran down under the gallery toward the north and the corral.

He had almost achieved the corner of the house when he heard someone pounding toward him in the darkness. He tried to swerve out of the way, but he was too late. He rammed into the man with a force that sent them both sprawling and drove the wind from his lungs.

And while he was lying there gagging, he heard Juke's voice lift up in a wild, cursing yell: "He's got away! He ain't dead! He's headin' for the corral."

Still fighting for breath, Dave heard in the gloom the puncher he had collided with moaning softly and stirring. Dave crawled over to him, raised his gun, and crashed it down on the man's head.

It was too late to move now, for a half-dozen men were running under the gallery toward him.

Dave put his face to the ground and sprawled out and lay there in the darkness, trusting to the night and their haste to miss him. They were running blindly now. The first man hurdled the two figures lying side by side on the ground, and the others split their ranks and pounded past.

And then he heard Wallace approaching, cursing like a maniac. Wallace paused beside him, put his hands to his mouth, and yelled: "He ain't got a horse. Surround the barn!" And then Wallace ran forward again, so close this time that the toe of his boot touched Dave's gun.

Dave lay immobile a moment, then came to his knees. He

faded into the shadow of the house, moved on past it into the cottonwoods, and then turned and ran. Within a few hundred yards he was brought up abruptly by a dry ditch. He dived into it, squatted down, and waited there, sucking great drags of breath into his lungs, hearing the ruckus over by the corrals.

He knew he would have to hurry now, for there wasn't much time. He turned west then, heading for the horse pasture at a dogtrot. He skirted the stand of cottonwoods, and when he finally reached the fence he climbed it and walked in the darkness toward the middle of the pasture. He lay down there in the grass, and presently he heard a horse pounding across the small field, searching for the loose horses. The man found them bunched down toward the far end of the field where the grass was better. Now the herd started toward the corral. Dave saw someone had lighted a lantern and hung it over the corral.

Wallace was smart. He knew, or guessed, that Dave didn't have a horse. Once his men were mounted he could beat the country inch by inch and sooner or later pick up a man afoot.

The herd pounded toward Dave, and he lay down again, watching the rider ride by him, hazing the horses into the open corral gates. Two men were by the gate, holding it open, and two more were guiding the horses into the corral.

Dave, clinging to the fence now, and crawling up on hands and knees, moved toward the corral. When the last of the horses was inside, the gate shut, and two more lanterns lighted to help in snaking out the mounts, Dave moved closer. He kept watching the man on the horse, holding his breath.

The gate shut; the rider swung off, tied his horse, took off his rope from the saddle, swung over the gate bars, and dropped into the corral. Men were cursing now as the horses milled nervously. It was slow work, cutting out horses, and these men were in a panic of a hurry. Wallace's voice goaded them with orders.

Dave, on his belly now, crawled along the ground next to the corral toward the lone horse. The milling horses inside cut off the light of the lantern, so that he was in darkness. He inched forward until he came to the gate. That was open, barred, and he would have to wait until the horses circled again. He lay there, peering into the dusty corral, watching the horses. A puncher made a cast, got his loop on his pony, then the horses broke and started milling. When they came around to him Dave, keeping them between himself and the lantern, raced across the length of the gate and dived in the shadow of the poles, right at the horse's feet. The pony snorted, but nobody paid any attention. Dave reached up, untied the reins, and slowly led the horse along the corral poles until they were outside the lantern night. Then he rose and walked the horse farther back into the darkness. When he was certain he was clear he mounted him and rode out toward the end of the pasture. There was a gate there which he went through, and then he pointed off toward the Corazon. Isolated shouts drifted down the cold night to him from the house, and he could still see the lanterns.

He put a hand to his shirt pocket, felt the deed and receipt there, and then lifted his horse into an easy lope.

He was smiling a little into the night, and he did not take his hand from the deed. Here, over his heart, in the palm of his hand, he held the key to the man behind Wallace, the man who killed Sholto, the man who ruined McFee.

XX

WITH McFEE's lunch on a tin tray, Ernie left the restaurant and headed for the sheriff's office, whistling cheerfully through his teeth. Each meal Ernie went through this same curious rigmarole of cutting McFee's food into small bits, slicing his bread thinly, and fishing around with a spoon in his cup of coffee just to make sure that no implements of escape were smuggled in to him in his food. That was funny, come to think of it. McFee, since his preliminary hearing, was too broken in spirit to even try to escape. He was too dumb to, besides. And beyond that, Dave would have him free in quick order —if everything went right last night at the Bib M. Ernie wondered about that and knew he was cheerfully expecting the impossible. But his new partner was a man who could do the impossible.

He kicked open the door to the office and saw Lacey Thornton in a chair talking to Beal. Ernie said howdy and went on through the corridor to the cell block. McFee's face was gray with worry and fright, and he didn't even look up at Ernie as he unlocked the door and put the tray in the cell.

Coming back to the office, Ernie wondered about Lacey Thornton. He was one of their suspects in Sholto's death, perhaps the man behind Wallace, and now Ernie, keeping this in mind, had his first chance to observe him.

He loafed into the office and said, "How's things, Lacey?" and sat down.

"Soso," Lacey said. The faint aura of bourbon whisky surrounded him, and his monkey face was its usual brick color. He suddenly seemed a little uneasy to Ernie, but then Ernie figured that might be his imagination.

"How's that murderin' coyote of a McFee?" Lacey growled.

"Holdin' up, sort of," Ernie answered, grinning.

Lacey turned to Beal. "You handed out that reward for his capture yet?"

Beal shook his head. "Nobody captured him. Me and Ernie was first out in the street, but when his horse throwed him a half-dozen other men was around too."

"What do you aim to do with the money?" Thornton asked.

"I dunno," Beal said.

Lacey Thornton cleared his throat and said, "That's what I come to see you about. This—this party that put up half that reward money, he claims that he ought to get it back."

Ernie regarded Lacey Thornton closely, and he was suddenly certain of one thing. The reward money Lacey Thornton had brought over and said was sent anonymously was his own. And now that McFee was jailed he wanted it back.

Ernie's lip curled in contempt. He said dryly, "What's the matter, Lacey? Gettin' pinched for cash?"

Lacey Thornton squirmed in his chair to face him, his lips forming words that were soundless. Suddenly he exploded: "Dammit, Ernie, you sayin' I'll keep that money instead of returning it?"

"Why return it? It's yours, ain't it?"

"Ernie!" Beal said sharply.

"Why, look at him," Ernie said stubbornly. "Hell's bells, his face give it away. What are you gettin' so red for, Lacey?"

"If I'm gettin' red it's because I got a prime notion to knock your head off!" Thornton bawled.

Beal got to his feet. "Ernie, I want to talk to you," he said ominously.

"Go ahead."

"In your room."

Ernie shrugged and went ahead of Beal into his room. He heard Beal say, "Stay here, Lacey. I won't take a minute."

Beal came into the room and shut the door and then regarded Ernie with pure bale in his eyes. He said with savage sarcasm, "Nobody's ever told Mr. See's son that Lacey Thornton owns one of the two newspapers in this county, have they?"

"Sure," Ernie said cheerfully. "What of it?"

"Listen," Beal said, almost choking with rage. "I'm sheriff here. I was elected! *Elected*, you hear? Lacey Thornton backed me in the last election, and he's goin' to back me in the next —if I treat him right! And now my deputy comes along and calls him a liar!"

"Well, he is one, ain't he?"

"What's that got to do with it?" Beal bawled, his cherub's face looking as if it was ready to burst into tears. "He could eat his kids for breakfast, but what's that got to do with tellin' him so?"

"All right," Ernie said.

"All right what?" Beal bawled. "You've already called him a liar! You can't call him one again!"

Ernie's face got a little red with anger. "Yes, I can. If you don't quit drippin' off at the mouth, I will."

Beal almost choked. Then he bellowed, "You're through, Ernie! Fired!"

"What? Again?" Ernie gibed.

"This time I mean it! By God, you and me are through! There's four more days to payday, and if you come back here on the fifth day I'll kick you across the street!"

Ernie sobered at this. In the past Beal had fired him in the morning, sulked through the day, and the next day, when Ernie showed up, it was forgotten. Ernie worked hard, and Beal knew it, and even if they argued and fought it was usually ironed out in time. But this time Beal meant what he had said. A kind of panic seized Ernie now. He couldn't be fired! Dave needed him here.

He said soberly, "Listen, Harve, maybe I shot off my mouth. I always do, I reckon. But I'm plumb sorry. I reckon I made a mistake."

"That won't work this time!" Beal said grimly. "You've put a noose around my neck for the last time! What I said goes. You're through come payday!"

Ernie couldn't hide the dismay on his face. His bluntness, his impulsiveness, his outspokenness had finally done for him. He'd pushed Beal too far. And what would Dave say now?

Beal said bitterly, "Keep away from Lacey and give me time to smooth it over." And he stalked out, his fat slack body ramrod straight.

Ernie sank down on his cot and stared at the floor. A faint suspicion began to form in his mind. Was Lacey Thornton really the man who had killed Sholto, and was Beal in with him? Ernie tried to put that out of his mind, but it wouldn't go. Suppose Lacey and Beal really were in cahoots to keep McFee in jail? That would explain Beal's easy acceptance of the killing of Sholto. And if Lacey was the man who tried to kill Dave the other night, then he saw Dave and Ernie talking. And if he saw that and reported it to Beal, wasn't this Beal's way of getting rid of his deputy before he interfered with them? Ernie had a sick feeling in the pit of his stomach. In spite of Harve Beal's bombast, his bluster, his timidity, his caution, his fence straddling, and his fumbling, bumbling bewilderment, Ernie liked him. No, Harve wasn't a crook. But how explain all this?

Ernie didn't know; he only knew that for once he had goaded Beal too far, and now he was paying for it with his job. The job didn't matter so much, but he had failed Dave. He had . . .

The sound of angry voices, many of them, in the front office interrupted his thoughts. He rose and opened the corridor door. He could hear someone shouting, and he hurried into the office.

There stood Tate Wallace, his riders crowded in behind him, facing Beal. Tate whirled at Ernie's entrance, and Ernie was appalled by what he saw on Wallace's face. Wallace looked berserk with rage.

"Dave Coyle stole the deed to the Bib M last night! He was hid in the house!"

"Stole the deed?" Ernie echoed blankly.

"Stole it! Killed four of my men and escaped!"

Ernie leaned back against the wall, relief flooding him. He didn't have to act as if he were surprised; he was, even if he knew it would happen beforehand. Dave had got away with it.

Ernie said softly, "Well, I'm double-damned!"

Wallace turned to Beal, who sat there with a look of stupefaction on his face. "And somethin' else! He told me he'd taken the record of the deed out of the county clerk's files!"

Beal gazed helplessly at Ernie. "So that's why the lock was broke the other day." He looked up at Wallace and said, "What do you want me to do?"

"Do?" Wallace yelled. "Find him! You're the law here, ain't you! Deputize every man in town! Comb the country! Take my crew and get all the men you can!"

Beal just stared at the floor. Presently he said, "That makes your title to the Bib M no good, don't it? You haven't got a deed, and there's no record of it ever bein' filed."

Wallace nodded and then said in a thick, wicked voice, "That's it, Beal! But if anybody tries to take that place away from me I'll kill 'em! I bought it!"

"Nobody said you didn't," Beal said hastily. "I was just figurin' out why he stole the deed."

"I'm goin' to get that deed back if it takes ten years!" Wallace raged. "Beal, I want you to send a man over to Sabinal with a telegram for the Governor, askin' for troops! I want you to put every man that can bear arms to huntin' Coyle!"

Lacey Thornton said, "There's somethin' better than that, Wallace."

Wallace looked at him for the first time. Ernie watched them, to see if anything passed between them. If there was he couldn't see it. Wallace's eyes were hot with anger, his face stiff. Thornton just wore his usual whisky flush, heightened a little now by the excitement.

Thornton said, "Beal has got ten thousand dollars here on deposit—ten thousand reward money that was supposed to be put on McFee. But it ain't been paid off, because McFee walked into the jail, almost. Why not take that ten thousand and put it on Dave Coyle's head—dead or alive—because he killed four of your men? He's got seven thousand on it now. That would make seventeen thousand dollars and——"

"I'll put three more to make it twenty," Wallace said.

"Good. That's twenty thousand dollars." He looked around the room. "Why, hell, every man in the county will give up his job or close his store to hunt Coyle. That's more'n a man earns in three-four years!"

"I'll do it!" Beal said, coming to his feet. "Ernie, get the word around town. Twenty thousand reward, and anybody can get it! And they don't have to capture him this time. They can kill him!"

Ernie, a little sick when he thought what a man would do for twenty thousand dollars, went out to spread the word around town.

In an hour all the stores except Badey's, all the saloons except Tim King's Keno Parlor were closed. The town was sold

out of ammunition, and horses were at a premium. In Yellow
Jacket's main street, there was a milling mob of riders, waiting to split up and start the biggest man hunt—and the long-
est—any of them could remember.

XXI

FROM THE hotel lobby window Carol, Lily Sholto, and Senator
Maitland saw the posse forming and watched it for an hour.
Finally, when it split up and rode out of town in all four
directions, Senator Maitland observed, "I wouldn't like to be
in Dave Coyle's boots."

"You think they'll get him?" Carol asked anxiously.

Maitland shrugged. "If there's any justice left in this world
they will."

"But, Uncle Dan," Carol objected, "he's helped us."

Maitland nodded somberly. His seamed face looked weary
today and stern, somehow. He was sitting between Lily and
Carol. He looked at them both and said, "I shouldn't be saying this, I know. I'm Bruce McFee's lawyer and friend, so I
should be grateful to Dave Coyle for stealing that deed. It
puts Wallace in the position of a trespasser now. He has no
right, no title to the Bib M now. The disappearance of the
deed and any record of it will defeat him in court. The Bib
M is still the McFee place." He shook his head and made a
wry face. "Still, I'm a man of conscience, I hope. I don't like
to win my court fights in that manner."

Carol laughed uncertainly. "Neither do I, Uncle Dan, but
it's been given to us, it seems."

"Certainly." Maitland looked gloomily out the window.
"Still, it doesn't change things much, does it, my dear? Your
father is still coming up for trial on a murder charge." He
said with sudden passion, "The ranch be damned. I want
your father free!" He looked at Carol. "Isn't that the way you
feel?"

Carol nodded mutely. Maitland looked at his watch. "It's
visiting hour now. Shall we go over?"

The three of them crossed the street, but at the sheriff's
office their way was barred by Beal.

"No visitin' today," he said firmly.

"And why not?" Maitland asked.

Beal glared at him. "Don't ask me, Maitland. Figure it out for yourself. Your little outlaw friend has made you happy enough for one day. You can do without the visit."

Maitland said angrily, "Are you insinuating, Beal, that I had any connection with the theft of that deed?"

"I'm not insinuatin' anything, Senator," Beal said shortly, angrily. "All I'm sayin' is that it looks as if you'd won your case out of court! I'm sayin' somethin' else too. I got too much to do today without herdin' relatives of a killer in to weep on his shoulder. Get out!"

Maitland took the girls out, and since there was nowhere else to go, they went back to the hotel. A sudden weariness overwhelmed Carol in the lobby. She was sick of this, sick to death. She hated the town; she hated the hotel; she was without hope, bored to tears, and helpless as a baby. She envied Lily Sholto, who was so calm that nothing surprised her. Why, when the news came that Dave Coyle had hidden in the Bib M house and stolen the deed Lily only smiled.

Carol said, "I'm going to my room, Uncle Dan. I think I'll try and sleep. If any news comes in wake me."

Lily looked at her and didn't ask what kind of news. It was in Lily's face that she knew what Carol meant by news. If Dave Coyle was caught or killed was what she meant. Carol flushed a little under that friendly stare of Lily's, then mounted the stairs, and sought her room.

She let herself in, closed the door, and walked slowly over to the bed. Halfway there she stopped, a small cry escaping her.

There, sound asleep on her bed, one hand folded under the pillow, was Dave Coyle.

Carol stood transfixed for a moment, then she tiptoed swiftly to the door and locked it. Oh, the fool, she thought, the reckless, headstrong fool!

She felt her knees go weak as she turned to look at him again. Twenty thousand dollars on his head, the whole of the county hunting him, and he was peacefully asleep on a bed in the hotel across the street from the sheriff's office!

And then Carol had a thought that warmed her and made her feel important again. He trusted her enough to come to her when he needed shelter and rest.

Carol sat down then in the chair. She wasn't going to waken him. He was probably exhausted. She sat in the chair still as a mouse for two hours, as the sun heeled over and the room grew dark.

She was sitting there in a kind of dreamy trance when
Dave's voice startled her.

"How long you been here?"

Carol started and then looked at him. He was propped up
on his elbows, grinning at her.

"Hours," Carol said. "Dave, why do you take the risk?"

"I wanted to talk to you," Dave said. He got up, stretched,
yawned, and went over to the washstand, poured out a basin
of water, washed his face, dried it, ran a hand through his un-
ruly black hair, then came and sat on the edge of the bed,
pulling out a sack of tobacco.

Carol said, calmly as she could, "Do you know there's a
twenty-thousand-dollar reward on your head?"

Dave lighted the cigarette and said, "Is that all? Wallace
is a piker."

"Oh, Dave!" Carol moaned. "You've done enough for us.
Can't you get out of the country?"

Dave grinned around his cigarette. There was none of the
insolence in his face now that Carol had seen before. He
looked friendly. He reached in his shirt pocket, brought out
a paper, and held it in his hand. "Here's the deed."

"You shouldn't have done it, Dave," Carol said.

"Aren't you glad?"

"Yes, yes, of course."

"Sorry you cussed me out the other night?"

Carol flushed a little. "I—I am. Dreadfully sorry."

Dave grinned and looked at the deed. "What are you going
to do with it?"

"Destroy it, shouldn't I?"

Dave shook his head and laid the deed on the bed. "I been
figurin'," he said slowly and looked levelly at Carol. "You
think your dad will be acquitted?"

He had said casually, almost brutally, the thing that Carol
had not even dared to ask herself these past few days. But now
that he had framed the question Carol knew that she had
already answered it in her mind. It was settled. She said softly,
hopelessly, "No, I don't."

"Neither do I," Dave said. "So maybe I better tell you
what I been thinkin'."

"You aren't going to try to break him out of jail!" Carol
said swiftly, alarm in her voice. "Dave, it won't work again.
Don't crowd your luck!"

"Listen to me," Dave said. He picked up the deed and held

it in front of him. "That deed will get your dad out of jail," he said slowly.

Carol stared at him, not understanding. "But—but he's in for murder, Dave."

"Forget that," Dave said. "I know what I'm talkin' about. I've found out some things. You haven't got ten thousand dollars to your name, have you, Carol?"

"Ten thousand? No," Carol said blankly.

"Has Senator Maitland?"

"No, he's poor."

"Ten thousand dollars will get your dad out of jail," Dave said, watching her.

"How?"

"Ernie See can be bought," Dave lied slowly. "For ten thousand dollars Ernie See will let your dad out of jail, give him a fast horse, and start him on his way to Mexico."

"Dave!" Carol said softly. She looked searchingly at him, trying to get a clue to his thoughts. Then she said, "How do you know?"

"Every man has his price," Dave said cynically. "I found out his. It's ten thousand dollars."

Carol looked wonderingly at him. "But what would Dad do in Mexico—providing he could get there?"

"What'll he do dead?" Dave asked brutally.

Carol shuddered. Dave had put it bluntly enough; it was either Mexico or the hang noose.

She said, "That's true. He should go. But where will we get ten thousand dollars?"

Dave, who had been holding the deed in front of him, simply waved it once and said nothing.

Carol, understanding, said swiftly, "You'll sell the deed back to the Three Rivers?"

"Not to Wallace himself. I don't trust him. I'm goin' to sell it back to the man behind Wallace for ten thousand dollars."

Carol felt an excitement pounding through her, and then it was dampened. "But do you know who it is?"

Dave grinned. "I don't. But I'll tell you how I can find out. You remember that night at your spread when you told me of the letter bein' stole?"

"Yes, yes!"

"I'll send a letter to each of those men who could have stole the letter. I can't send one to Will Usher because he's

dead. I won't send one to Ernie See because I've found ou'
he can't be the one. But I'll send a note to Sheriff Beal and
one to Lacey Thornton." He paused. "I'll also send one to
Senator Maitland."

"But——" Carol began and then smiled. What difference
did it make if Uncle Dan got one? He'd just be bewildered and
wouldn't understand.

"What will you say in the notes?"

"I'll say the same thing in all of them," Dave continued
"It will read like this: 'If you want the deed to the Bib M,
follow these directions. Get ten thousand dollars in bank
notes. At seven o'clock tonight ride south out of Yellow
Jacket three miles until you come to the big cottonwood by
the ford. There will be a fire burning there. Dump out your
bank notes by the fire, so I can see them. Then walk twenty
feet south, lift the flat rock, and the deed will be under it.
If your bank notes are just paper you will be shot by me. If
they are really bank notes you can ride off unharmed.' I'll
sign my own name."

Carol nodded, then said, "But what if it's Sheriff Beal and
he brings men with him?"

"Seven o'clock is just after dark. There's a butte behind the
cottonwood. On top of it I can see whether one man comes
or a dozen. If it's more than one I grab the deed and run. If
it's one I stay there." He grinned. "It can't fail."

Carol thought a moment, then said bitterly, "Whoever it
is, they'll send a messenger. We'll never know who is behind
Tate Wallace and the Three Rivers outfit."

Dave shrugged carelessly. "We got to give that up. We
don't care who it is, just so your dad goes free."

"That's true. That's all that matters. Only—we'll never
know."

It was almost dark in the room now. Dave said, "You got
any paper and a pen?"

"Are you going to write the letters?"

Dave nodded. "You go downstairs. It's almost suppertime.
Leave me here. When you come back there'll be four letters
for you to mail. Take them out and mail them."

"Four?" Carol asked. "Who is the fourth one to?"

Dave smiled faintly. "It's a man. He's got nothin' to do
with this. His name is—let's see." He scratched his head.
"George Bemis. He's comin' to town soon. I'll mark his letter 'Hold till called for.' You mail 'em all right after supper."

Carol nodded. "And when will Dad make his escape?"

"Two nights from now," Dave said.

Carol stood up and got the paper and pen and envelopes. Dave pulled the curtain, and she lighted the lamp. Then she stood by the desk, and Dave pulled the chair over.

"Be careful, Dave," she said softly. "Be awfully careful." She hesitated, then said passionately, "Oh, Dave, are you sure it will work?"

"Why won't it?" Dave asked absently.

His very indifference encouraged Carol. She walked to the door and said, "You'll be careful?"

Dave didn't look up. He had already started to write, and still writing, he said "If you tell anyone about this—anyone, understand—your dad will hang."

"Who would I tell?" Carol asked resentfully.

Dave didn't even answer her. He was writing. She closed and locked the door and went downstairs, feeling a little angry that Dave thought she'd tell. She'd show him.

XXII

BY six o'clock the next evening Dave's stolen horse was tied to a small cedar in the dry wash behind Alamo Butte. The road stretching across the sage flats to Yellow Jacket was empty. Dave, standing under the cottonwood, shivered a little in the chill air, for when the sun went down now the nights were immediately cool. Soon winter would be on them, and he would drift down into Mexico again, aimless and footloose, following the sun. For some reason that thought didn't cheer him up now.

He set about gathering brush and stacking it under the big cottonwood. Fuel was scarce around here, and he worked fast to get a big pile. Finished, he hunted up a big flat rock, paced the ten feet south of the fire, and put the rock down. He did not place the deed under it; he kept that in his pocket.

Then he climbed the face of the butte. It was dusk now, but he could see for miles out on the flats on either side. Presently, riding the road from Yellow Jacket, he picked out a pin point of black that soon materialized into the shape of a horse and rider. Nothing moved anywhere else, except a scattering of cattle off toward the east.

Satisfied, he climbed down again. It was getting dark fast. He lighted the fire, picked up his rifle standing against the tree, then crossed the dry gulch, and bellied down amid the tall sage on its far bank.

Darkness came suddenly, and the night breeze fanned the flames. Dave listened, keening the wind for any sound of more than a single rider. But there were only the night sounds about him, the scurrying of a mouse in the brush, the deep tearing sounds of the bull bats as they cruised and dived for their food overhead.

And now there was the sound of a horse approaching. Dave lay there watching. He heard the horse stop, and he knew the man riding it was looking over the place before he ventured into the firelight.

Then Tate Wallace rode up to the cottonwood and dismounted. Dave knew it would be Wallace and was not surprised. He saw Wallace carrying a canvas sack, step over to the fire, kneel, and dump out fat, tight-packed sheaves of bank notes. One bunch, picked at random, he untied and fanned out, so that anyone watching from the darkness could see they were bank notes. He waited a moment, standing away from the fire and giving an observer time to look, then he walked over to the stone and lifted it.

Before he had time to curse Dave called easily, "Wait a minute, Wallace. I'll bring it over to you."

Dave came down the bank and crossed the arroyo. Wallace was standing with his hands in the air.

"I haven't got a gun," he said quietly.

"I didn't think you would have," Dave said. "Come on over to the fire."

They walked into the circle of firelight, and Dave reached in his shirt pocket and brought out the deed and receipt. He handed it to Wallace, who hesitatingly accepted it, then opened it to make sure it was the deed.

"I throwed in the sheet I tore from the county records too," Dave said.

Wallace folded the deed and put it in his pocket. "Thanks."

Dave said, "Don't thank me. Just write me a receipt for that deed."

"Receipt?" Wallace asked curiously. "Why a receipt?"

Dave looked at the fire and said idly, "When you're in my business, Wallace, you learn to cover your back trail. I don't aim to get another reward plastered on me for stealin' a deed I ain't got. Write me a receipt, I say, so I can show it to the next tank-town sheriff that throws down on me for stealin' the Bib M deed."

Wallace regarded him with speculation and then said, "You're gettin' pretty cagey, Dave."

Dave looked up at him and answered simply, "Well, you know what I'm fightin'. I got to be." He reached in his shirt pocket and brought out a slip of paper and a stub of pencil. "Write the date, the amount you paid, and the place—here at Alamo Butte."

Wallace took the pencil and paper and scribbled a receipt. Dave took it, looked at it and nodded, and then pocketed it carelessly.

Wallace said, "Don't you want to look at the money?"

"No. I reckon the count is right," Dave said easily. "You're smarter than that."

"Can I go now?"

"Sure," Dave said.

Wallace walked a few steps toward his horse, then paused, and looked back at Dave. Dave was still staring absently at the fire.

"Mind my talkin'?" Wallace asked.

Dave glanced up at him and shook his head. "Go ahead."

Wallace's long lean face almost broke into a smile. "You said something about tank-town sheriffs. You driftin'?"

"That's right." Dave almost grinned too. "Mind tellin' me who's been backin' you, Wallace?"

Wallace only smiled and shook his head.

Dave shrugged and yawned. "Well, I don't give a damn," he said quietly. "It's a nice, smooth job, Wallace. You're considerably slicker than when you tried to cold-deck me in Dodge."

"I'm older," Wallace said.

"Yeah. Nothin' like practice, I reckon," Dave said idly.

Wallace said, "You sure raised hell with me for a while there."

"I had to have money. Might's well get it from the gent that's makin' it, hadn't I?"

"Well, you got it," Wallace said dryly. "And, mister, you sure earned it the hard way."

Dave chuckled. "But I got it."

"Well, so long."

"So long," Wallace said.

He and Dave faded out of the firelight at the same time, neither wholly trusting the other. Dave turned then and walked back toward his horse. He was whistling cheerfully, softly and off key.

It was all over now but the shouting.

He knew the man behind Wallace, the man who had shot Sholto, the man who had framed McFee—knew for dead certain. Tomorrow the rest of the world would know.

XXIII

SHERIFF HARVEY BEAL always walked to work because his horse, which he seldom used, was stabled at the feed stable below the office. When he swung into the main street this morning he was struck by the absence of activity in the town. For a moment it puzzled him, and then he remembered that most of the stores were closed, the men out hunting Coyle. The street, usually busy at this early-morning hour, held mostly women and children and only a scattering of men. He could have counted on both hands the number of saddle horses, buckboards, and spring wagons at the tie rails.

Ernie See had drifted in with his crew at an early hour this morning. They had combed one slope of the Corazon fruitlessly and had come back for rest and grub before they started out again. Most of them, Beal guessed, were still in bed.

He passed Tim King's Keno Parlor and said good morning to the swamper, who had already swept out and was stacking empty beer barrels on the boardwalk in front of the saloon. This irritated Beal a little, as it did every morning, because he had warned Tim not to clutter the sidewalk with the barrels. But this morning it was only a minor irritation. He had lots more to think of.

Approaching the office, he was fumbling in his pocket for the keys when he noticed the horse at the tie rail in front of the office.

It stood there with its stirrups tied over the horn, the cinch loosened, and its bit slipped.

Beal suddenly hauled up with an abruptness that was surprising. He stood there looking at the horse, like a hunting dog pointing, as the significance of it came to him.

Only one man left a horse like that—Dave Coyle.

For a moment Sheriff Beal was panicked. The last time this had happened was in Sabinal—and Sholto had been kidnaped.

He looked uneasily around him, as if he expected to see Dave Coyle watching him. No, the street was almost deserted. Slowly, then, Beal moved to the door of his office. He unlocked the door, then, still looking up and down the street, he backed into the office and locked the door. He moved swiftly to the window and peered out again. The horse was standing there patiently, a symbol and a threat and a puzzle.

Beal lifted his Stetson and scratched his head, then turned around. What he saw then almost stopped his heart.

Dave Coyle was asleep on his desk top!

A cold clawing fear seized Beal, and he held his breath. Then he heard the deep slow breathing of Dave as he slept.

Ever so softly Beal tiptoed over to the door, unlocked it, and stepped out, locking it after him. He went on tiptoe past the office, then ran.

In the saloon he bawled to Tim King and his bartender, "Tim, send a man to wake Ernie! Tell him to get all the men he can and come down to the office! Here, gimme that greener from behind the bar!"

He took the shotgun from the amazed bartender, yelled, "Get on with it, man!" and ran out of the saloon.

He took up his position across the street in front of Badey's store. Every man that passed—and there were half a dozen—Beal ordered into Badey's to pick up a gun and ammunition. Slowly, minute by minute a crowd congregated on the boardwalk in front of Badey's. Beal hadn't told them what he was arming them for, but they, too, had seen the horse across the street and knew what it meant.

In ten minutes Ernie, with a dozen more men, drifted up and said, "What the hell is the fuss?" His hair wasn't combed; his eyes were bleared with sleep, and his shirt was buttoned crooked.

For answer Beal pointed to the horse and said, "He's asleep on my desk in the office."

Ernie cursed softly, levering a shell in his gun. Beal said quietly to the crowd, "Surround the place, back alley and all. Tell the women to get off the streets. Ernie, you and about four others come in with me."

Beal gave his posse, which was swelling by the moment, time enough to pick their vantage points, and then he and Ernie started across the street, walking slowly, carefully, rifles slacked just off their shoulders.

Beal unlocked the door, pushed it open a way, peered in, then waved the others in after him. Dave was still asleep. The awed townsmen filed in on tiptoe and locked the door behind them.

They stood in a half circle around Dave, watching him, while Beal signed Ernie to take Dave's gun.

Ernie reached over and gently edged the six-gun out of Dave's holster, and then Beal signed to the others to raise their rifles and cover him.

Small beads of perspiration had formed on Beal's forehead. Gingerly he reached over with his gun barrel and poked Dave in the ribs.

Dave woke at once. He opened his eyes, glanced coolly at the men covering him, and then sat up slowly. He yawned, and when his mouth closed again his face was insolent, his eyes jeering. His lip was lifted faintly in a sneer as he looked at Beal.

"Took you long enough," Dave said to Beal.

"Don't you move!" Beal said.

Dave sneered and slipped to the floor and hitched up his pants. The men moved backward a step.

Beal said, "Ernie, unlock that corridor door."

Ernie did and stood aside. Dave looked at him and said, "I want four eggs for breakfast. No cream in the coffee."

He turned and walked into the cell block. McFee's guards, who waited each morning to be let out of the cell block by Beal, were standing by the door when Dave walked in. Dave marched past them, stopped, and looked at McFee.

Carol's father had lost ten pounds during the time he had been in jail. All the fight had gone out of him, and now his face looked gentler, less like a bigot's.

Dave said, "How they treat you here, General?"

"All right," McFee said quietly. "So they got you, eh?"

"For a while," Dave said, indifferent. He turned to Beal and said, "Don't stand there like a knot head, Beal. Give me a room. And hurry up with that breakfast. I'm hungry."

Beal made an inarticulate noise, and Ernie laid a hand on him. "Just get him in a cell before you blow up, Harve! What about that one across from McFee?"

Dave was put in the cell opposite his partner, and then Beal relaxed. The others crowded around Dave's cell and looked at him. This was the man with the twenty-thousand-dollar reward on his head. The rest of the town, men, women, and children, were pouring into the cell block now, for the word had spread like a grass fire. Beal did his best to keep them out, but there were too many of them. They flocked into the narrow way between the cells, fighting for a chance to see and insult Dave Coyle, the famous outlaw. The kids jeered at him, and the women shouted angry insults, while the men mostly stared and then smiled in a superior way. While Dave Coyle was fighting them and licking them he was some sort of god, but when he gave himself up they concluded he was just a man like themselves. He was scared. Too much bounty had put the odds against him, and like a wise man he had decided to face the music and trust his life to a jury instead of his guns.

Ernie and Beal fought for half an hour to clear the crowd out, and while Beal didn't fight too hard, since these people elected him, he finally succeeded in making his authority felt. The cell block was cleared, and a man was sent for the breakfasts.

Dave sat on his bunk and yawned, partly out of sleepiness and partly out of boredom. He observed McFee from time to time, but they did not talk. All the bluster and the truculence in McFee was gone. He was just a patient, soft-spoken old man.

Ernie and Beal brought in the breakfasts and watched their two prisoners eat. Ernie kept watching Dave for some sign of success, and finally, when Beal had turned to say something to McFee, Dave nodded imperceptibly. Ernie felt a vast relief flood him. It had worked.

Dave, finished, said, "Beal, come here."

Beal and Ernie came up to the bars. Beal had a look of smug self-satisfaction on his cherub's face.

Dave said, "You figure I done you a favor?"

"Favor?" Beal echoed. "How?"

"By givin' up. By not shootin' you. I was awake when you came into the office alone this mornin'. I could have gunned you."

Beal flushed. "All right. Maybe you did, only we'd of caught you anyway."

"But you admit I done you a favor?"

Beal nodded cautiously.

"Then do me one."

"Depends," Beal said skeptically and added, "I don't see why I should be doin' you any favors, Coyle. You've kept this damn county in a holy hell of an uproar for too long."

"I want my preliminary hearin' today," Dave said.

Beal just stared at him. Ernie said, "Why?" truculently.

"I want to git it over with, that's all."

"Why, damn your gall!" Ernie blurted out. He knew Beal well enough to know that Beal would invariably take the opposite side he took in any argument. His cue was to object, and Beal would be contrary enough to contradict him. "Why should we be doin' favors for a coyote like you?" Ernie asked hotly.

"Wait a minute," Beal said pacifically. "Judge Warburton's here now, Ernie. Why not?"

"Why not?" Ernie glared at him. "Hell, just because he asked us to, if for nothin' else!"

Beal said grimly, "The sooner it's over, the sooner he hangs."

"Why, I wouldn't——" Ernie began. Beal laid a hand on his arm and took him over to a far corner.

Beal said sternly, "Remember our talk the other day, Ernie? You're through tomorrow."

"I remember," Ernie said glumly.

"Just so you do," Beal said. "Now, since you're still deputy, I'll tell you why I agree with Coyle. The longer we keep him here, the more chance there is of him breakin' out. The sooner I get him in Sante Fe for the trial, the happier I'll be. No sir, I'm goin' to talk to Warburton."

"He's your prisoner," Ernie said sulkily. "I'd keep him here till he rots, if I was doin' it."

"But you ain't!" Beal said emphatically.

Beal walked over and said to Dave, "You'll get your hearin' just as soon as I can arrange it."

At that moment the corridor door opened and a man poked his head in. "What about Miss McFee seein' her old man with Maitland?"

Beal felt magnanimous now. "Bring them in."

Carol came in. Dave could tell by the dazed expression on her face that she had heard the news. Senator Maitland, beside her, looked with firm disapproval at Dave. Ernie, down at the far end of the corridor out of earshot, smoked in silence.

Carol spoke to her father, but she came to Dave's cell. "What happened?"

Dave said, "It's so simple you wouldn't believe it."

"Tell me."

Dave said bitterly, "I slept out last night. I got cold. Then I got to thinkin' of all the other nights I'd have to sleep out, waitin' for a shot in the back, hidin' out, goin' without food and sleep, tired and hungry and broke. I—just decided to give up."

Carol didn't say anything, and Dave thought she was going

to cry. "I got the money," he said softly. "It's hid. Your dad will get out, so don't worry."

"Oh, I'm not worrying about him. What about you?" Carol cried passionately.

Dave only shrugged carelessly and said, "I'll break out when I'm rested up." He rose and called, "Senator."

Maitland came over to the cell. "I'm havin' my preliminary hearin' this mornin'. I want a lawyer or I'll get framed for a dozen things I didn't do. You figure you'd take the job?"

Maitland's kindly face sagged in amazement. Then his mouth clamped shut, and he said emphatically, "I would not!"

"Oh, Uncle Dan, why not?" Carol cried.

"Here's one reason," Maitland said bluntly. He pulled out the letter from Dave offering the deed for sale. "This shabby little piece of blackmail is mainly my reason for objecting." He ripped the letter in small pieces. "On behalf of my client I wouldn't consider paying ten thousand dollars for a deed that was never legal. It's cheap and ugly blackmail. I suppose you sold it."

"To Wallace," Dave said. "If you'd been smart you'd of bought it for McFee."

"Quite right," Maitland said coldly. "If McFee had had the money, if I'd had the money, if I could have raised the money, I would have bought it back from you. But you see, Mr. Coyle," he added with elaborate sarcasm, "McFee is broke and I am poor, so the deed goes back to that band of robbers."

Carol was about to say something to Maitland, but the warning light in Dave's eye stopped her. She said instead, "Uncle Dan, Dave helped us once, or tried to. This isn't much I'm asking you, but please, won't you be Dave's lawyer? Don't let them frame him with every crime that's been committed in the county for the past three years."

Maitland looked undecided.

"Please," Carol said.

Maitland's face softened. "I suppose I could. It's just a formality."

"I'll pay you," Dave said.

"I won't take it," Maitland said coldly. "It doesn't change my opinion of you. You're still an outlaw, a bad one, and I won't represent you after today."

"*Bueno,*" Dave said softly, and in a way that made Carol look sharply at him.

When they had gone out Ernie strolled down from his end of the corridor. "Well?" he asked softly.

"It'll be easy," Dave said. He was smiling in anticipation.

XXIV

WHEN THE eleven o'clock stage from Sabinal rolled in the crowds were milling in the street. Sheriff Beal and Ernie See were forming a double line of heavily armed men that stretched between the sheriff's office and the stairway to the courtroom above Badey's store.

Lacey Thornton got out of the stage and asked the first man he saw what was happening.

"Hell, they got Dave Coyle," the man said. "He's havin' his hearin' now."

Lacey Thornton's bloodshot eyes gleamed with anticipation, but there was something he wanted to find out. He found Beal bawling orders to the men and asked him to step aside. Beal, always courteous to the editor of the Sabinal Clarion, came over out of earshot of the crowd. First Lacey asked how they had captured Coyle, and Beal explained it. Then Thornton reached in his coat and brought out a paper. "Read that," he said.

Beal did and then grinned. "Hell, I got one too."

"He was tryin' to sell you the deed, too, was he?" Thornton asked.

Beal nodded, and they looked at each other, faint suspicion in their eyes. Beal put the letter in his pocket. "I went out with a bunch of men, but he didn't show up."

"I didn't do anything," Thornton said. "He probably wouldn't have showed up if I did."

"Well, we got him now, anyways," Beal said. "Come on up to the courtroom and see how he takes it."

After much more shouting the lines stiffened, and Beal went into the jail. As he was going in Tate Wallace, standing by the door, said, "Be damn careful, Sheriff. He's dynamite."

Beal nodded and went inside. Three minutes later he and Dave Coyle, handcuffed together, stepped out between the waiting lines.

Dave walked with an arrogant, cocky tread. His lean face was shaded by a dark beard stubble, which turned his eyes an even paler gray. The old sneer was on his face, and he looked at the crowd contemptuously. He carried his jeering arrogance like a banner. To an uninformed onlooker it would have appeared that Dave was the confident lawman leading Beal, the prisoner, to trial. The crowd shouted and hissed, but Dave paid no attention.

They mounted the steps, and the crowd streamed in after them. The courtroom was small, containing benches for seats. In a cleared space at the rear of the room there were two tables and some chairs in front of a raised stand on which the judge's bench sat. The prosecuting attorney, a mild-appearing, studious man, was seated at the table talking to the judge when Dave entered.

Afterward there was a fight to get seats. Ernie and Beal sat on either side of Dave, and now his handcuffs were removed. Presently Senator Maitland took a chair at the table behind him; the crowd was seated, and the hearing was about to start.

Dave looked at the crowd. He picked out Wallace in the front row near the window and Lacey Thornton and Carol back in the mob.

The judge rapped the desk and called the court to order. He was an old man, kindly and frail-looking, and Dave liked his looks.

When the courtroom quieted the judge cleared his throat and picked up a paper.

Dave suddenly stood up and strolled over to the judge's bench.

Beal came to his feet, as did Ernie, and pulled his gun. Dave turned his back to them and said, "Judge, I want to ask some questions."

"All in good time," Judge Warburton said gravely.

"No, now!" He turned to face the courtroom, which was hushed now. He said to the prosecuting attorney, "What'll I be tried for?"

"If you'll sit down," the attorney began, "we'll conduct——"

"What am I?" Dave rapped out.

"For the killing of Jim Sholto, if you want to know!"

Dave turned to Judge Warburton. "You know who killed Sholto?"

Judge Warburton said patiently, "My good man, sit——"

"I didn't kill Sholto. But the man who did is in this room. And I can prove it!"

There was utter silence.

Beal came up and said quickly, "Let him talk, Judge. We'll get it straightened our later."

"Do you want to know who he is—with proof?" Dave asked Beal.

Beal said swiftly, "I do."

"Do you want me to prove to you that McFee's been swindled, that Wallace is a crook, that the man backin' Wallace is a killer?"

There was uproar in the courtroom.

Dave raised his voice and called, "Ernie, go guard that back door."

Ernie lunged for the aisle and hurried down it to the back door. Judge Warburton whacked his gavel on the bench, and slowly the room settled into silence. Someone in the crowd called, "Pin him down, Harve!"

When there was silence once more Beal said, "If the court will let him talk we may find out something of value."

Warburton nodded.

Beal said, "Go ahead."

Dave said, "Sheriff, this whole thing hinges on one letter. That letter is in the post office below. It's addressed to George Bemis. There ain't any George Bemis. I wrote the letter. If you go get it you'll learn somethin'."

Beal looked perplexedly at Warburton, who said, "This whole thing is against any known rules, so we might as well break another one. Go get the letter, Sheriff."

"Get McFee too," Dave said. "I need him."

The judge nodded at Beal again, and Beal went out with two men. Dave stood in front of the judge's bench, hands on hips, arrogantly facing the crowd.

Soon Beal returned with McFee and the letter, which he gave to Judge Warburton.

"And now what?" Judge Warburton asked. The crowd was utterly quiet.

"I'll start out with the night me and McFee broke jail," Dave began, talking to the crowd. "We was bein' held for killin' Sholto, me for shootin' him, McFee for payin' me to do it. Sholto wasn't dead. You know that now, because we brought him back to town."

He looked at Warburton, and Warburton nodded.

"The night after we broke loose we stopped at the Bib M. We gave Mrs. Sholto a note to give to Miss McFee. Is Mrs. Sholto here?"

Lily, sitting next to Carol, stood up. Dave said, "Did Mc-
Fee give you a note?"

"He did," Lily said.

"Do you know what was in it?"

"No."

Dave waved her down and said, "Sheriff, you followed Miss
McFee out to the Bib M with Lacey Thornton and your
deputy. When you went into the house, did Miss McFee
have a letter in her hand?"

Beal looked blankly at him and then pursed his lips. "She
did. I remember."

Dave saw Thornton. "Did she, Thornton?" he asked.

Thornton said, "Yes, I think so."

"Did she, Ernie?" Dave called.

"I never saw it," Ernie said truthfully.

Dave turned to Maitland. "Did she, Senator?"

"She did," Maitland said.

"All right," Dave went on. "Beal wanted to search the
house. Miss McFee put the letter she hadn't had time to
read on the hall table and helped the sheriff search the house
for us. When you came back downstairs what had happened
to the letter, Miss McFee?"

Carol said faintly, "It was gone, stolen."

"Now remember," Dave said, "only five people could have
stolen it. Only four, really. Lily Sholto didn't steal it, or she
would never have given it to Miss McFee. That leaves Sheriff
Beal, Lacey Thornton, Ernie See, and Senator Maitland." He
turned to the judge and said, "Is my count right, Judge?"

Warburton nodded. He was leaning forward now, listening
closely. Beal only looked puzzled.

"Now," Dave went on, "I want McFee to tell what was
in that letter he'd written to his daughter."

McFee was puzzled, too, but he stood up. "Why, I told her
I was safe. I told her I'd see her the next night, because Dave
Coyle and myself were bringin' Sholto back to the sheriff's
office the next night. Sheriff Beal would naturally free me,
because I was being held on the charge of helping to kill
Sholto."

Dave nodded and McFee sat down. Dave said, "Then whoever stole that note—one of those four men—knew Sholto
would be brought back to town the next night." He looked
at the judge again. "Am I right?"

"Yes, obviously."

Dave turned to the crowd again. He said flatly, "Beal said

McFee killed Sholto there in the street. But when he caugh
me he claimed I killed him. So he's not sure who did. Bu
he's got to admit that four other men could have killed Sholtc
because they knew he'd be brought into town." He looked a
Beal. "That right, Sheriff?"

"It could be, except you did," Beal said.

Dave shrugged and turned to the crowd. "Wallace, yo
feel like answerin' questions?" he asked.

"No," Wallace said meagerly. He shifted uncomfortably i
his seat, which was next the window.

Dave smiled. "I don't blame you, so I'll answer my ow
questions. I knew Wallace three years ago. He was a tin
horn gambler that couldn't pay his debts back in Dodge City
That right, Wallace?"

Wallace didn't answer.

"And now, two years later, he had fifty thousand dollars t
buy the Three Rivers outfit. Where'd the money come from
Wallace?"

Wallace didn't answer. People were looking at him now
and he was squirming under their curious gaze.

Dave said jeeringly, "He doesn't want to answer. All righ
it's his own business, he thinks. But since he won't answe
let's suppose somebody loaned him the money to buy th
place, somebody backed him."

"You're guessing now!" Warburton said sharply.

"I'll prove my guess," Dave said.

"Go ahead then, only stick to facts. You have so far."

"This is a guess, then," Dave said flatly. "Somebody backe
Wallace. McFee is bringin' a suit against Wallace becaus
McFee claims he never signed a paper deedin' his place over t
Tate Wallace. He claims it was forged. You all know tha
Wallace claims it wasn't forged, and he had a witness t
prove it. But this witness was kidnaped. McFee was jailed fo
helpin' in it." He paused, for effect, then said, "Now liste
careful, you people; you're the judge."

There was a murmur of interest. The crowd really was li
tening, some against their will and their better judgment, bu
nevertheless, they were listening.

"If that deed was forged, as McFee claims, then it prove
that Wallace wanted McFee's range and his place." H
turned to the judge. "Don't it, Judge?"

"It would seem so—if the deed was forged."

"All right," Dave said flatly. "If it could be proved tha
Bruce McFee killed Wallace's witness, Jim Sholto, then Mc

ee would hang. If he was dead he couldn't contest the deed,
ould he? And Wallace would get the Bib M, wouldn't he?"

There was a ripple of laughing assent through the crowd.

"So," Dave said, spreading his palms, "Sholto was killed,
nd it was hung on McFee."

Wallace came to his feet. "Hung on him? Hell, no, he did
: or you did it! I didn't do it! Me and my crew was drinkin'
n the saloon when it happened."

"Hear that?" Dave asked ironically. "He didn't kill Sholto.
hat's a fact. Either I did it—nobody knows why—or Mc-
ee did it because he wanted to hang——"

Here the laughter interrupted him, and he waited for it to
ie, and then went on: "—or—and this is a big 'or'—one of
hose four did it—Beal, See, Thornton, or Maitland—be-
ause they knew Sholto would be in town."

He ceased talking and looked around at the judge. "How
bout it, Judge?"

"I follow you," Warburton said. "But I still don't see what
ou're drivin' at."

"You've got it," Dave said calmly. "Who stood to gain
nost by Sholto's death, Judge?"

"Why—Wallace, if it could be proved McFee killed
holto. McFee, dead, couldn't contest the deed."

Dave said, "Let it ride there. Wallace stood to gain by Mc-
ee bein' hung—Wallace or the man behind him. And since
Wallace didn't kill Sholto, would you say the man behind
im did?"

Warburton said sharply, "If there's a man behind him."

"There is," Dave said. "He's in this room with me, with all
f us."

There was a stirring of interest in the crowd, some cries of
oubt, some of "Get on with it," and "Let's hear him out."

When it was quieted Warburton said, "You've got a lot
o prove. This is just guessing. Set about giving proof now."

Dave nodded and placed his hands on his hips. "I stole the
eed from Wallace's place. You all know that. That left Wal-
ace without any legal claim to the Bib M."

There were nods of assent.

"I knew Wallace had to have the deed back if he wanted
o keep the Bib M. I wanted to sell the deed—*but I also
vanted to prove there was a man behind Wallace.*"

There was utter silence now. Finally Warburton asked
keptically, "Did you prove it?"

"I did," Dave said. "There's a letter in your hand, Judg.
What day was it mailed?"

Warburton picked up the letter. "The fourteenth."

"Two days ago," Dave said. "Remember that. Two day
ago. Now open the letter, Judge. Read it out loud."

Judge Warburton did. When he had unfolded it Dave hel
up his hand. "Listen careful. This is it."

Judge Warburton read in a firm voice:

"I didn't kill Sholto. I know that. McFee didn't kill hir
either because he wouldn't hang himself. Who did? One c
four men: Beal, See, Thornton, or Maitland, because the
knew Sholto would be in town that night. Because Wallac
is the man who stood to gain by Sholto's death, I think on
of those men is backing Wallace.

So I'm doing this. I am writing notes to all four of thes
men. I'm offering them the deed for the sum of ten thousan
dollars. They won't show up in person to buy the deed back
because they don't want to be connected with Wallace. In
stead they'll send Wallace to get the deed.

So I am sending notes to all four—but each note names .
different meeting place. Beal's note told him to meet me a
twelve o'clock at the Wagon Mound post office on Tuesda
night. Thornton's note tells him to meet me at the Minter'
stage station at ten o'clock Tuesday night. Maitland's not
tells him to meet me by Alamo Butte at seven o'clock Tues
day night.

First I will go to the Alamo Butte. If nobody shows u
with the money I'll ride to Minter's stage station. If nobod
shows up there I'll ride in to Wagon Mound.

But one thing I will know. Wherever Wallace shows up t
buy back the deed, I can tell by the time and the place h
turns up who sent him.

DAVE COYLE"

Warburton looked up, excitement in his eyes. "And di
Wallace turn up?"

Dave nodded.

Wallace lunged to his feet. "I never bought it back!" h
shouted.

"At which place?" Warburton asked swiftly.

Dave drew out a piece of paper from his shirt pocket an
handed it to Warburton. "Read it out loud, Judge," Dave
said dryly.

Warburton read, " 'I, the undersigned, received the deed o the Bib M in return for payment of ten thousand dollars n the night of September 15 at the big cottonwood by Alamo Butte. (Signed) Tate Wallace.' "

Warburton raised his eyes from the note and looked down t a man and said, "Senator Maitland, you were the purchaser."

XXV

FOR A MOMENT there wasn't a sound in the room, as everybody looked at Maitland. He was sitting behind the table, his kindly face suddenly gone very unkindly and gray and drawn-looking.

It was Wallace who acted first. He lunged out of his chair, a gun in each hand, and faced the courtroom and the sheriff.

"Maitland," he drawled, "it's time we left this party, I reckon."

Maitland suddenly got a hold on himself. He stood up, not looking at Bruce McFee, and bowed ironically to Dave and then said grimly, "Not before I finish a little business, Tate. Give me a gun."

"Git back of me and open the window!" Wallace said harshly. "I'm goin' to take care of him myself."

Maitland stepped swiftly behind Wallace and threw open the window. It looked out on a sloping roof of a store that adjoined the courthouse.

"Jump," Wallace said.

"Not till I see you kill him," Maitland said harshly.

At that moment Dave moved. Or rather he exploded. He dived for the shelter of the judge's bench, and at the same moment a gun roared out. The bench boomed with the slap of the slug.

A woman screamed, and Beal dropped on his face. Warburton cringed away, and the prosecutor dived under a table.

Maitland said savagely, "Go over and get him!"

Wallace started for the judge's bench.

And then Ernie's voice bawled out, "Catch, Dave!"

His gun went lobbing over the heads of the standing crowd the whole length of the room. It hit the front wall and caromed down behind the bench.

It didn't strike the board floor, and Wallace, as well a every man in that room, knew that Dave had caught it.

Wallace didn't hesitate. He turned and ran for the windov Maitland jumped; Ernie ducked out the back door. Wallac achieved the sill, and then Dave's voice rapped out, "Tur around and take it, Wallace!"

Wallace wheeled, standing in the window, to send on snap shot at Dave before he jumped.

And then Dave's gun opened with one sustained roar. Wa lace screamed and tried to grab for the window frame. Bu the bullets from Dave's gun, all five of them, had broken hi arm and smashed into his body. He toppled slowly over, bloo already gushing from his mouth, and then he fell. They hear the heavy, lifeless thud of his body on the roof, heard it slide then heard it drop dully to the ground, like a sack of droppe oats.

Ernie piled out onto the stair landing just as Maitland le the window for the roof. Ernie vaulted the railing and hit th roof thirty feet from Maitland just one second later. Maitlan rolled, fell, landed on his feet in the passageway between th two buildings, then ran for the alley.

Ernie raced along the roof. When Maitland broke out int the alley he turned left, coming in behind the building Erni was on. Ernie, hauling up at the edge of the roof, saw Maitlan below. Scarcely pausing in his stride, he jumped. Five sho racketed out from the courtroom in quick succession.

Maitland took four full steps, and then Ernie landed astrid his shoulders with the impact of a ton of rock.

Maitland didn't even cry out. He simply caved in unde Ernie's weight. And Ernie just sat on him and bawled, "Com and get him!"

They found Ernie that way, sitting on Maitland's head yelling at the top of his lungs.

Maitland was carried to the jail, and Beal, with Dave an McFee on either side of him, Judge Warburton behind him and Carol and Lily lost in the howling mob somewhere be hind, followed. Ernie had Maitland slung over his shoulder and he marched through the office into the cell block an deposited Maitland on a cot.

This time Beal and Ernie really had a fight to keep th townspeople out. But this time Beal was serious, and it didn' take long.

When the howling mob was on the other side of the steel door Beal came back to the cell where Ernie was working over Maitland, throwing the water from the drinking pail in Maitland's face in measured slops.

McFee, Dave, and Beal stood over him, and Ernie slapped Maitland's face.

Maitland's eyes opened, and he looked gravely at the four of them. Then his eyes rested on McFee a long moment and then slid away.

"I'm sorry, Bruce," he murmured. "I almost had you."

"But why?" McFee cried. "Why did you do it?"

Maitland shut his eyes and said softly, "Money, money, more money, power, everything. Why does a man want what he wants?" He opened his eyes now, and they settled on Dave. "I—I misjudged you too. I should have killed you. I almost did, when you were talking with Ernie. I should have known."

Beal said tonelessly, "Want a doctor?"

Maitland made a wry face and whispered, "It's too late—too late for everything."

He suddenly sighed, and his head rolled over, and he looked as if he were asleep, at peace with all the world. He was dead.

Ernie shuddered and turned and went out. Beal, Dave, and McFee followed. Once in the corridor the four of them looked at each other.

"Who starts first?" Beal asked, and his cherubic face broke into a smile. He said to Dave, "If you'd look at me just once without sneerin' I'd ask to shake your hand."

Dave grinned then, and Beal put out his hand. "Hell, I been wrong. Been wrong most of my life, I reckon. But I'll promise you one thing, Coyle. I'll git that reward lifted from you if I have to hold the Governor up to do it." They shook hands on that.

McFee said quietly, "This last reward is lifted automatically. As for the seven thousand, I put three of it on him myself." He smiled at Dave. "That's off now. And if I know my politics, the rest will come off."

"Politics?" Ernie echoed.

McFee nodded and smiled gently. "Governor Johns and Maitland hated each other like poison. I know that, because I'm a friend of both. And now that Maitland is gone—well, Johns steps in to take over the territory. I think Johns will be properly thankful for the man who turned up Maitland's crooked work."

Ernie looked at Dave and grinned. "How does it sound?"

Before Dave could answer there was a hammering on the door, a persistent hammering. Ernie broke away and went to the corridor door and opened it.

Carol and Lily Sholto, the crowd in the corridor shoving them, came in. Their dresses were ruffled, and Carol's cheeks were flushed with excitement.

"Dad!" she cried. She ran into McFee's arms and hugged him, and he hugged her, close to tears.

Carol broke away from him and looked at Dave.

McFee said, "Don't thank him yet, girl. I haven't had my say."

He looked over at Dave and smiled wryly. "Well, youngster, you've called me a jug head, a knot head, Grandpa, thickheaded, bullheaded, stubborn, hardhearted, a miser, a bully, and a fraud. I'd like to shake your hand." He extended his hand.

Dave looked at it and then at him, and he said suspiciously, "You would? Why?"

"Because I was all of that and considerably more too. I'm goin' to spend the rest of my life makin' up for what I spent most of it doin'. I'm goin' to hunt up Lacey Thornton first and offer to throw in with him again. Then I'm goin' to hunt me a new foreman." He looked steadily at Dave. "You lookin' for work?"

Beal said quickly, "Just a warnin', Dave. You can't leave the county until this reward business is settled."

"But——"

"I know," Lily said, a faint teasing malice in her eyes. "You can't just drift now, can you, Dave?"

Dave glared at her.

"Better take it," Ernie said. "We mean business when we say that, don't we, Harve?"

Beal looked at him and laughed. "Did you say we?"

Ernie's face fell. He remembered that tonight he was through, fired. "Well, I can say it up till midnight," he said truculently.

Beal laughed. "Ernie, you can say it till next year and the year after, so far's I'm concerned."

Ernie, grinning, looked at Lily and nodded his head to Dave

and Carol, and Lily said, "I feel very faint," with astonishing abruptness.

"Why, lady," Ernie said, "it's hot in here. Let's get out of this jail before you faint."

He took Lily's arm and McFee's arm and started out with them, saying to McFee, "You look faint too, Mac. How'd a drink go?"

And that was the way Lily and Ernie, more observant and considerably more understanding than Beal and McFee, at last left Carol and Dave some privacy.

Beal, at the door, turned and had his mouth open to call Dave, when Ernie yanked him through the door and slammed it. "This is my night to howl," Ernie said pointedly. "I'm doin' it. Man, I don't see why I work for such a dumb man." And he grinned—and Beal did too.

In the cell block Carol said, "Well, we'd better go too."

Dave said nothing, only looked at her.

Then he said abruptly, "You reckon all women are alike, Carol?"

Carol looked at him strangely. "What a queer question. I don't know. Why?"

"Lily claims they are," Dave said. It was hard for him to talk, but he was slogging away at it.

"Does she?" Carol said blankly.

"You take her," Dave said. "She married a murderer. She knew it. You think she's crazy?"

"Why—not if she loved him, no."

Dave gulped, and his hands were fisted until the knuckles were white. "You think Jim Sholto had a right to ask her to marry him?"

"What are you talking about?" Carol said impatiently.

"Oh hell," Dave said miserably. "I dunno myself."

"But what were you trying to say, Dave?"

Dave took a deep breath. He said swifty, agonizingly, "Lily married a murderer. Did you—could you—do you think a woman—well, does a girl——"

"You mean," Carol said quietly, "If Lily would marry a murderer, do I think I could marry an outlaw?"

"How'd you know?" Dave blurted out.

"Oh, Dave!" Carol said impatiently. "You've shied all around it for ten minutes. Can't you speak plain?"

"Sure. Will you marry me?"

"Of course. Why didn't——?"

Dave didn't wait for the rest. He had done a lot of unorthodox things in a jail, but this was the first time in one he had ever asked a woman to marry him. And been accepted.

"REACH FOR THE SKY!"

...md you still won't find more excitement or more thrills
...han you get in Bantam's slam-bang, action-packed
westerns! Here's a roundup of fast-reading stories by
some of America's greatest western writers: